Conan could endure a city whose streets did not turn into jungles between sunset and sunrise. But the last thing he wanted tonight was the Guardians inviting themselves to a personal fight, when he was ready to meet his enemies with his own strength and steel.

Vandar shrugged. "Reza's at the gate. If he smells a bad fish—"

From inside the palace, a shrill scream tore into the night. Conan and Vandar whirled, swords leaping free in a single gesture. The scream came again, and found an echo from another part of the house.

Now, if the watcher on the inn's roof was just half as sober as he should be—

A woman wearing only a night shift ran from the bushes, eyes wide but unseeing. Conan held out a massive arm in her path. She struck it and rebounded as if she had struck the branch of an oak tree. Then she collapsed, sobbing.

Vandar knelt and shouted in her ear. "What's happening, you witless sow? Answer, or I'll—"

The Adventures of Conan
Published by Tor Books

CONAN

THE GUARDIAN
—BY—
ROLAND GREEN

A TOM DOHERTY ASSOCIATES BOOK
NEW YORK

CONAN THE GUARDIAN

Copyright © 1991 by Conan Properties, Inc.

A Tor Book
Published by Tom Doherty Associates, Inc.
49 West 24th Street
New York, N.Y. 10010

Cover art by Ken Kelly

ISBN: 0-812-50961-7

First edition: January 1991

Printed in the United States of America

0 9 8 7 6 5 4 3 2 1

THE
GUARDIAN

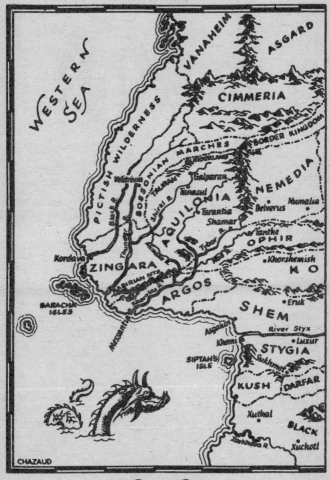

WESTERN SEA

PICTISH WILDERNESS

VANAHEIM

ASGARD

CIMMERIA

BORDER KINGDOM

MARCHES

BOSSONIAN

Venarium

Black R.

NEMEDIA

Galparan

Numalia

Belverus

Tanasul

Tybor

Shanki R.

TAURAN

Tarantia

Shamar

AQUILONIA

Tybor

OPHIR

Tanthe

Khorshemish

Kordava

ZINGARA

KO

ARGOS

SHEM

Eruk

ZAMBOULA ISLES

BARACHA ISLES

Mezzamolus

Alemalon

Asgalun

River Styx

Luxur

Khemi

STYGIA

SIPTAH'S ISLE

Sukhmet

KUSH

DARFAR

Xuthal

BLACK

Xuchotl

Zarkheba R.

CHAZAUD

Tundras

Haloga

HYPERBOREA

Deserts

Steppes

BRYTHUNIA

KEZANKIANMTS

HYRKANIA

CORINTHIA

ZAMORA

KHITAI ➡

KARPASH MTS.

Shadizar
Arenjun

Sultanapur

TURAN

VILAYET
SEA

T H

KHAURAN

Isle of
Iron
Statues

KHORAJA

Deserts

Akif

Aghrapur

Zamboula

Saman

Zaporoska R.

Kuthchemes

Khawarizm

Sungara

Kajur

Preion

Ilbars R.

KESHAN

Kassali

PUNT

Keshia

VENDHYA ➡

KINGDOMS

ZEMBABWEI

IRANISTAN

PROLOGUE

Argos lies next to Ophir, the oldest of all lands inhabited by men since the oceans swallowed Atlantis. Not so venerable, Argos is yet of respectable antiquity.

In the days when the dark empire of Acheron seemed about to sweep all before it, men fleeing from Ophir reached a fine harbor on the shore of the Western Sea. Some continued their flight, taking ship beyond settled lands and indeed beyond human ken.

Others vowed that they had fled far enough. Where swamps and hills made defense easy they built a fortress that commanded the harbor. Unless the hosts of black Acheron learned to swim, that harbor would let the fortress be supplied until time itself ended.

Generations passed, and Acheron went down into the darkness that it had vowed for others. The fortress now stood above a town with its own walls and towers. It also bore a name of its own—Messantia. (Tales disagree

1

whether the lady Messana was the daughter or the mistress of the first captain of the fortress.)

After the passing of more generations, there was no more room on the shore. Men settled inland, found good land, forests rich in timber and game, lakes and rivers abounding in fish. Farms grew into villages, and the villages into towns. The whole land from Messantia as far inland as the Ophirians would allow came to bear the name Argos.

Other realms took form around Argos—Zingara, Nemedia, Koth, and Shem all had common borders with it. None of these had so many merchants, skilled in finding how a craftsman of Asgakin in Shem might pay for ingots of copper dug from the hills of Bossonia.

In time the merchants became the rulers of Argos. They ruled with a lighter, or at least a steadier, hand than the kings of neighboring lands. So Argos was no easy prey when monarchs whose greed outstripped their wits sought to seize her.

Her citizens learned the rudiments of arms from boyhood. Not formidable in the field, behind their own walls they could prevail against anyone except the mighty hosts of Aquilonia. In times of peace, the merchants also paid for the Guardians, men chosen by lot to serve in arms for a term of years. During those years they watched the borders, guarded against bandits in the country and thieves in the towns and cities, and if need be stood in the field against invaders while the citizens rallied.

Five times Guardians paid with their blood to buy the time the citizens needed. Thrice they fought so well that the invaders did not wait for the rallying of the citizens, but fled with empty hands and bloody wounds alone to show for their efforts.

When a boy named Conan was born to a blacksmith in distant, windswept Cimmeria, it had been the best part of a century since anyone sought to conquer Argos. No doubt captains in every land moved wooden pieces about on maps, showing how they might bring her down. Perhaps when they were drunk enough, they even believed in their plans.

It was always the sober men who prevailed, and Argos was left in peace.

No land grows as old as Argos, however, without secrets growing upon it like moss upon the stump of some ancient oak. And some of these secrets are matters that wise men speak of only in whispers, or not at all.

When Conan of Cimmeria fled from Turan to become the captain of a Free Company, most of those secrets were known to only one man in Argos. He called himself Lord Skiron, although it was as certain as the sunrise that Skiron was not the name his mother had given him. It was almost as certain that he likewise bore a different face than the one given him by nature.

Akimos of Peram shivered at the damp chill of the cave and drew his brocaded robe of Khitan silk more closely about his stout frame. It was padded, as was the tunic under it. Both together seemed as thin as a dancing girl's veils against the damp chill of the cave.

Skiron had certainly led him far underground, deep into the maze of tunnels that once served as the last refuge for the Messantians. Here no light had ever shone save the flickering glow of torches, fighting an unequal battle against the darkness. Here they might be under the moat, under Lake Hyrxa, under the River Khorotas, or even under the sea itself!

3

The last thought made Akimos look uneasily upward, as if the rock ceiling might suddenly crumble and gush green water, crushing and choking him at once.

A faint cough drew his eyes downward. Skiron stood by the bronze brazier, a faint smile on his thin lips. Beside him knelt the tongueless, deaf slave who bore his apparatus.

Akimos flushed, as he realized Skiron knew of his employer's unease. The merchant prince roughened his voice, lest he betray himself more,

"Well, man, get on with it! Or do you have a spell for the rheumatism and lung fever I will surely carry away from here, if I wait much longer?"

"It is prudent to address me as Skiron," the sorcerer said. "If you can shape your lips to the word 'Lord' as well, so much the better."

He made a swift pass with both hands over the brazier. The thin red smoke curling up from it writhed, thickened, and took form. Akimos saw his own face in the smoke. First it bore a coronet, in no style he recognized but heavy with rubies and emeralds cut in the Vendhyan manner.

Next he saw himself bare-headed. Then his face took on a look of the most dreadful agony. His mouth was open, and the silent screams of the illusion seemed to echo within the living man's skull.

At last Akimos beheld his severed head, picked eyeless by the birds and rotting on the spike thrust up through it from neck to crown.

He swallowed. "I think—"

"You thought you might allow yourself impatience, Lord Akimos. I thought it best to show you where that impatience might lead you."

"I am grateful for the lesson, Lord Skiron," Akimos

4

said. He decided that he would gladly call the man King of the Sun and the Moon if it sped today's work onward!

But Skiron was passing on to other matters. A peremptory gesture, and the slave handed him two vials of powder the color of dried blood. Another gesture brought forth more charcoal for the brazier.

Skiron cast the charcoal onto the coals already glowing in the brazier. Heat rose in waves almost at once. Sweat dripped from Akimos and the slave, but Skiron seemed unaffected, for all that he was the closest to the heat.

A final gesture by the sorcerer, and the slave brought forth a simple brass box, such as a woman of no great rank might use to hold lip salve and face powder. To see an object so commonplace here amid shadows and sorceries made Akimos want to laugh. The desire passed at once, as Skiron's ancient eyes turned toward him.

Could the man read another's thoughts? There were tales of sorcerers in other lands who could do so, Akimos knew. But all with such powers had been cast out of Argos three generations ago, in the Archonship of Hipparos the Great. And Skiron was an Argossean born—

The sorcerer's hands moved with the speed of striking adders. The two vials of crimson powder seemed to leap into the braziers. Akimos held his breath, anticipating vast bellowing clouds of smoke to follow on the heels of the heat.

Instead, even the thin gray smoke of the charcoal vanished, as if sucked into a huge mouth. Akimos gaped in surprise. Even the smell of the smoke was gone. In its place was a pungency, like half a score of herbs and spices, mingled together, well rotted, then set afire.

Akimos hastily closed his mouth, and fought the urge to clap his hand over his face.

Again Skiron's hands darted toward the brazier. This time they cast the brass box toward the coals. Instead of falling among them, it *floated* gently downward, like a soap bubble. A hand's-breadth above the coals, it stopped.

"For a street entertainment, well and good, Lord Skiron," Akimos said. He spoke as much to the fear coiling in his bowels as to the sorcerer standing by the brazier, feet apart and long-fingered hands now clasped behind his back.

Something that was both smile and sneer crossed Skiron's thin face. He raised both hands over his head, brought them sharply downward, then shouted a single word in no tongue Akimos knew or wished to learn.

The box changed. First it grew, trebling its size in an eyeblink and going on, until it was the size of a shepherd's hut. It changed color, from the yellow-brown of plain brass to crimson, then aquamarine, then an eye-searing emerald hue that seemed to glow, then a midnight blackness that made the cave seem as bright as noonday—

Akimos tried to look into the blackness, felt both his vision and his soul being drawn out of his body into the box, and squeezed his eyes shut. The nightmare sense of being sucked dry vanished.

The merchant prince licked dry lips and opened his eyes. The box had returned to its normal color, but not to its normal size. It still loomed man-high over the brazier, and now strange signs and stranger figures writhed serpentlike across its surface. Akimos fought fear by seeking to put a name to the signs and figures, with indifferent success.

It took more than recognizing a curse in Old Kothian to ease his fear of what Skiron had unleashed here. What Skiron had unleashed at *his* bidding. . . .

The last signs and figures writhed off the box, hung in the air for a moment, then vanished. As they did, Skiron cried out again, this time uttering no words but only a hideous mewling sound like a cat in mortal agony.

Before Akimos' eyes, the box flew open and the lid *grew teeth*. Teeth that would have dwarfed a lion's, teeth half as long as Skiron's arm.

One of those arms gestured. The box leaped into the air, plunged on to the slave, and clamped those nightmare teeth shut on his neck.

In the cave was utter silence, the silence of the world beyond the grave. The slave could make no sound, for all that blood trickled from his neck, and Akimos dared make none.

Skiron waited until Akimos could not even hear his own breathing. Then as if he had been calling a watch dog off a visitor, he walked over to the box and slapped it with the flat of both hands.

It sprang open, releasing the slave, who collapsed at his master's feet. Then between one breath and the next the box shrank to its former size, and fell to the slimy floor with a clang.

Skiron passed both hands over the brazier, drawing forth a cloud of bluish smoke the size of a baby's head. Holding it as if it were an eggshell, he carried it to the prostrate slave and let it fall on his bloody neck.

The gashes from the box's teeth and even the blood on the slave's skin vanished. The slave opened his eyes, felt his neck, and seemed about to fall senseless again.

"Up, you fool!" Skiron said. "If I must carry my

7

apparatus myself, the next time I may let you bleed awhile." As he spoke the words for Akimos's ears, he also signaled the same message with swift-moving hands.

The slave leaped to his feet, to douse the brazier and gather the rest of his master's apparatus into the leather sack on his back. Skiron came to stand before Akimos. In one hand he carried the box.

"Better illusions than I have ever seen in the street, certainly," the merchant prince said.

Skiron's smile was that of cat to mouse. "Illusion, you who would be greater than any in Argos? Look at this box, as you would at one of your clerk's ledgers."

Akimos looked—and of their own will, his hands began making gestures of aversion. The box still had teeth, and the tip of each tooth gleamed with fresh blood.

"When do you wish me to begin my work, Akimos?" the sorcerer asked. "And in which House?"

"Lady Livia first," Akimos said. "It is a house of girls and old men, weak of spirit or limb or both."

"I have not heard that said of Lady Livia," Skiron said.

"You earn your gold as a sorcerer, not a counselor!" Akimos snapped. "I will grant you that Lady Livia is no fool. But what can one girl do when her household is in a panic? What can the wise do, surrounded by fools?"

Skiron looked to see that his slave was ready to depart, then looked back to the merchant.

"Akimos, I think you had best hope you will never learn the answer to that question."

He turned and strode off after the slave, before Akimos recovered his wits, let alone his tongue.

Skiron did not give way to laughter until he was far on the way down the tunnels toward his house by Menephranos's Gate. Then he sat down on the damp stone and laughed until his ribs ached as if a mule had kicked him.

The folly of Akimos, doubting his powers! The horror of the merchant prince, when he saw those powers displayed! And the fate that lay in store for the man, when Skiron no longer needed him.

That would not be for some time, however. The thought of how much time sobered Skiron. Time for Akimos to subdue half a dozen of his rivals, to become the greatest merchant of Argos. Time for him to have the Archons and the Guardians eating from his hand. Time for him to endow the school for sorcerers that Skiron sought to found. And time for all those promising lads—yes, and lasses—who would come forward, to learn what Skiron would gladly teach.

Then Skiron and his pupils would bring sorcery back to Argos. Men whose only art was clinking coins together would give way before them. And the sorcerers of Koth who had told Skiron to "go and teach yourself what you can" would be bound to admit that he had done their bidding, and not without effect.

They would all be dead by then, those men whose dismissal had left scars yet unhealed on Skiron's soul. But from the shades they would watch him rule Argos, and they would know that they had been wrong.

Skiron laughed again, softly, and beckoned to his slave. Together they ascended the last fifty paces of the tunnel, to a crack in the rock. The slave passed within the crack, while Skiron turned, raised one clenched fist, and spoke three short words.

Around the footprints on the floor, the dust danced and swirled. In a moment there was no trace that men had ever passed this way. Darkness swallowed the tunnel, as Skiron vanished into the crack, lantern in hand.

CHAPTER 1

"**C**aptain! Armed men on the road!"

Helgios, Captain of the Guardians of House Ossertes, took both his helmet and his feet off the guardroom table. Clapping the gilded helmet onto his balding head, he ventured to the window.

The sentry had spoken the truth. A motley crowd of men was ambling down the hill toward his end of the Great Khorotas Bridge. They seemed of every race, having in common only ragged clothes, unkempt hair, and steel ready to hand.

One man stood out from among them, and not only because he was the tallest by half a head. He was broad in proportion across the shoulders, but he moved with the lithe grace of a great cat. Long black hair brushed shoulders clad in a short coat of mail, and a well-used broadsword swung in a leather scabbard at his waist.

Helgios's conviction that he faced bandits wavered.

That man did not look like a bandit chieftain. But then, neither did the flame-haired wench Karela, and all Ophir had been abuzz with her deeds not long since. A band of free lances, perhaps?

"Posts!" Helgios shouted.

He heard the cry pass across the bridge and to either side. The gates at both ends swung down. Archers scrambled up ladders to perches on top of the guardhouses, cursing as splinters tore flesh and clothing. In the shadows below the bridge, a half score of men hastened with oil and tinder, ready to set fire to the wooden midspan of the bridge.

Helgios had not grown old enough to gain his paunch and lose his hair without some care for his duty. Though all the hosts of Aquilonia might be marching up to the bridge, they would not find Helgios son of Arthrades unfit to defend the Great Bridge.

It had been no part of Conan of Cimmeria's plans to approach the borders of Argos in the company of two score men. He was a seasoned soldier, for all that he had yet to see his twenty-fourth year, and no fool as well. It had not escaped his knowledge, that Argos had scant use for bands of free lancers.

One man, seasoned to arms and also an experienced captain, might have a better chance. With a place in some merchant's house, he could provide for those of his old company who might come by.

Some would, he knew. The new rulers of Ophir were cleansing their land of free lances with a ruthless hand. He would see again some of those he had left, that dawn on the slopes of smoking Tor Al'Kiir, where an evil god had gone to his last rest. When Conan saw those men, Conan's Company would march again, under new colors and doubtless with a share of new faces, but once again a force to be reckoned with.

Instead, Conan had marched less than two leagues from that grim battleground before he found himself no longer alone. Twin brothers, hardly more than boys, who had served in Blezuis's Company, joined him. In their eyes Conan saw hunger, fear, and the memory of seeing too many comrades who had survived the civil wars impaled by the command of Iskandrian the Eagle.

He could not have sent those lads back to face the stake in their bowels any more than he could have struck a woman. Using well-learned and well-remembered skills, he stole a chicken from a farm and gave them their first decent meal in some days. At cock-crow the next morning, they were on the road together, the three of them.

Four days later, Conan's Company had seventeen men. Four days after that, it had a score and a half. Two days further on, Conan glowered at them as they devoured venison poached from a royal forest and roasted on a fire of royal trees.

"Crom! I'd thought to slip away to Argos unseen. Now I'll stand out like a beard on a eunuch!"

The men laughed, but sobered quickly as the Cimmerian continued.

"Now, we're not three days' march from the Argossean border. The Eagle's like as not to have the borderlands swarming with men like fleas on a jackal. So we'll go on as an oath-bound band of free lances, or not at all. Swear to follow my orders and guard your comrades as you want them to guard you. Swear that, by whatever you believe in, or don't let me find you here at dawn."

It took every god that Conan knew of and a few he did not to finish the oath-binding. But it was done, and

13

only two men were gone when Conan's Company began its march to the border.

That march passed without hindrance, at least from the soldiers of Iskandrian the Eagle. Perhaps it was prudence on the part of the man, not to move a mighty host toward the border of Argos while the crown of Ophir still rested lightly on the youthful head of Moranthes II.

The Argosseans themselves had only their Guardians and their walls, but their friends in other lands had more, much more. They would not be slow to set soldiers marching and gold flowing, to discomfit the Ophireans—and perhaps to snatch some bits of land from Moranthes's unseasoned hand.

Conan more than half wished that Iskandrian might be moved to such folly. Then the Argosseans might swallow their distaste for free lances, swallow it unsalted and raw. And their allies would surely give him a place in the host marching on Ophir.

Then he could pay a few blood debts, for fellow captains and comrades already impaled. Conan had few kind memories of the lordlings of Ophir, who had used free lances as pieces in their bloody games of intrigue. Half of them held the life of a free lance lower than one of their hunting dogs.

But Conan put his dream aside by nightfall on the third day, with the border in sight. At dawn of the fourth day, he ordered his men to make themselves fit to be seen, or at least to not frighten children into fits. They obeyed, with moderate success, and he led them down the hill on to the road toward the Great Khorotas Bridge.

The water dragon was neither the oldest nor the largest of its kind. But it was without doubt the hungriest.

When magic departed from Argos, the spells that vitalized it also departed, and it slept in the mud of the bottom of the Khorotas for two centuries.

Now the faintest of vitalizing influences from the spells Skiron cast so freely had crept down through the water to the resting place of the dragon. It woke, and found itself hungry. Fish satisfied the ache in its belly, but not the ache in its tiny mind.

There lay the memory of warm-blooded, two-legged prey, dragged down as they splashed across fords or leaned too far out of flimsy boats. That memory brought it upstream, to where it had once lain in wait.

Yet something was not as it had been. There was not so much prey afloat in boats, and hardly any at all fording the river. Where the prey had walked, a monstrous pile of stone rose, twisting the current in undreamt-of ways.

The dragon cast up and down the river, and from time to time it fed, on a child playing too close to the river or a woman washing clothes knee-deep in the water. But always it returned to the pile of stone, for it sensed that atop it lay what it sought.

It could not climb the stones. Not yet, at any rate. But it remembered how often the two-legs stumbled and fell, plummeting into the water. Then a single snap of fanged jaws would finish matters.

Unbreathing, unblinking, and infinitely patient, the dragon waited below the bridge.

"Who comes here?" one of the bridge guards shouted at Conan. The man wore a red tunic with breastplate and high-crested helmet of bronze, and held out a long spear with the point toward Conan.

The Cimmerian stepped forward until the spearpoint

15

was a finger's breadth from his chest. Then calmly he rested one large hand on the spearshaft and pushed it downward.

"Conan, Captain of Free Lances, and his company," he said, as if he had been asking the price of a room at an inn.

Behind him, some of his men laughed at the look on the face of the guard. Conan silenced them with a glare. He could see more guards with a mounted captain leading them, approaching across the bridge.

The captain rode up, and Conan raised a hand in formal greeting. "Honor and glory to you, Captain. Whom have I the honor of meeting?"

"Helgios son of Aranthes, Bridge Captain in the Guardians of Ossertes, greets you—ah—?"

"He says his name is Conan," the guard interjected.

Conan's black brows met and the guard took two steps backward from the sheer force of the look. "It is *my* custom to speak the truth, Captain Helgios."

"As it is mine, Captain Conan," the Guardian said. "Since this is so, I will tell you more of the truth. There is no place for free lances in Argos. Not when we are at peace, certainly, and seldom when we are at war. As long as the Guardians do their duty. . . ."

By the time Helgios finished, Conan had learned nothing he did not already know and heard his men beginning to grumble behind him. He shrugged, then crossed his arms on his massive chest.

"Well, then, Captain Helgios," he said. "Are we free to enter Argos in search of other work, lawful in the sight of gods and men?"

"You may enter, yes, if a citizen of Argos gives bond for each of you that you will not become beggars or thieves."

"Captain," Conan said, speaking as he would have to a small child, "few if any of my men have ever been in Argos before, let alone become known to its citizens."

"At least known as men worthy of a bond," Helgios amended. His gaze raked the company. "The men of Argos have better things to do with their gold than go bond for unbathed Cimmerians and their beggarly followers."

Without turning, Conan silenced the angry growl behind him with gestures. He had seen the archers posted in all the towers of the bridge and on the far side of the Khorotas. At a word from him, this guardroom soldier and his men would feed the fishes of the Khorotas, but the victors would not live to enjoy their victory.

He was glad that he had posted four men in the bushes at the Ophirian end of the bridge. They could see and hear without being seen or heard, and would bear the tale of what happened to other free lances if they sought safety in Argos. This much at least Conan owed his fellow fugitives from the Eagle's impaling squads.

"Of course, men such as yourselves, who have made a good life as free lances"—Helgios almost kept a straight face—"should not be so poor as you wish to seem. It is also lawful to post your own bond."

"Indeed," Conan said. He could smell a man seeking a bribe a league upwind. They always made a midden-pit smell sweet by comparison. But no harm ever came of asking a man's price.

"What is the bond?"

"Two drachmas a man, and four for yourself, without the right to bear steel. If you wish to bear steel—"

"Do we look like hod-carriers?" someone shouted.

17

"Move your tongue faster, little captain, or by Erlik's brass tool I'll have it out of you!"

"Silence!" Conan roared, then looked at Helgios. "Without being so ill-spoken as that man, Captain Helgios—?"

"Seven drachmas a man. Five to the Treasury, two to the funds of the House of the Guardians. I have the right to collect for the House."

Conan swallowed a laugh, which was more than some of his men could manage. "You must think the air of Argos is nectar and its water sweet wine, to ask so much for letting honest men into the land."

"We think it is a peaceful land," Helgios said stoutly. "We *know* we intend to keep it that way."

"We have no quarrel, then," Conan said.

He would also have small trouble meeting Helgios' price or even a rather greater one. He had enough jewels from Karela's loot to buy a small town. He also had enough knowledge of the world not to show them to Helgios. The captain would not be content with the customary bribe, if someone showed him a vision of more wealth easily gained.

He turned to his men. "Very well. It seems the Argosseans have lean purses and want to fatten them off ours. All of you should have a few coins put aside, if you're worth the leather of your boots! I can spare a little from my own purse, to make up the bond of anyone who's been truly unlucky.

"So step forward, men, and pay what you can. Finish with this, and we can be drinking decent wine under a real roof by nightfall."

A few of the men hung back, more cursed by an astonishing variety of gods, and all shot black looks at Helgios. The Guardian sat his saddle with a careless grin as though all this was no more than water off a duck's back. No doubt it was, to him.

Conan cast his gaze over his men as one by one they came forward to offer their bond coins. A few he noted as men to be watched, lest they seek to slit Helgios's throat some dark night. A few years ago he would have been among them, but those few years had shaped Conan into a very different man from the youth who joined a company of Turanian irregulars.

The pile of coins on the cobblestones at the feet of Helgios's mount grew steadily. Conan began to think that he might have to show at most the smallest of the jewels, a rough-cut opal that Karela said once adorned an idol in Kush. (But then, Karela was almost as lively a tale-spinner as she was a bed partner.)

A man who called himself Trattis stepped forward, holding up an empty purse and patting his ragged clothes. Both man and clothes looked as if they had been used to scrub pigsties.

"Forgive me, my lords," Trattis whined. "But my luck has been ill—"

"Bugger your luck!" shouted someone behind Conan. The shouter thrust the Cimmerian roughly aside as he advanced on Trattis. "I saw you counting those pearls, the night after you joined—"

"Pearls?" Helgios said. He looked down at Trattis and the man now looming over him, a stout-thewed axeman who called himself Raldos. Then the Guardian's eyes widened, and in a single movement he drew his sword and shouted:

"Seize that man!"

Unfortunately for Helgios, but fortunately for Trattis, this command gave the other Guardians no clue as to which man they should seize. While they looked from one to another of the free lances before them, Trattis drew a knife and leaped backward. Raldos lunged for him, and met the knife in his belly. Helgios slashed wildly downward, but his dress sword was ill-suited for mounted work; it cut only the empty air.

Trattis dashed to the railing of the bridge, leaped on it, and sprang out into the air. Conan reached the railing just in time to see the man cut the water cleanly and vanish. He unbuckled his sword belt and started unclasping his mail shirt, while watching for Trattis to surface. No man could hold his breath forever, or swim upstream against the current of the Khorotas.

By the time Conan had his boots off, he knew the breath in Trattis's lungs must be near its end. Had he plunged straight to the bottom and buried himself in the mud like an anvil? Or was it not entirely Conan's fancy, that shadow in the water under the bridge, and a ripple as if something large was moving just below the surface?

Fancy or no, the Khorotas would not have those pearls. Conan sprang on to the railing, aimed just downstream of where Trattis had gone in, and dove.

The water dragon was startled for a moment when the falling body broke the surface almost on top of it. The sensation passed as swiftly as anything could in the creature's sluggish mind. One leg of the body brushed its crest, and it recognized what it had almost within its grasp.

The first of the two-legs to fall off the bridge had come. The dragon rolled on its back, opened its mouth, and lunged.

Trattis had little breath left in his lungs, having knocked most of it out of himself when he struck the water. He still tried to scream as the jaws came out of the murky water to close on his chest. He only inhaled water, so that he was already drowning when the finger-long teeth pierced his heart and lungs.

The dragon shook the two-legger's body hard, several times. Nothing tore loose. It seemed that this two-legger was not ready to eat. The dragon remembered, however, that time would solve this problem. Now to find a place to hide the two-leg, and leave him for the time needed—

The water above the dragon burst again, as *another* two-leg plunged into the river. Water dragons were not keen-sighted save with magical assistance, but it took no very keen sight to make out limbs churning the water.

This two-leg was surely alive. If allowed to stay that way, he might escape. The thought of enough flesh to truly fill his empty belly drove everything else from the dragon's mind.

The dragon opened his mouth, Trattis floated free. Then the scaly jaws turned toward Conan.

Unlike Trattis, Conan entered the Khorotas with breath to spare and his wits about him. A moment later he wished he had also entered it with his sword in hand.

What came out of the brown-green murk of the river was nothing worse than he had fought in Vendhya, Khitai, and more other lands than he could count on his two hands. But it was *huge*, and he had no doubt it would be very tenacious of its life, natural or otherwise. It had this much at least in common with a Cimmerian.

Conan bent double to draw his dagger. Then he kicked hard at the scaly nose, to distract the beast and push himself clear of it. The nose must have been a sensitive area; the water churned as the beast writhed. Conan saw it roll over on its back.

This exposed an area that looked not only sensitive but vulnerable, a broad stretch of wrinkled white skin under the throat. Conan's dagger tore through the skin into the flesh beneath, dark blood misted the water, and the beast writhed again.

Conan could not deny the speed of its turn, as it rolled upright and lunged at him again. Teeth ripped at his clothes and grazed his skin, without tearing his flesh.

The beast's lunge allowed the Cimmerian to grip the crest on the great head with one hand. With the other hand, he thrust the dagger deep into the red eye that glared at him from below the crest.

He might have been caught in the eruption of an undersea volcano. The beast's death throes battered at every part of his body. He gripped the crest and the dagger's hilt, knowing that if he parted company with the beast he would be shattered by flailing limbs or tail.

Conan was sure that the beast's death throes lasted long enough for him to drown several times over, if not indeed for the world to end in the march of the Frost Giants. He was vaguely surprised when the writhings ended and he still had breath in his lungs. Powerful kicks drove him to the surface and an even greater surprise—warmth and sunlight. He took a great gasping breath, then another, then reached for his dagger's sheath.

"Crom!"

The sheath was gone. So was what was sewn into the back of it—the jewels from the sceptre of Ophir. The jewels, which would have bought entry into Argos for an entire host of free lances, let alone a single company!

Conan invoked several other gods besides Crom, then gave over cursing. Crom gave a man the wits to devise plans and the courage to carry them out if luck was with him. He did not give a man the right to whimper if the world did not always go as he wished it.

The jewels were gone. But if Trattis really had pearls—and from the way he fled for his life from Raldos's accusation it seemed that he might—the next best thing to find would be Trattis's body.

That took a while, and when Conan found the body it was neither intact nor alone. The current had washed it up on a gravel beach some hundreds of paces downstream from the bridge. What seemed like half a village's worth of farmers was standing on the beach, gaping at it.

When Conan rose out of the Khorotas like some sea god, the gapers took flight almost as one farmer. The only folk left behind were a small boy, who stumbled and fell, and a girl somewhat older, who ran back to help him up.

As Conan loomed over them, the girl scooped up gravel in one grubby hand and bared her teeth.

"If you touch my brother or me, you'll be—"

Conan smiled. "I'll be what?"

"You'll be picking gravel out of your eyes, you big—" What followed suggested that Conan's ancestry included quite a variety of beasts, mostly unclean.

Conan finally laughed out loud, which brought the girl to an abrupt silence. "My lady, this is poor thanks I get for wrestling with river monsters."

The girl's mouth gaped. She looked from Conan, with his bruised side, to Trattis's mangled corpse. Then she looked at the river.

"You fought—you fought the river demon? You—alone?"

Conan jerked a thumb at Trattis. "No fault of his, but he was in no condition to be much help. As for the demon, I not only fought it, I'd wager a good sword I killed it. If you want to doubt my word and go diving for the body, it's just downstream from the Great Bridge—"

The girl ended the discussion by fainting. Her brother set up a howl like a lost soul. Several villagers came rushing down the bank, waving scythes and pitchforks, ready to rescue the children from whatever the river had thrown up.

Conan had to spend a tedious time explaining that yes, he had slain the creature they called the river demon, and no, he was not a sorcerer nor had he used magic.

"All I used was a knife in the beast's eye," he growled. "Magical or not, that'll do for any beast with its eyes anywhere close to its brain. Which makes you witlings safe enough, for Crom only knows if you *have* brains."

After a while, Conan realized that the villagers were not witlings, merely stunned at the sudden end of the menace of the river demon. Also, perhaps, doubting that it could have been ended without sorcery—which meant that the "demon" itself must be a creature of magic.

Which would be neither here nor there, except that Conan loathed and distrusted sorcery. Part of Argos's charm for him was that it was a land where magic was scarcely known, let alone practiced. In this as in other matters, it began to seem that he had more to learn about Argos.

It took another while to persuade the villagers to let him examine Trattis's body. As a victim of the river demon, it seemed the thief needed to have some hedge-wizard's ritual muttered over him, then be burned with herbs gathered by the dark of the moon by a seventh son of a seventh son or some such nonsense. Conan didn't care if they roasted Trattis's body for a village feast, as long as they let him search it for the pearls first.

About the time the villagers let Conan near the body, Helgios rode up with a score of his Guardians, Conan's own men following at a little distance. Conan met them at the top of the beach, and briefly recounted his adventures in the Khorotas.

As one man, the Guardians drew back. All except Helgios, who would not let the villagers see a Captain of the Guardians showing fear. But Conan noticed that the captain's face was pale under its tan, he was sweating more in the riverside shade than he had on the sunlit bridge, and one hand was moving in rites of aversion.

By the time Helgios was finished, Conan had done with Trattis's body, and a half-score of the Cimmerian's men had joined him. He did not curse this time, but he had as much reason to as before. The pearls had vanished as utterly as the Ophirean jewels, no doubt down the river or at best into the maw of the dead beast.

Conan imagined what Helgios would say if asked to dredge up the monster from the bottom of the Khorotas, then let Conan rummage about in its guts. But there was something else that he could ask of Helgios, that the man might grant. At worst, it could do no harm.

"Captain Helgios," Conan said. "Have you the money for our bond?"

"You are short—oh, at least two drachmas for each man," Helgios said.

"Just the amount that would stick to your fingers," Conan did *not* say. Instead he shrugged. "As you wish. But I would remind you of this. The beast I slew—"

"That you say—"

"That I slew," Conan repeated. His tone said all that was needed about Helgios's fate if he again named the Cimmerian a liar to his face.

"The beast I slew," Conan went on, "seems to have left its mark on your riverfolk here. They won't forget, or be ungrateful. Also, I shed a bit of my own blood, and one of my men lost his—"

"One of your men was a common thief, with a price on his head even before he joined Karela!" Helgios growled.

"I know nothing of any of that," Conan said blandly. Helgios seemed ignorant of the Cimmerian's own association with Karela the Red Hawk, and it seemed best to leave him that way.

"But I do know that the man was oath-bound to me. I'm owed a trifle for him. What do you say that slaying the beast counts as the rest of the bond, for me and all my company?"

"I say you insult the laws of Argos," Helgios snapped. "They are strict and plain."

"So are the villagers' notions of justice," Conan said. "They'll hear about us being turned away like beggars, after ridding them of that monster. They won't like it, and what they don't like they'll talk about, to any man with ears.

"So any man with ears in Argos will hear about Captain Helgios and the Great Bridge Guardians. Do you think you'll like what they hear, Captain? Do you think your House will like hearing it?"

Greed and common sense fought a desperate battle,

back and forth across Captain Helgios's broad face. Finally he slapped the pommel of his saddle. He looked as if he would have spat at Conan's feet, if he'd dared.

"Very well," he said finally. "You need offer no further bond now. But I warn you. You may well be judged as owing that bond within one year of your entering Argos. You may also be banned from certain kinds of work."

"As you wish," Conan said. "But if so, then I'll ask something more. Any of my men who wish to stay here in the village can do it." He'd noted the looks some of the men were giving the younger village women, and knew some of them would be asking to stay. He also knew that if they did, they would be well placed to hear any news from Ophir, and pass it on up the Great Road to Argos.

Helgios shook his head, half angry, half amused. "Captain Conan. I thought Cimmerians had all their wits in their swords. Never did I think to see one bargaining like a merchant in a bazaar of Shem!"

"You doubted Cimmerians washed, either!" Conan replied. "Shall I stay and teach you even more about my folk?"

Helgios at least had it in him to laugh at himself. "Captain Conan, I doubt my dignity could stand any more such lessons. Gather your men, those who are bound for Argos, and make them ready while my clerk draws up the bond testament."

Conan made the open-palmed Iranistani gesture of respect. "I hear and obey, Captain Helgios."

CHAPTER 2

Lady Livia, head and heiress of the House of Damaos, awoke to the knowledge that something was amiss.

She did not know what it was, and the gray light filling her bedchamber showed her nothing. She burrowed under the light quilt until only her eyes showed above it, then again cast her gaze about the chamber.

This was no small task. The master bedchamber of the Damaos palace would have made a great hall for lesser dwellings. Its ceiling with the frescoes of clouds and eagles rose as high as the mast of a fishing boat. The windows giving on the garden had screens of Vendhyan teak inlaid with ivory, not only from the Black Coast but the rarer ivory of Vanaheim. Where Iranistani carpets did not hide the floor, it was intricate mosaic work, flowers that no garden ever grew and beasts unknown to nature, in a hundred hues that caught and held the eye.

Livia would have preferred the homey comforts of the room in the children's wing of the palace where she'd spent her girlhood. Instead of making her feel like the true head of House Damaos, moving into this echoing tomb of a bedchamber had only reminded her that she was barely more than a child.

"I must forget that, to do my duty as head of our House," she had urged Reza, the chief steward. "Would it not be wise to let me stay where I feel comfortable, so that I may keep my wits about me?"

"Tongues would wag that your wits were straying," Reza had assured her, with the familiarity of a old servant. "That would be a black mark against you, along with your youth."

"I am a full nineteen years, of age to be head of this house," Livia had snapped.

Reza had not quite smiled. "But you just said, my lady, that you were barely more than a child?"

"Oh, you—!" she had burst out, trying to find a name that would shock Reza. After a moment, she knew this to be futile. Iranistani by birth and once a sergeant of Turanian irregular cavalry, Reza could not be shocked by anything a well-born lady of Argos could call him.

In the end she had done as Reza thought the dignity of House Damaos required, and remained in the great chamber. She even slept in the bed that had been her father's, although it was chill sleeping, one young woman in a bed with room for six.

From beneath the quilt, Livia completed her study of as much of the room as the hangings of the bed allowed her to see. She had just concluded that her suspicions were unfounded when the squeal of metal on tile made her stiffen.

Now the dawn let her see through the hangings. At

29

the foot of the bed stood a great mirror, silver in a frame of gilded bronze. Now the mirror was moving, wobbling and squealing, but advancing steadily around toward the right side of the bed.

Livia's wits sought to deny the message of her eyes. They did not slow her hands, which darted in under the silk pillows. They emerged with a night shift of the palest yellow linen and a stout-bladed dagger, a Turanian blade fitted in an Aquilonian hilt made to the measure of her hand.

Only her two chief maids knew that Livia slept naked with a dagger under her pillow. What Reza did not know he could not question.

Livia sat up, her long fair hair flowing over her bare shoulders, dagger held low in the right hand and shift wrapped lightly around the left. Thus had one of her father's old caravan guards taught her to bear steel.

The mirror continued its steady progress. Livia felt her hands growing slick and licked sweat from her full upper lip. Now she knew more than that something was amiss. Magic was at work.

The mirror squealed and grated to a stop. Livia could have sworn that it made a little bow to her. Then its silvered face began to swirl with shadows, crimson, cobalt, and gold. The shadows had no form, but seemed to tug insistently at Livia's mind, inviting her to see in them what in her innermost heart she wished.

Without taking form, the shadows reached out from the mirror, like wisps of fog. The bed hangings lifted from their path, rising as if in a strong breeze. Livia felt more cold sweat prickling her skin, but not a breath of air moved.

Magic, beyond any doubt. And not wrought by any

friend of hers or her house. She could not have said how she knew this, but it was certain knowledge.

How to fight it? She remembered her stepmother one night, babbling in her cups after her miscarrying.

"So much magic works on the imagination. If you imagine there is no magic about, chances are there will not be. Or at least you may weaken it a fair bit."

Her stepmother had done little to make either her life or her father's happier, but the woman's kin were from far back in the mountains, hard upon the Aquilonian border. There the folk of the villages kept customs that were their own, far older than any of the realms that claimed to rule them. They recked little for kings or archons, and much for the ancient knowledge of their wisewomen.

Livia would see if for once the babblings of her stepmother held wisdom.

She closed her eyes and told herself that she was lying in bed, between sleeping and waking, and that nothing whatever had happened in her chamber. It was not happening. It would not happen.

It had not happened. It was not happening. It would not happen. . . .

A force that seemed neither within her nor outside, but some of both, drew her eyes steadily open. The many-hued shadows danced before her, closer and faster than before. Now they seemed to paint images within her mind, instead of before her eyes. Images of her own face, eyes glazed and mouth slack with weariness.

Mortal sickness, even death? No. She felt a tingling in her breasts and a warmth in her belly. Although maiden still, she knew what *that* meant.

The shadow-images were herself, sated with passion like any animal. Passion that the sorcerer now sought to make her feel. Passion that he hoped would disorder her wits, leave her weakened for his next attack—

Livia could no longer close her eyes, but she fought against the image in her mind. Against the desire, she conjured up pictures of the bedchamber empty save for swirling dust, ablaze from floor to ceiling, even flooded with filthy water from the Khorotas—although it would take a flood like the one that brought Atlantis low to flood the Damaos palace on its hill.

The desire neither left her nor swallowed her. She had to fight, but she could. Now able to command her limbs, she climbed out of the bed and took two swift steps onto a rich Vendhyan carpet. The deep wool wrapped her toes in soothing warmth.

How long the battle continued, Livia could never be sure. She only knew that gray dawn had turned to rosy sunrise when the shadows suddenly left her. They vanished like the smoke they so much resembled. She staggered and would have fallen to the rug if she had not gripped the bedpost with her free hand.

Then she reeled again, as a nightmarish din of screams and cries erupted from deep inside the house. Livia pushed herself away from the bedpost. She had taken three shaky steps toward the door when it flew open. Her two maids plunged through it, sprawling on the floor with their skirts lifted to their knees.

After them rolled the cart on which they had been bringing her breakfast. No human hand touched it as it rolled up to the maids, then over them. It lurched as it passed over their writhing forms, and hot herb water spilled from the tray. One of the maids screamed.

The same caravan guard who taught Livia the use of a knife also taught her some wisdom about fighting. "When somebody or something unknown is moving, the first thing you do is stop it. Then maybe you can guess what it is.''

Livia lunged at the cart, throwing all of her weight and strength against it. She was not a small woman, and from much riding and swimming not a weak one either.

The cart shivered and seemed to fight her. She pushed harder. The cart shivered more violently. Then at the same moment it fell apart and fell over. Livia's breakfast deluged her maids, who screamed again and leaped up, beating at scalds and spots on their gowns.

Livia gripped the nearer maid by the hand. ''What ails you hen-wits?'' she shouted.

The maid stared, mute. Livia drew back her hand for a slap. The other maid jumped forward.

''My lady. You are unclothed!''

''Oh, trolls fly away with clothing!'' Livia shouted. ''Has the magic struck everyone in this house mute and witless?''

The maid swallowed. ''Then you know . . . ?''

''I have been fighting magic in this chamber since before dawn. I could not cry out until moments before you entered. *What has happened?*''

The watch aboard ships out to sea could have heard the question. Livia glared at the maids, who gaped back at her like dead fish, and then she turned toward the door.

A long broad shadow fell across the carpets, and Reza entered. Not so much as the twitch of a muscle betrayed awareness of his mistress's nudity. He drew himself up, then put his hands together.

''Lady Livia. Spells are being cast upon this house and objects within it. Some have been changed in shape,

33

others in substance as well, to be able to do injury to the unwary.''

''How many are hurt?''

''Few, and none of them likely to need a doctor. There is great fear and the house is quite unfit to receive guests, but little worse than that.''

Livia's strength left her in a long sigh of relief. She reeled to the bed and sat down with her head in her hands.

After what seemed a century, she became aware that Reza was standing over her. She was also aware that she was still naked, and that the night shift was no-where in sight.

She snapped her fingers at the maids. ''A night shift and chamber robe, at once!'' They seemed able to obey. As they fumbled in her wardrobe chests, she turned back to listen to Reza.

''I have given instructions that the injured are to be put to bed over the old stables. The grounds appear uninjured, so I have ordered the gardener's apprentices to help clear away damaged goods. The kitchen is in some disorder, but none of the food seems lost or spoiled. If the cooks can be set to work again, we shall be in a fit state to entertain Lady Doris of Lokhri and her son.''

''Gods be merciful!'' Livia exclaimed. ''I had completely forgotten about Lady Doris and Lord Harphos.''

Reza's face was eloquent of what he would never put into words: that he wished they could all forget about Lady Doris and her callow son. House Damaos was not so fortunate. As the wealthiest unmarried woman in Argos, Livia was also the finest marriage prize. Since coming of age the year before, the fingers of two hands could hardly number her suitors or would-be suitors.

Gangling, pimply Harphos was only the latest of them. Unlike some of the others, however, he came with a formidable ally—his mother, Lady Doris. Harphos might say nothing if Livia put him off today. His mother was another matter.

She would not only speak, she would ask questions. If she found no answers by fair means, she would not be above using foul ones. Livia had no doubt that Doris could find the price of a good many of her servants, perhaps any except Reza.

So the choices were simple. Receive Lady Doris and her son as if all was well. Put them off, and tell them the truth. Or put them off, and tell them a lie that would surely be found out within a month.

The last did not bear thinking about. If she put them off, never would Lady Doris believe that the magical attack was a small matter.

There was nothing to do, but let the meeting go forward as agreed. If the visitors were curious, Livia would do her best to satisfy them.

Perhaps Lady Doris might even have some advice and counsel. No one in Argos ever called her foolish, although many said she had not bred her wits into her only son.

She would give no advice without asking a price for it. Perhaps even a betrothal agreement that could not be broken without much gold and a greater scandal than the magic.

Livia felt a sudden chill, remembering that a betrothal would also give Harphos bed-rights. The chill passed, as she remembered the desire the sorcerer had cast into her. Could she bed a man—still more, a husband—who could not awaken that desire, then satisfy it?

And could she be ready for Lady Doris and Harphos, if she spent more time fretting herself over what could not be helped? Livia looked at the shadows on the rugs and shook her head wearily.

"Reza, is my bath chamber fit for use?"

"If you will garb yourself, my lady, I will summon a messenger to learn."

"Very well." Livia clapped her hands, then pulled on the shift the maids handed her and held out her arms for the chamber robe.

Lady Doris and her son were expected about the fifth hour. With everyone in the house working like galley slaves, the Damaos palace was in fair order by then. Any witling could tell that something was amiss, but it no longer looked as if a troop of Kozaki bandits had camped in it overnight.

As she stood in the shade of the portico, Livia knew that she owed her household much. Forgetting their fear, they had stood to their posts like soldiers. Even her maids had worked so hard putting her chambers in order that she had to remind them to change their soiled gowns. And Reza—well, she had neither words nor rewards great enough for him.

Livia put up a hand to pat a fugitive curl into place. Her hair, unbound at dawn, now rose two hands' breadth above her head, brushed to a high sheen and held up by her mother's great pearl and gold combs. Her gown was of the finest blue Khitan silk, in a shade matching her eyes, and at her throat she wore the great ruby necklace of the House of Damaos, with the Secret Star, large as an infant's fist, hanging in the middle.

It would do no harm to remind Lady Doris that the House of Damaos *needed* no alliance with her house, nor with any other. If she refused even a betrothal to all her suitors alike, nothing would come of it save the need to live a chaste life. That would not be the best way to live, as she remembered desire shaking her, but better than being at the whim of a man like Harphos.

A trumpet sounded at the foot of the hill, then a second. The horn of her gatekeeper answered it. After a weary interval, the trumpet sounded again. It seemed no closer. Livia cocked her head, and thought she could hear shouts, perhaps curses, and certainly the braying of asses and the lowing of cattle.

She uttered a brief unseemly prayer that Lady Doris would be trapped among the farmers bound for market until nightfall, then rang for Reza.

"Is all in readiness?"

"All that gods or men could ask has been done, my lady."

"Ah, but will that be enough for Lady Doris? She is no man, and I sometimes wonder what respect she gives the gods."

Reza's face was eloquent in disapproval of this levity.

"Forgive me, Reza. You know that I am more my father's daughter than my mother's."

"They both made you what you are, my lady, and I think both would be proud of what that is."

"Bless you for those kind words, Reza, and—oh, Mitra, here they come!"

A veritable caravan was passing through the gate— four mounted guards, two sedan chairs, each borne by eight sweating slaves, a half score of servants on foot, and four more mounted guards bringing up the rear.

"The groom *was* told to examine the horses while he fed and watered them, was he not?" Livia asked urgently. It would tell her much, if Lady Doris's guards rode their own horses or hired ones, and if their own horses were well or ill fed. That House Lokhri was declining was no secret. How fast and how far were matters yet to learn, and the horses might have something to say.

"That was the first order you gave for the groom, my lady," Reza said consolingly. Livia could not remember for the life of her giving any such order. She suspected that Reza had given it himself, but if he had, it would be obeyed as if it came from her, or indeed from the very gods.

Sorcerers might terrify her servants and disorder her house. The spell was not known to man that could make anyone of House Damaos disobey the chief steward.

The caravan was now marching up the winding path toward the portico. Reza lifted a hand, and from the roof another trumpet gave its silver-throated cry. The horses began to curvet and prance, and their riders to look uneasy.

As the stablehands rushed out to attend the visitors' horses, the litter bearers halted and lowered their burdens. Lady Doris was the first out. Her son was by law the head of House Lokhri, but Lady Doris recked little for the law and less for wagging tongues. Her own was such a trenchant weapon that even those men who called young Harphos friend would not speak up for him, lest they be flayed alive as by bandits on the Silk Road to Khitai.

Harphos dismounted next. As always, he looked as if he were about to sprawl on his face in the dust. As always, he spared himself that indignity. This time, Livia saw, he did so without clutching the roof of the litter like a drowning man clutching a log. He was as crop-headed as ever, a style which did not suit his long face, but his tunic and robe and boots were not only new but almost matched.

"The blessing of our house to yours, Lady Doris," Livia said formally.

Lady Doris took her eyes off the statues behind the path long enough for good manners, then stepped up on to the portico beside Livia. She was not as tall as Livia, but rather fuller of hip and breast. In her youth she had been accounted one of the finest-looking women of Argos, and even now her blue-black hair showed not a thread of gray.

Harphos walked up to the two women with his eyes so fixed on Livia that he nearly stumbled. His mother had to remind him to return her greeting. Livia turned her face briefly aside, not sure whether she would be hiding tears or smiles. Harphos was not much of a man, but no one deserved being under the thumb of Lady Doris as he was!

"I see you have one of the new castings of Polyemius's 'The Runner,' " Lady Doris said. "A fine work for those whose taste runs to such things."

Livia's hands did not quite curl into claws. No meeting with Lady Doris since her father died had passed without some such sharp remark from the older woman. In truth, House Damaos had one of the oldest castings of Polyemius's masterwork, if not indeed the original. But Lady Doris would rather be laid on the rack than admit it, since it was some years since her house had been able to buy even a casting of a lesser Polyemius.

"We can discuss taste and much else at more leisure and in greater comfort within," Livia said. "The Rose Chamber has been prepared for our pleasure." *And if so much as a splinter of porcelain remains in view, may*

39

the gods have mercy on the servants, because Reza will have none!

She held out her arm to Harphos. "Come, my lord. We have a new vintage from Nemedia on which I would value your opinion."

Harphos drank little, but she had to say *something* to the poor antic. Her reward was a faint smile from Harphos and wide eyes from Lady Doris as her son took Livia's proferred arm.

Lady Doris's eyes grew no smaller as they proceeded through the battered palace. Livia trusted to Reza's judgment and the servants' hands, and made no effort to guide her guests through undamaged rooms. Lady Doris had been here too often not to be suspicious of that.

The Rose Chamber was as clean as it needed to be, and the climbing rose that wound upward to the sunhole in the middle of the ceiling had opened several new blossoms since last night. Their delicate scent fought without great success against Lady Doris's heavy perfume.

Servants brought trays of fruit and cakes and a great jug of the Nemedian wine, cooled in snow. Livia was lifting the jug when she halted, holding it at arm's length.

A chip the size of a child's hand was missing from the rim of the cooling pot. One of the kitchen servants had overlooked it, and even Reza could not be everywhere.

Since this was so, Livia vowed to say nothing of the matter. But her halt had drawn Lady Doris's eyes.

"Your servants seem less polished than I remember them," the older woman said. "Has ill luck in finding good ones finally overtaken even the House of Damaos?''

She looked and sounded ready to dance on the table if this was so. Livia's own reply was as cool as the snow.

"No. Only accidents that might have happened to anyone, while we made the house fit for your reception.''

"Quite a lot of accidents, I would say,'' Harphos put in. "I could see where things had been cleaned up—very well, but still—''

He broke off as Livia let slip a word ladies of her rank and station were not supposed to know. Then he laughed nervously.

"Sorry, Livia. If it is something you would rather not speak of—''

"It is nothing shameful,'' she said, smiling. That was the most intelligent thing she had heard him say in years, and now he was actually apologizing to her—without the prompting of his mother, and, to judge from her expression, possibly without her approval!

"Then by all means let us speak of it,'' Lady Doris said briskly. "We of the archonal Houses must stand together against the follies of servants, or our very palaces will tumble about our ears.''

If bumbling servants ever did bury Lady Doris in the rubble of the Lokhri palace, Livia would call for a day of public rejoicing. Since the woman was both alive and a guest under her roof, she kept this thought to herself.

They rambled over a weary stretch of tales of dropped vases, burned food, and spilled chamberpots. "I wonder if there is magic in all this somewhere, spells cast to addle our servants' wits?'' Doris concluded.

Fortunately she said this as she turned to help herself

41

to more grapes, so she did not see Livia flinch. Commanding her voice with an effort, the younger woman inquired, "Magic? As well blame Atlanteans!"

"Magic has not been gone from Argos so long as that," Doris replied. "And when I dined with Lord Akimos two nights ago, I overheard the Fourth Archon say that he would not spend public money to hire witch-seekers."

"Who? Lord Akimos or the archon?"

"The archon, of course. Although now that I recall it, Lord Akimos seemed to be of the same mind. He came to the house as though he was weary and cast down, but . . ."

By the time Lady Doris had finished reciting what every one of her fellow guests wore, ate, and said, Livia was fidgeting openly and Harphos looked as if he would if he dared. Livia smiled at him again, and he ventured to reply in kind.

"I wonder if the archon and Lord Akimos have the right of it," Harphos said. "There was that river dragon they killed a few days ago, by the Great Bridge on the Khorotas. The fisherfolk had lost a half score of women and children to something, but no one imagined it was a river dragon. First one seen in the Khorotas in a century, or so I heard."

"You cannot have heard the truth at a drinking party with Guardian captains," Lady Doris said sharply.

"But, Mother, they certainly talked like it happened. It was a captain of free lances who killed the beast. He dived into the river after one of his men fell off the bridge, and found it feeding on—"

"Remember you are at the table of a lady, Harphos," Lady Doris said. "Do not forget what I taught you, as to what may be spoken of there."

Livia was greatly tempted to use that unladlylike word again, or even several of them. With Lady Doris shocked into muteness, perhaps Harphos would find his tongue again.

And perhaps pigs would fly. More likely, Lady Doris would recover both wits and tongue and wonder why Lady Livia was so curious about this matter of the river dragon.

A century ago was the time when magic was cast out of Argos, or so the scrolls said. A century without either magic or river dragons—and now within a few days her house was disordered by magic and a river dragon roamed the Khorotas.

She would not waste her breath praying that this was coincidence. Instead she would speak to Reza. He seldom needed to buy his own drink in any of several taverns, but if he did, tongues might wag. Perhaps he could even have a word with that captain of free lances.

Livia turned her thoughts back to her guests. Half her mind would suffice for Lady Doris, but to ignore poor Harphos would be like kicking a puppy.

CHAPTER 3

There were hotter suns than that of Argos. There was thinner air than a man breathed on the slopes of the Rabirian Mountains. There was much harder work than cutting timber in those mountains.

Conan had endured all three, and not as a free man, either. But he had never endured all three together, when he had a band of free lances to lead, or at least keep out of trouble.

Earning the extra two drachmas of their bond had put Conan's Company to no small difficulty. Except for the handful left in the village on the Khorotas, Conan wished them to remain together.

He knew the look in the eyes of too many Argosseans; if one of the company made trouble, all would suffer for it. The more they were under his eye, the less trouble they would make. Or so Conan judged.

He understood that few Argosseans would hire an

entire company of free lances. Few had the gold, and fewer still had work that demanded so many fresh hands *and* would last long enough to let the men earn their bonds.

Days went by, and there was no work. There were, however, Guardian captains (and not only Helgios) who more than hinted of the company's fate if it did not find work soon.

"You lose your own silver, for a start," one said to Conan one night over some wine only a trifle short of vinegar. "Then it may not be long after that before we ask you to please go back the way you came."

Back across the Argossean border, into Ophir—into borderlands where the campfires of Iskandrian's men now sparkled from hilltops within sight of the Khorotas. Conan and his men would not escape discovery this time, even if the Argosseans did not courteously warn the Ophirians of their coming! Having seen the Argosseans now, Conan would not have trusted any one of them to guard his sister's virtue, if offered the right price for selling her to a tavern.

"And if we do not choose death in Ophir?"

"Then you will be choosing it in Argos, Captain Conan. How many Guardians can you fight?"

"More than you seem to think, if you're fools enough to force the battle on us!"

"Ah, but the folly will not be ours then. Or at least it will be divided between us. What the gods will say of that, I leave to you to learn. You will most probably be meeting them before I."

Conan fought the wish to prove the Guardian a liar in that at least, by snapping his neck on the spot. But more than a score of men oath-sworn to the Cimmerian

45

would die of slow hanging or slower impalement if he did that. His hands only twitched.

"We have drunk together, Cimmerian," the Guardian went on. "So I owe you a favor."

"On Argossean favors, a man could quickly grow thin," Conan growled.

"Not on this one, I think. If your men are stout enough for hard work, seek it in the Rabirian Mountains."

"What sort of work?"

"Mining, quarrying, road-mending, timber-cutting, who knows? It changes with the seasons, likewise the whims of the merchants."

Conan could believe that. His experience of merchants led him to believe that they could contend with the gods themselves for honors in the matter of whims. As to the rest—it made as much sense as anything he had heard in Argos, and more than most.

So he bought more wine, and thanked the captain, and the next day sought and was given the right to take his men into the mountains. They grumbled and cursed, and two of them deserted, but the rest were still with him when the jagged peaks pierced the northern horizon and the sound of felling axes echoed down the glens.

Lord Akimos twisted from the waist in a vain effort to ease the pain in back and buttocks. He also loosened the thong of his riding cloak, which seemed ready to saw his head from his shoulders.

Nothing could alter the fact that he was too old to be riding up into these mountains at all, let alone in disguise. A disguise, moreover, which demanded that he ride with scant escort on horses reprieved from the knackers.

He had no choice, however. If it was noised about that he had ridden north to speak with the dragon-slayer, it would reach Skiron's ears sooner rather than later.

Then he might quickly be worse off than before. Skiron might well cast down the dragon-slayer in a duel of spells. Even if he was defeated, Akimos would still have only one sorcerer and be at the man's mercy, instead of having two whom he could play one against the other.

He reined in and raised a hand in signal to those behind him.

"Time to let the horses blow. And for Mitra's sake, hand me the flask."

Enough wine to dull the pain would topple him from the saddle. But a mouthful or two would wash the grit from between his teeth and remind him of the world outside these mountains.

As Akimos lifted the flask, he heard the sound of axes borne on the breeze. Then abruptly the axes gave way to angry shouting. He thrust the flask into his belt and put spurs to his horse. They clattered up the path, with guards drawing swords and unslinging bows as they rode.

Conan needed no warning from Talouf the Shemite that the twins were at the end of their tether. He had been watching them for days, as sharply as the little knifeman he had made his sergeant.

So when he heard an angry shout from Jarenz, he turned. When he saw the youth dancing about on one leg, holding a bloody foot in both hands and cursing, he started downhill. When he saw guards approaching, he broke into a run.

Talouf was right behind him, but he had learned something in his few days as a sergeant: his knife was still in his sheath. The Cimmerian and the Shemite reached the fallen log from uphill at the same moment as Jarenz's brother Vandar reached it from below.

The guards whirled. One raised his club, the other a short whip. The whip cut the air, an arm's length in front of Vandar's nose.

"Back to work, you!" the guard snarled. "We can see to your brother."

"As you did with a rope as rotten as the food in the hall?" shouted Vandar. His voice almost broke in his rage. He stepped forward.

The whip cracked again, this time coming down across his shoulder. Vandar made an animal noise in his throat and leaped for the guard.

He never contemplated the leap. As he began it, Talouf dove between the two men, flinging himself under Vandar's feet. The tall youth went sprawling. The guard raised his whip, to lay it across Vandar's back.

The whip never fell. A long Cimmerian arm shot over the guard's shoulder, catching the whip in mid-air. A quick twist, and the lash was wound around a massive Cimmerian hand.

The guard whirled, and a booted Cimmerian foot hooked around his ankle. He went on whirling, lost his balance, and crashed to the ground as the whip dangled from Conan's hand.

"I'll give this back when you know enough not to use it on free men," Conan said.

"Who says you pack of apes are free?" the guard with the club asked. He still had the club raised, but he had backed away from the fight to what he clearly hoped would be a safe distance.

"It was written in the bond-scroll—" Conan began.

"What? You can read? First a Cimmerian who can read, and then one who makes jests? This day is full of—ekkhh!"

Conan dangled the guard from one hand while plucking the club from his limp hand with the other. "This day will be full of broken bones and missing teeth for you, if you don't mind your tongue. Call your captain. I'll have words with him about this matter, and *now*!"

The guard could hardly have left more swiftly if he had been fired from a siege engine. The whipman rose, looked at his whip, then contemplated Talouf. The Shemite had one hand on the hilt of his dagger. Vandar had no weapons, but his face would have sent demons to flight.

Conan jerked his thumb downhill. "You go to the leech. If he's too drunk to climb the hill, bring his salves and bandages yourself. I've tended a few wounds in my time."

"You—"

Conan stretched the whip between his two hands, his muscles writhed, and the tough leather parted like thread.

"Go, or the next wound I tend after Jarenz's will be yours."

The guard found obedience wise, although he did not leave quite as fast as his comrade.

Conan turned to Jarenz. "Now, let's see to that leg."

"Thank you, Captain. Thank you," the youth stammered. "I will never be able to thank you—"

"Yes, you will," Conan said. "Thank me by keeping your mouth shut when the captain comes uphill. We may end this day without another fight, if matters stay between him and me."

49

"Yes, Captain. Of course, Captain. I will be silent as—"

"Start now."

Jarenz's mouth opened, then shut without a word. Talouf and Vandar laughed.

Conan wished he could find something to laugh about. From the stir of movement downhill, the captain of guards was already on his way up, and with a mounted escort.

As Akimos rode uphill, he heard trumpets and drums sounding. Guards ran past, carrying clubs and short-swords, passing Akimos as if he were riding a turtle.

The guards vanished around the bend in the trail, to be greeted by more shouts. Akimos almost spurred his horse, before he remembered its condition. The next time he wore a disguise, he vowed, it would be as someone who traveled well-mounted!

Around the bend lay a clearing, recently cut from the forest. A pile of dressed logs lay ready to be rolled to the river and sent downstream. Atop the pile stood a giant, tangled black hair sweeping broad shoulders. Huge hands danced in signals, sending ragged men with axes and mauls scurrying about.

Akimos had been neither Guardian nor caravan guard nor yet free lance, but he had seen all three in action. He knew that he was seeing a war captain readying his men for a fight.

The camp's guards' faces told plainly of the same knowledge. They gripped their weapons, but even those with bows were pale and sweating. All kept their distance, even the captain.

That worthy turned to Akimos. "Lord—"

"Hsstt! Guard your tongue, fool!"

"Councilor, then. Best stay back. That mad Cimmerian and his men have struck down two of my guards. They refuse to submit to justice."

Looking at the men the captain had to enforce that justice, Akimos found his sympathies with the Cimmerian. He would not have trusted the captain's notions of justice either.

Memory flickered in Akimos, then glowed brightly. Had not it been said of the dragon-slayer that he had the look of Cimmeria about him?

"Ho, Captain," Akimos called. "I am a councilor to Lord Akimos. He seeks the sorcerer who slew a river dragon by the Great Khorotas Bridge. Do you know where he might be found?"

Something that might have been amusement passed over the face of the Cimmerian, but the blue eyes remained as cold as the northern sky. "I might. If I did, I might even tell you, if you made it worth my while."

Akimos kept his face straight with an effort. The guard captain looked on the verge of a seizure.

"How much would that take?" Akimos said. "My master knows the value of information. He also knows the value of a drachma."

"How many drachmas will it take to pay the fines of my men?"

Akimos looked a question at the guard captain. The man shrugged. "That depends on the timber merchant's judgment and the hurt to the guards."

"How long must we wait for that?"

"More than days, less than a month."

"And meanwhile, I must return to Lord Akimos and tell him why I have not been able to find the sorcerer?"

Had the captain dropped dead on the spot, Akimos would not have been surprised. He was beginning to find this entertaining. Bargaining was in his blood, an art he had mastered so well that he could do it equally well in a dungeon, aboard a ship, or here where the mountain peaks gnawed at the northern horizon.

"No—that is, I can name a price. But if my master does not think it sufficient—"

"My master will make it up to him. Indeed, he has already agreed with your master to give me the power of judgment in such matters as this."

The captain's face now showed more greed than fear. Akimos dismounted and clapped him on the shoulder. "Come, my friend. Our masters have already agreed. Why should we quarrel?"

The captain snapped his mouth shut, then jerked his head. "No reason at all, if you have a hundred drachmas."

"A hundred!" Akimos's voice squealed like a fresh-gelded pig's. "My master will have my blood if he must pay more than sixty."

"Mine will also have blood, if his guards desert because they have not had justice!"

"A hundred drachmas is not justice for two hurt guards. It is a ransom for the Crown Prince of Aquilonia!"

"Well, perhaps seventy . . ."

Akimos turned away to smile where only his horse could see him. The man had agreed to bargain. Now let him learn what it was to bargain with a merchant prince of Argos!

Conan watched the bargaining with thinly veiled amusement. Talouf did not even bother to veil his. The rest of the company did not take their eyes off the guards. If it came to a fight, the guards' archery would do much to balance their lack of numbers, at least until the archers fell.

Conan had no particular stomach for a fight. If he had been alone, he would long since have been on his way across the mountains. Zingara and Aquilonia both lay that way, and neither made such a fuss as the Argosseans about whence came a man with a good sword arm.

But more than a score of men oath-bound to him was too many either to leave behind or to lead across the mountains. He must settle their fate here in Argos, and just maybe the gods had sent him a way, in this Lord Akimos. (If the man was the lord's agent and not the lord himself, then he, Conan, was the High Priest of Set!)

At last the captain of the guards grunted and nodded. "I will take that offer. But if my master repudiates it, you had best flee to the Pictish Wilderness to escape me!"

"Oh, have no fear," the other man replied. "I am too old and fat to wish to leave my lord's service. What I have told you is only the truth."

Conan waited, arms crossed on his chest, as the drachmas changed hands. When the man climbed over the stumps to stand before him, the Cimmerian gave an open-palmed greeting.

"Now, Captain. I hope my—my master's gold—has bought something worth having."

Conan grinned. "Would you believe that *I* am the dragon-slayer?"

The other's surprise was transparent. "You are a sorcerer?"

It was Conan's turn to be surprised, but he hid it with care. What game was afoot, that Lord Akimos needed a sorcerer? That they were rare in Argos was was one of the few good things the Cimmerian knew about this land so far! Best say something that sounded well, truth or not.

"I have some small power over weapons," Conan said. "I can't say if that helped me with the dragon or not. I've certainly heard that they're creatures of magic, so those powers couldn't do the dragon any good or me any harm."

"Very surely," the robed man said. He looked about him, to see who was within hearing. "Captain—"

"Conan."

"Ah, the same who commanded free lances in Ophir?"

"Your master seems to have spies everywhere."

"He can afford them, and knowledge can bring more wealth. Nor is this true only of merchants. It can be true for you as well."

"What kind of knowledge?"

"Your magic."

"My—" Conan closed his mouth, deciding that what he had heard was really what Akimos had said. This did not mean that neither of them was mad, but it made Akimos even more interesting.

"Yes, your magic," Akimos went on. "You will be richly rewarded, if you use it on behalf of a young lady, a friend of mine direly in need of help."

Conan had to fight the urge to laugh in Akimos's face several times during the merchant's tale. But as the story of Lady Livia's magic-wielding enemies drew to an end, a thought leaped unbidden into his head.

"I'll serve the lady as best I can," Conan said. That at least was the truth. "But I'm captain as well as wizard. These men are oath-sworn to me. I'll not leave them at the mercy of the likes of that guard captain.''

"Your old company can certainly come with you—" Akimos began. Conan let the man babble a welcome, before explaining about the amount yet to be paid on his men's Argossean bond. The merchant's face promptly lost some of its color, and he found himself briefly speechless.

He was not long finding his tongue again. "Of course, Captain Conan. Not all of Lady Livia's foes may strike at her by magic. Good men with steel in their hands may be needed as well. How many of your men were you thinking of bringing?''

"All of them.''

"All?''

"All who wish to remain with the company, and that's a score at least.''

Akimos appeared to be doing sums in his mind. Conan grinned and clapped the merchant on the shoulder, hard enough to make him reel. "Come on, man. Your master's been good for a hundred drachmas. A hundred more won't empty his coffers.''

"A hundred—?''

"Our bonds, and something to put decent clothes on our backs and decent boots on our feet. Lady Livia won't thank any of us if we land on her doorstep looking like the pick of Aghrapur's beggars!''

"No-o-o," Akimos said.

The bargaining went quickly, but put a smile back on Akimos's face. At last the merchant returned to his horse to count out more money. Conan sat down on a handy log and struck it three times with his fist.

From a hollow in the ground under the log, Talouf

arose, brushing wood chips and dirt from his clothes. "Well, Talouf?"

"Well, Captain. If I'd seen that in the bazaar, I'd wonder where he stole what he was trying to sell."

"My thought too. But pretending to be a sorcerer for some wealthy old harridan is no bad way out of here. At least it gets our bond paid and takes us to Messantia. After that—well, being a free lance makes the wits and the hands quick."

"Almost as good as being a thief, eh?"

Conan decided that Talouf was referring to his own previous career, not his captain's. Between lifting other men's purses and bedding other men's wives, Talouf had earned death sentences in more lands than his native Shem.

"We need to send a messenger to the men in the village," Conan said. "Who's best?"

"Vandar."

"Jarenz doesn't need him?"

"He's lame but not crippled. And Vandar would walk through fire for you now. Best put him to work before the fit passes."

"When was the last time you trusted anybody, Talouf?"

"It was on my fifth—no, fourth naming-day—"

Conan made a disgusted sound and rose. "See to the men, Sergeant. I'm going to see if our merchant friend knows a decent wineshop within a day's ride!"

CHAPTER 4

Livia of Damaos lay face-down on the couch in her bath chamber while her maids massaged oil scented with Vendhyan incense into her skin. The air of the chamber was fragrant with the oil and warm and moist from the bath. If she could simply drift off to sleep, and when she awoke find all the problems facing her House a thing of the past—

A familiar knock rattled the door.

"Reza?"

"My lady, there is urgent news."

"A moment."

She sat up and took the lemon-hued robe a maid handed her. A cap pulled hastily over her hair, and she called, "Enter."

Reza entered, with the catlike tread that was not the least remarkable thing about the man, considering his

57

size. He wore his working tunic and a face like a thundercloud.

One look at that face sufficed. The maids gathered the oil jars and fled as if the room had caught fire. Livia wished her dignity permitted the same. But it did not, nor did putting off the hearing of bad news make it any better when it came.

"Lord Akimos is doing us a favor," Reza said heavily. "Or at least that is what the letter says."

"If I may . . . ?" Livia held out her hand, and Reza put the parchment in it.

"No scribe wrote this one," she said. "This is his very own scrawl." She read swiftly, and felt her eyebrows rising and her hair crawling on her scalp.

"How did he hear of the attack?"

"Do you wish me to ask?"

"Was it through Lady Doris, do you think?"

"Most likely."

Livia shook her head. "If we ask, she will know that we are uneasy, and that she has made us so. I would not give her that pleasure. Besides, it may be Harphos's tongue that has wagged, not hers."

Reza's face said what he thought should be done about the young man's tongue. Livia shook her head. "To do anything would be to shame him before his mother. What has he done to deserve that?"

"He has thought himself good enough for you!" Reza burst out. "Atlantis will rise again before that is true!"

"If there is magic afoot in Argos, then who knows what may happen?" Livia said, but she had to smile at Reza's outburst. The man had no children, and with both her father and her keeper-father dead he had begun to keep a fatherly eye on her.

"One of the things that will not happen is Harphos

being a fit husband for you," Reza said doggedly. "Perhaps left to himself he might mend, but will his mother let him out of the nursery while she lives?"

"You may be speaking wisdom," Livia said. "But let us return to Lord Akimos. He speaks of sending us a sorcerer who is also a captain of free lances, or a captain who is also a sorcerer. *With* a score of his company. And not just any hedge-wizard, either. It is the man who slew the river dragon at the Great Bridge."

"There are no river dragons for him to slay in Messantia," Reza said. "And I like not taking a band of strangers among us, whatever magic their captain commands."

"If a sorcerer is attacking us, then a sorcerer may defend us," Livia said. "Nor are sorcerers so common in Argos that we can afford to throw one away like a rotten cabbage. If we must send to Shem or Koth for one, it will take longer and reveal our danger to even more strangers."

"True," Reza admitted. "Then this—Captain Conan—will be allowed into the house?"

"Yes, and even some of his men."

"Not all?"

"Only as many as you think you and the other men can overcome if needful. Nor will they have any secrets from us for long."

"Ah," Reza said. His face seemed to glow, and Livia could swear that his nostrils flared, like an old war horse who hears a distant trumpet.

"Yes. I will trust you to devise ways of ferreting out those secrets." She smiled. "If you cannot, I shall wonder if you were truly a sergeant in Turan, or only a midden-cleaner!"

* * *

Lord Akimos's drachmas did not reach to providing horses for Conan's whole company. They had a five-day march before the walls of Messantia rose white by the bay ahead of them.

It was not one of the easier marches Conan could remember. The roads were splendid, the weather equally so, and the countryside all about rich and inviting. But there was more than one wineshop between the mountain camp and Messantia. In fact, there was more than one wineshop on each day's march.

Keeping his men on the march or at least on their feet taxed Conan's powers and patience to the utmost. By the halfway mark of the journey, he would gladly have left them to drink themselves senseless while he went on to Messantia.. Once he had taken his place in Lady Livia's house, he could summon those sober enough to understand the message when it reached them.

The only flaw in that plan was the Argosseans. Conan had little reason and less instinct to trust them. They would surely find that his men had broken one or several of their fine-spun laws. Then Conan's Company would be back where they had been, and no doubt with Lord Akimos turned against them for spoiling his grand gesture.

The last league to Messantia was all downhill and even men with aching heads and dry mouths could make good time. Conan rode at the rear on a piece of crowbait barely equal to his weight, while Talouf headed the line, leading the company mule. Across the mule's back were sprawled the two men who could not be routed to their feet that morning.

A mounted patrol of Guardians rode up, studied the company and Conan's letter with Akimos's seal, then let them pass. This happened twice more before they reached the Orchard Gate of Messantia, and at the gate-house itself the Guardians dallied until it was well past noon.

"A pox take these mincing children," Jarenz muttered. "What could they do against us if we drew steel?"

Conan wanted to laugh. Some of the Guardians looked old enough to be Jarenz's grandfather.

Talouf shrugged. "I have counted five score of them at this gate alone," the Shemite said. "I would wager that many could do a good deal to twenty free lances who were none of them sober last night."

The walls of Messantia were also enough to sober any man. They were five men high and three men at least thick, apart from the protection provided by the Guardians. Though the streets inside the walls might be paved with gold, any man with his wits intact might still think twice about seeking to breach the walls.

In time they were given a pass, a finer piece of parchment than Conan's old commission as a captain in the hosts of Turan. They were given no directions to the Damaos palace, but how could they lose themselves, in a city not half the size of Aghrapur?

The answer was; far too easily. They contrived to do so thrice at least, and the last time cost them the mule. It seemed they had wandered into an area where folk were allowed only on foot between dawn and dusk.

"It seems we ought to be wanderin' back out of this gilded jakes of a city," muttered one of the men who'd been forced to walk when the mule was confiscated. "They're keepin' the dung off the streets, but puttin' it between their ears!"

Conan was beginning to agree with the man when they finally reached a gate and wall that would have

61

served for most of the cities in Ophir. Lemon trees in bloom barely rose above the gilded spikes on top of the wall. A large bell hung from a silken thong, with a padded hammer on another thong beside it. Conan gripped the hammer and pounded on the bell until its clanging seemed about to raise echoes from the distant mountains.

"Who goes there?" came a voice from inside the gate.

"Captain Conan and his company, to enter the service of House Damaos at the behest of Lord Akimos."

"His seal?"

It was a command. Conan chose to obey, displaying the parchment with its impressive blue wax seal. A moment later the outer gate of ironbound logs opened in response to the command of some unseen sentry. Then, the inner gate of gilded bronze did likewise, with a faint sigh. A path of white gravel ran arrow-straight up to a house of blue and white marble.

House? Palace, rather. No noble in Aghrapur would have refused it as his seat, and the royal palace of Ophir was hardly larger. None of them, however, had standing at their front door the woman who greeted Conan as he led his company up the path.

Wealthy the Lady Livia was, beyond doubt. But harridan? In another forty years, perhaps, but Conan doubted it. With the gods' favor, she would not lose those sea-blue eyes nor that fine carriage, and with those alone she would still turn men's heads. Now, when she had to be younger than Conan himself, she was a woman for whom men might sack cities.

Hair the color of ripe wheat, held in place by combs each worth a noble's ransom, rose atop a perfectly oval face. Her white gown of Khitan silk covered her from throat to ankles, but Conan could read the curves where it stretched tight over breast and hips.

She reached out a long-fingered, cream-skinned hand whose wrist bore a bracelet of gold and tiny rubies, and spoke in a voice like the flowing of a clean spring.

"Welcome to the service of House Damaos, Captain Conan. I am the Lady Livia. Our steward Reza will see to your men."

For the first time Conan became aware that Livia had a shadow, a man grown gray but nearly his own size and with the look of an old soldier about him. He also wore a white robe, but of fine linen with a blue border, and though his belt was studded with seashells it supported a long curved Iranistani dagger.

"Your coming finds us unprepared to fitly quarter all your company," Reza said. "We can find places for ten and yourself. For the rest, we shall provide the price of rooms in a good inn not far from the harbor."

Divide the company and then—what? Suspicion rose in Conan. He crossed his arms on his chest, to keep his hands from the hilts of his blades, and bowed.

"If that is your wish, my lady, then it is our command. But we have lived harder than beggars, on campaign. If we can have tents, we would gladly find a place in your gardens."

"I would gladly give it to you," Livia said. "But if I did, my father's ghost would haunt me and the gardener would fling himself into the sea. No, give us time, and we shall have better than a tent in a garden to offer all of you."

She turned away. Conan knew dismissal when he saw it, and a woman who had made up her mind. He also saw Reza watching him intently, except when the big steward's eyes flickered to right and left. Conan's gaze followed Reza's, and he detected men ready and waiting, thinking they were hidden.

This house might be a trap. But the streets of Messantia were certainly one. For the moment, the company had no clear path of retreat.

But he would find one. Conan vowed that, hoping some helpful gods would listen, but not much caring whether they did or not. If he had to find that path by carving it from the living flesh of Livia's men with his broadsword, he would do it. For his own honor, he could do no less.

"Talouf," he said softly. "Is there a man you can trust, to lead at the inn?"

"Kirgesthes is shaping well, but I really need him—"

"Not half as much as I need you, if we're going to be wrestling serpents in their nests."

"Serpents?" Talouf grinned. "That wench doesn't look much like a serpent, although I'd wager wrestling with her—"

"Is no jesting matter," the Cimmerian said, gripping Talouf's beard and twisting gently. "Remember that, and pass the word to any of the men who may forget."

"Yes, my lord," Talouf said, unrepentant.

"Good. Now, Kirgesthes will lead at the inn, you and I will lead here, and as to the rest we'll let the men draw lots."

That would be fairer. Not to mention that Conan had no idea which men besides Talouf would be more useful in each place, until he had answers to a few questions.

He made another vow, that he would have those answers before another sunset, or else have his men on the way out of Messantia.

* * *

From behind the curtains of gauze Lady Livia watched the ten men chosen for the inn march out the gate. They marched raggedly but kept their eyes roaming about them and their hands close to their well-used steel. A few started to talk, but the sergeant quickly silenced those.

Reza came up silently behind her. It was a measure of his unease that he had not knocked.

"I wish your keeper-father was still alive."

Livia turned and smiled. "Reza, the last time I said that, you told me that wishes were the death of wisdom."

"Also of good soldiers, and it is true. Forgive me, my lady. I meant no insult."

"Reza, you would not know how to insult me if you meditated on the matter for a year. I thank the gods for this. Now, what do you make of our Captain Conan? In truth, I had expected someone your age."

"Free-lancing is a way of life for young men, my lady. By the time a free lance reaches my years, he is usually either retired or dead. Only those lucky in battle but unlucky in loot are still soldiering at fifty."

"I am not sure you will not be soldiering again, if Conan proves no friend to House Damaos. He has the look of a man hard to either deceive or kill."

Reza nodded, his face sour. "Much my own thoughts. But we can either do as we intended, or remain ignorant until Conan choses to tell us the truth. Or shows it to us, by carrying out his master's orders."

In spite of the heat of the afternoon, Livia felt a chill. Even when her keeper-father was fighting for her inheritance in the courts, she had not needed to fear being murdered in her bed. Now she could not sleep easily—at least until Reza had finished his work.

CHAPTER 5

Conan walked in the gardens of the Damaos palace. He wore his sword belted on over a linen tunic in the Argossean style, and carried a long ashwood staff in his hand.

He had been offered sandals, but his soles were no bad substitute for leather. As for the tunic, some of his men scorned it as womanish, but he himself held his peace. It was what free men wore in Argos, where trousers were the mark of the barbarian.

It also left a man free to move against his enemies and wield his weapons. Conan asked no more of any garb, be it breechclout, armor, or royal robes.

As he walked, he listened for any cessation of the cries of the night birds and the *chirr* of insects. He also probed the ground ahead of him with the staff.

Before him spread a patch of lawn that might have been worked by a barber, so neatly trimmed was each blade of grass. Too neatly trimmed, Conan thought, and remembered Reza's warning. He thrust his staff hard into the ground. At the fourth thrust the ground gave way with a soft sigh. There was nothing soft about the clank of iron meeting ashwood, as the expected mantrap below snapped shut on his staff.

Very surely, Reza and his men knew their work. This was not the first cunning contrivance to keep unwanted visitors from disturbing the palace. Conan doubted it would be the last.

Best he learn a little more of Messantia, including secret ways out of the city, and that quickly. When Lady Livia found that he was no more a sorcerer than he was a priest, dismissal from her service was the best he and his men could hope for. She needed twenty more armed men as much as she needed a bout of the flux—

Conan stepped back from the lawn and behind a tree in one flowing movement. The night birds no longer sang, and he now realized they had ceased their song before he sprang the mantrap. From behind the tree he stared toward the wall.

A dark shape appeared, bobbing and weaving as it threw a padded arming doublet over the spikes. Softly, Conan gave the call of the Ophirian black owl. He was about to draw his sword, when the dark shape replied with the same sound. A moment later, Conan was guiding the man who called himself Belgor behind the tree.

"How are you doing at the inn?"

The lean, crop-eared man frowned. "Oh, it's fine enough. Vandar rode in this afternoon. But there's two men who seem to be hangin' from the rafters like bats. Men Kirgesthes says were with that Lord Councilor or whatever he was, up in the mountains."

Lord Akimos's men, at the inn. Watching Conan's men. Waiting for something.

"Have they come to any of our men?"

"Not that I'm rememberin'—no, wait a bit, Captain. It's last night that I saw one of them, talkin' to Douras."

"Does Douras still think he should have been sergeant, in Kirgesthes's place?"

Belgor made a gesture of aversion. Conan glared. "Crom, man, I'm only asking if Douras's tongue is still wagging the way it was on the road!"

"Well, he won't thank me for tellin'—"

"I'll do worse than not thank you if you don't."

"Yes."

The one word seemed to exhaust Belgor's powers of speech, but it was enough for Conan. It seemed that Akimos was doing just what the Cimmerian would have done in his place. Find a discontented man in the ranks of the company and turn him into a spy. Perhaps groom him to lead the company, if the need arose to find someone besides Conan. . . .

Belgor now looked ready to talk more, but the Cimmerian cut him off with a sharp gesture. The night birds were not only silent. Ears sharpened by a dozen hair's-breadth escapes told Conan that some of them were taking flight.

"Back over the wall, and tell Kirgesthes to watch Douras."

"Captain—?"

"Climb the wall, man, or I'll heave you over it and hope you land on your empty head! Did they crop your wits along with your ears?"

Belgor now heard the same as Conan—footsteps approaching through the gardens. The men seemed to be attempting silence, but Conan had heard less noise from elephants in Vendhya. Belgor sprinted for the wall, scrambled up the rope he had left hanging, pulled it up after himself, and vanished down the street side.

Conan drew his stout-bladed Aquilonian dagger and left his sword sheathed. Against these men he wanted surprise, best gained in the shrubbery where a short blade was the master of a long one. Then he settled down to wait.

The tree was not the best of all places to wait that he had seen in the garden. But he was there, and he could wait without moving, as silent as the stepping stones in the reflecting pool a hundred paces nearer the house. The men had to move to close with him, so could not be as silent even had they the art.

It was not a short wait. The men seemed to know at least that they should move slowly, and they had a fair distance to travel. From the rear wall to the rear of the house was more than two hundred paces. In many lands, Conan had seen smaller plots of land supporting whole families.

The men continued their clamorous approach. It seemed as if they *wanted* to be heard. Conan would have set that notion aside, but it had begun to seem that in Messantia nothing was too twisted to be the truth.

Returning to Ophir began to seem less foolish than hitherto. At least there a free lance would know who his enemies were and how to fight them. Also his fate if he lost, so he would have no reason to do other than die sword in hand. In Argos, matters seemed like the boxes Conan had seen in Khitai, where inside each box nestled a smaller one, until in the heart of the whole affair lay something the size of a pea.

Between one breath and the next, silence fell across the garden. Conan had to strain his ears, even to hear the breathing of the men. So that uproar had been a trick! Well, perhaps it was time to teach these tricksters a few things they seemed not to know about Cimmerians and free lances.

Not a leaf stirred as Conan crept toward where he had last heard the men. He knew they had to be behind a rose hedge, but not exactly where. He made a wide half-circle around one edge of the hedge, to come in well behind it. Even in the darkness of the garden, he could then see along its whole length—and he would wager that no Argossean had his own cat's-eyed night sight.

He barely breathed as he crept past the end of the hedge, dagger in hand. He lay flat on the dew-damp grass for a moment, to be sure he remained unseen and unheard. Then he began his crawl again.

As he did, footsteps thudded on the grass to his right. Conan rolled, dagger leaping up like a striking snake. A dark figure rushed in, loomed above Conan, and stretched out empty hands toward the Cimmerian.

Conan saw those empty hands with a heartbeat to spare. He struck with his clenched left fist instead of his steel-laden right hand, and the breath *wssshhed* out of the man. He doubled up, holding his belly, and staggered back into the path of his comrade.

The second man leaped to one side and closed with Conan. That leap cost him time. It might have cost him more, had Conan not seen that the second man's hands were also empty. The Cimmerian rolled on his back, and legs like tree trunks thrust and lifted at the same moment.

The second man rose like one of the fleeing night birds, soaring over Conan. He twisted in mid-air, enough to save skull and neck. He did not save himself from the roses. He crashed down into the man-high tangle of thorn-studded branches.

The silence of the night ended in the man's cry of pain, surprise, and outrage. Springing to his feet, Conan saw lights suddenly blossom on the roof of the house and in hedges and pavilions.

The man in the hedge seemed too entangled and thorn-gouged to be a menace. The first man, however, had regained his feet. As his hand groped toward his belt, Conan punched him again, this time on the jaw. He flew backward so far that he plunged into a reflecting pool. Conan gripped one foot and heaved until the man's head was clear of the water. Then he set his back against the nearest stout tree and cupped his hands.

"Ho, men of House Damaos! Turn out, turn out, turn out! This is Captain Conan! We have thieves in the garden. Turn out, all men of House Damaos!"

He heard the alarm echoing from the garden wall to house wall and back. Then he shifted his dagger, drew his sword, and readied himself to meet whatever might be coming at him behind those lights.

After what seemed half the night, Conan realized that the light bearers were not going to approach him. He saw dark shapes bending over the two senseless men, whispering briefly, then dragging them off. He thought he heard more whispering, but he saw no one. The light bearers might have been ghosts or demons, bearing off the fallen men to snatch their souls from them—

For a moment, the garden seemed full of a darkness that was not of this world. Conan felt his flesh crawling, doubted that there was need of it, but could not be sure. Had he been tricked beyond his worst doubts into serving a house where sorcery reigned and served the treacheries and stratagems Argosseans seemed to love as some men loved wine?

If he had been, he would know for certain before long. At least he would know if Talouf and the others kept their wits about them and remembered the instructions he had given them last night—

From the roof of the house, one of the lights started blinking. Then the other three suddenly went out. From closer to hand, the owl-hoot sounded.

Conan wanted to roar with laughter. Instead, he replied with a hoot of his own. Then he shouted.

"Men of House Damaos! Come out and end your tricks. Come out before I count to ten, or I might just decide to end you!"

Whispers started again, giving Conan a clear notion where the tricksters stood. A couple of men raised their voices loud enough for Conan to make out words. Then someone—it sounded like Reza—spoke a single harsh word. Silence returned.

This time it lasted no longer than a man might take to drink a cup of ale. Conan began to count, and reached five before he heard Reza's voice.

"Very well, Cimmerian—"

"Captain Conan!"

"Very well, Captain Conan. We will come out."

"With your lanterns in hand, and nothing else. The archers among my men have arrows nocked and a clear shot at any of you."

That was the way it was supposed to be. Conan was prepared to wager that Reza would not put the matter to a test.

The big Iranistani was not. As he emerged at the head of half a dozen of his men, Conan realized just how big the steward was. He might be old enough to be the Cimmerian's father, but a grapple with him would be no easy victory.

"Captain Conan," Reza began. "You must explain—"

"I must do nothing of the kind," Conan snapped. "You're the one to do the explaining. Starting now, and leaving nothing out. Including why you were ready to have a pair of your men end up ghosts. They came cursed close, you know, and if I hadn't been quick enough—"

"How much of you is quick, besides your tongue?" a man in the rear shouted.

Reza silenced the man with a glare, but Conan heard the men Talouf had in the bushes shifting about, ready to attack. The Cimmerian stepped forward, until he was just outside sword's reach of the steward.

From this close, he could be in among his opponents before they could move. Then he would have the edge that always came to one man fighting a number not trained as a team.

Also, any witlings among his archers would be slow to shoot, if they might hit their captain. Whatever tricks had been played on him tonight, if blood flowed it would not be he who began the fight.

Reza and his men gave way before the Cimmerian's advance. Conan's eyes flickered from one face to the next, trying to pick the man who might be readiest to draw shortsword or dagger. Reza carried only a staff much like Conan's, but his grip showed that he knew its use as a weapon.

Now the House Damaos men were moving out into a half-circle around Conan. Soon the advantage would pass from the Cimmerian to them. Conan decided that his duty to keep the peace would end in that moment.

As the half-circle formed, a clear light voice sounded from the direction of the house.

"Reza! Captain Conan! Enough! Keep the peace, or it will be the worse for both of you."

In the flickering lanternlight, Conan could have sworn the Iranistani was turning red. To ease minds, the Cimmerian sheathed his dagger. A moment after that, Lady Livia stepped into the light.

She wore a short white tunic that left well-turned legs bare from just below the knee, gold-stamped sandals, and a pale green mantle with a red border and a hood thrown back from her unbound hair. The blue eyes were cold, but she had a smile for both big men as she stepped between them.

"Captain Conan. I think you have the right to know what has been done here tonight, and why."

"And an apology, at least for the sake of my men!" Conan growled.

Reza's reply was one of the fiercest glares. Instead of stamping her foot, as Conan had expected, the lady gripped both men by the wrists. Either could have shaken her off as easily as a fly, but her grip seemed to have the force of an iron shackle.

"Reza, enough. Captain Conan, hear us out first. Then if you feel that you need an apology, it will be given. But I want you to *listen* first."

It seemed to Conan that he had been doing rather too much listening since he entered Argos. It also seemed that Lady Livia might tell him more than some of the others. Certainly, not listening to her could only mean a savage fight, and perhaps not even against his real enemies. It was not in Conan to hold back from a fight, but he did like to know if he was fighting the right people!

* * *

"I did what?" Akimos exclaimed. "Who has been filling you with nonsense?'"

This protest of innocence fell on deaf ears. Skiron glared at the merchant prince.

"I have ways of learning anything that may be known, not given to common men."

"You also seem to have conjured up fancies that are not known to anyone because they are not true."

"Do you deny that you sent a sorcerer to House Damaos? A sorcerer who may choose to oppose rather than aid me?"

Akimos started to laugh. "Skiron, did your—ways, or wine, or whatever talked to you—?"

"These insults are unbearable!"

"If you cannot bear them, you can doubtless find some way of living out your last years without my aid."

"Indeed, there is the fee I would earn, by informing the archons—"

"Of what? Can you say anything they would believe, coming from a man *I* will denounce for practicing unlawful magic?"

The two men stood facing each other across Akimos's table for a moment, like two billygoats on a narrow path. They might wish to fight, but both had seen clearly the long fall into the swift-flowing stream below.

It was the sorcerer who lowered his eyes, and the sense of victory made Akimos magnanimous. With his own hands he poured wine and set out a golden plate of cheese and pastries.

"Come, friend Skiron. You have wearied yourself with your labors for our plans. You need not weary yourself with fear of what exists only in your fancies. Drink, and I will tell you the truth."

"Or as much as it is in you to tell," Skiron grumbled, but he clutched at a piece of cheese like a starving man.

Akimos told of his scheme to have men grateful to him in the bosom of House Damaos. As Skiron listened, ate, and drank, his thin face seemed to gain flesh and lose weariness.

At last he nodded. "Can we trust a Cimmerian's gratitude?"

"We can trust it for part of what we need. As to the rest—I have yet to meet a Cimmerian who knew how to find the jakes when he needed to piss. Conan will never think to ask the questions that would reveal our plans for him."

Skiron made a gesture of aversion. "Then will you still want your men disguised?"

"Are you too weary?"

Skiron glared. "I have all the strength—"

"I meant no insult, Skiron. Truly, if you lack the strength—"

"I can shadowface half a dozen men with ease. More will take time that we may not have."

"That will be enough. House Lokhri would surely hire knifemen off the streets for much of its work. Its own men would be the leaders only. Have you faces for that half-dozen, from the ranks of the Lokhri men?"

"How many times have I gone with you to the Lokhri palace, and endured that cow Lady Doris pretending that she is a bull, and her bleating calf of a son?"

"More than you have enjoyed, I am sure."

"The gods know that is the truth!" Skiron said, gulping wine. "I will not need to go again. Give me two days, and also some knowledge of the size and strength of your chosen men. Then we may go on."

Disguising the attackers on House Damaos as minions of House Lokhri would sow confusion enough. Having Captain Conan letting the attackers pass freely would sow even more. It would probably also end the Cimmerian's place and even life, but one needed only a single arrow if it struck a vital spot.

And the Cimmerian's blood would go some ways toward keeping the peace with Skiron. That, the gods knew, would be no small gain, considering the sorcerer's manners even when he was *not* in fear of his position.

Conan sat at the small ebony table in Lady Livia's dressing room. Reza stood or rather loomed at the door, and the lady herself reclined on a couch also of ebony but inlaid with walrus ivory. She had donned a blue gown, but two long-toed feet and one slender arm were bare.

He sipped at his wine and listened to Reza finish the story of how the men of House Damaos had been set to bait him into a fight, to reveal his true allegiance. Had he slain them, it would have seemed wisest to put him and his men out at once, for they clearly served another master.

Conan listened to this babble for as long as his patience lasted. The wine helped. It made almost every other vintage he had ever tasted seem like vinegar. When Reza broke off to refill the Cimmerian's cup, Conan realized that this was his fourth cup and he felt as if he had been drinking weak ale.

He lifted the cup, drained it in a few swallows, then brought it down with a bang that silenced Reza.

"Enough!" Conan said. "I accept the apologies

you've made and all the ones you haven't made but are thinking of wasting our time with.''

''Now, Captain—'' Reza began, in spite of a warning look from his mistress.

''Reza, take your turn listening or I'm taking my men out of here. I don't know or care where, so long as it's away from this house.''

Conan took a deep breath and spoke quietly when he wanted to roar. ''What made you think the way I fought your men would tell you anything? Did you think I was an ox, to respond to the goad any time you used it?''

Reza seemed beyond speech, but his mistress was of a different fiber. ''Conan, that was indeed an error, and it was mine. I thought—forgive me, but I thought that a Cimmerian—''

''You thought that a Cimmerian was an ox? And no doubt Lord Akimos thought the same?''

Livia nodded, then her full lips twisted into something that might have been a wry grin. ''Captain Conan, that cup was a wedding gift to my mother.''

Conan looked at the wine cup in his hand. It was silver inlaid with turquoise, the metal a finger's breadth thick. Unknowing, he had squeezed the cup as flat as an oyster.

''Well, my lady. Here's a gift to you. Don't think a Cimmerian a fool until he's proved it. Otherwise he may think *you* one, and in Cimmeria fools are set out for the wolves and the blizzards.''

Livia swallowed and nodded, then smiled again. ''I will remember. But you must know this. In Argos we know other folk mostly by their traders, and Cimmeria sends few our way.''

''Then at least don't listen to what others say. Use your own eyes and ears.''

"I will," Livia said. "But consider, if Lord Akimos had done so, where would you and your men be now?"

Conan was still too close to rage to smile back, but he nodded. "Let's call tonight fair fight and no harm done. And what about another cup and some wine in it?"

"Captain, it is late—" Reza began.

"It's cursed near dawn," Conan growled. "But *I* don't want to sleep until we've planned how to deal with Akimos. A man doesn't treat me like a fool to have me do his bidding, not me, not anyone under me." If he had not already crushed the cup, his grip on it would have finished the work.

Livia brought another cup—plain pewter this time—and the wine jug with her own hands. Then she sat, with the gown falling away so that one leg was bare to the knee. It was as shapely as every other part of her that Conan had seen.

"I suppose you will want to bring your men from the inn—" Livia began.

Both Conan and Reza shook their heads. "How many men can Akimos send against us, if he trusts steel more than spells?" the Cimmerian asked.

"Not above three score," Lydia said.

"Then my ten and Reza's fifteen have the edge over any lesser number," Conan said. "We're defending, we know the house, and we won't let ourselves be surprised."

"Conan, you speak like Captain Khadjar," Reza said.

"I served under him for the best part of a year," Conan replied. Reza's face twisted, then turned red.

"Who is Captain Khadjar?" Livia asked.

Reza started a long description of the Turanian captain who had taught Conan much of the art of civilized warfare. After a time, Livia raised a hand.

"I will grant that he is the greatest captain since Kull of Atlantis," she said, smiling. "And I will thank all the gods that a man he taught has come to us. Join me in that, if you wish."

"My lady—"

"Enough, as Captain Conan said not long ago. What of defending the house against sorcery?"

At last Conan could laugh. "My lady, I do have power over weapons, as I told Akimos. I can wield anything made by man, and few men can face me and live. As for spells over weapons or anything else—I couldn't cast one to save Messantia from falling into the Western Sea." His smile faded. "I've never yet met wizard or sorcerer who didn't ruin everything he touched, himself included. They're dung and belong on dunghills."

"I'll pray that you can put any sorcerer in Akimos's service where he belongs," Livia said. "But as to your men—do you fear to warn Akimos, by uniting them under my roof?"

Conan looked at the young woman with new respect. No lessons from Khadjar for her, but a good head for war nonetheless!

The Cimmerian nodded. "Surprise will let us take prisoners, not just beat off the attack. I don't know what the archons say about this kind of game, but I'll wager one thing. Akimos won't like it if we have his men singing like birds to the archons."

They ended by agreeing to put a reliable man with a lantern on the roof of the house. Another reliable man would be posted on the roof of the inn. From there he could see any signals from House Damaos. On the proper signal, the free lancers at the inn would come at a run.

"The gods willing, we can put them in the rear of any unwanted visitors and sweep up the lot," Conan said. "If our luck's out, we can still beat them off. That will make Akimos pause. While he's rubbing his head, it'll be our turn to move."

They toasted this strategy with wine for all, and Conan departed to see to his men.

CHAPTER 6

Once more Conan walked by night in the gardens of the Damaos palace. He was not far from the place of his mock fight two days ago, but he was clad quite differently. He wore boots on his feet, mail under his tunic, and a mace swinging from his belt opposite his broadsword.

He also carried no staff for seeking out mantraps, for there were none to seek. That was Conan's advice, and it had not gone down well with Reza. Indeed, the steward had at first looked like a man called on to drown his children.

"I *want* anyone coming in through the garden to be close to the house before the alarm's given," Conan explained. He tried not to use the tone he would have with a child or a woman—or at least a woman with her wits less in order than Livia.

"Then it will be easier for them to enter," Reza urged.

"Also harder for them to leave," Conan replied. "They'll have to cross all those fine open lawns with my archers and yours sitting on the roof with loaded quivers and lighted torches."

"I suppose the danger is worthwhile," Livia said.

"May my sword and manhood both fail me if it isn't," Conan said. "We don't want to just drive off—whoever comes." Even among themselves, they did not use the term "Akimos's men."

"We don't just want to scare those bog-trolls' sons away. We want to eat them for a midnight snack and throw their bones back in their masters' faces. It's the masters we want to scare, not the men!"

Reza glared at the Cimmerian. No doubt it was the language Conan had used. In spite of everything, Reza seemed to think that his lady's ears were innocent and virginal, and must be guarded from soldiers' language.

Before the steward could speak, Livia nodded. "Yes. I do not want a long, weary battle before House Damaos is safe. As long as we are fighting, I will have few suitors, except those who wish to protect me for a price I may not wish to pay."

Conan had heard of Lady Livia's present crop of suitors. One matter where he and Reza saw alike: none of them were worthy of her. If they kept to their own houses for a time, House Damaos would lose nothing thereby.

But Conan knew that it was not his place to say *that*. "Place" was a word he'd learned well since he came to Argos; it seemed to loom over a man's daily uprisings and downsittings as "face" did among the folk of Khitai.

83

After a few days he had learned that it meant mostly sitting and listening to others do the talking. As often as not, they told him more than they wished him to know. So he had less quarrel with the idea of "place" than he had expected.

"You're the judge of your own value, my lady," Conan said. "I'm just a soldier. I judge the value of frightening an enemy into being foolish. I also judge the value of not getting any of my men snapped up in those mantraps."

"Your men should know the grounds by now," Reza grumbled.

"Some do, some don't," Conan said. "The ones from the inn surely don't. Besides, if there's a spy in the house"—Reza coughed and Lydia made a silencing gesture—"he'll send word that the mantraps are gone. The garden's safe. Any attack may come over the walls and walk up to the house where our men on the roof can practically piss on them!"

Livia smiled, then giggled, then laughed out loud. It was a good laugh for a man to hear, just as the lady herself was good to look at.

"I wish we really could do that," she said at last. "Can you imagine what the poor fools would say to their master when they went home? If they dared go home, and didn't just run off to Kush and change their names?"

Reza finally smiled. "Well, Conan, once again I learn how well High Captain Khadjar taught you."

"Let's not sell the wool before we've bought the sheep," Conan said. They all drank to a fine fat sheep wandering in within the next few nights.

* * *

The black-owl cry sounded from the roof of the palace. Silent as a hunting tiger, Conan hurried to the meeting place for messengers. Vandar ran up as the Cimmerian settled his back against a tree.

"We have armed men in sight from the roof."

"Any badge?"

In most cities, it would have been work to tell men from apes at night, let alone read house badges. But in the wealthy quarters at least, torches lit Messantia's streets bright enough to read the stamped date on an Aquilonian tenth-crown.

"None. But the Damaos man said that they had the look of Guardians to them."

"Erlik bugger the Guardians!"

Conan could endure a city whose streets did not turn into jungles between sunset and sunrise. He'd given over the profession of thief some time since, when he saw it led only to short rations and a short life. But the last thing he wanted tonight was the Guardians inviting themselves to a personal fight, when he was ready to meet his enemies with his own strength and steel.

Vandar shrugged. "Reza's at the gate. If he smells a bad fish—"

From inside the palace, a shrill scream tore into the night. Conan and Vandar whirled, swords leaping free in a single gesture. The scream came again, and found an echo from another part of the house.

The two men ran for the house. Conan stopped twice to give the hunting cry of a leopard, the signal to the lantern-bearer on the roof. As he caught up with Vandar by a splendid marble statue of a nude woman, Conan saw the lantern beginning to wink. Now, if the watcher on the inn's roof was just half as sober as he should be—

A woman wearing only a night shift ran from the bushes, eyes wide but unseeing. Conan held out a massive arm in her path. She struck it and rebounded as if she had struck the branch of an oak tree. Then she collapsed, sobbing.

Vandar knelt and shouted in her ear. "What's happening, you witless sow? Answer, or I'll—"

Conan gripped the boy by the collar of his tunic and pulled him upright. Then he gripped the woman by the arm and did the same. "What *is* happening in there?" he asked, more gently.

The woman gaped, then shook her head like a horse beset by flies. "Sorcery again! Oh, we thought we'd seen the last of it. But it's abroad again. Worse than before. Oh, sir, if you've any magic in you at all—"

Conan shifted his sword to his left hand and tucked the woman firmly under his right arm. As he did, her shift caught on a bush and tore free.

So Conan reached the palace to greet Lady Livia with sword in one hand and a naked woman under the other arm. The head of House Damaos was herself clad only in her night shift and her face was milk-pale, but she managed a smile when she saw Conan.

"I thought you were one for keeping your hands off the women of the house, Captain."

"Not when they run to me babbling of magic. Is that tame sorcerer at work again?"

Livia nodded. "Lights, sounds, foul smells, jars and barrels cracking and leaking. All in the cellar, for now. I've ordered everyone out of—"

"Gods, woman!" Conan roared. "That's just what our enemies want!" He dropped the woman unceremoniously to the grass and took the stairs two at a time.

Vandar was hard on his heels as they thundered through the door.

"Which way to the cellar?" Conan bellowed.

A manservant pointed, with a shaking hand. "There. But demons are loose—"

"Demons fly away with *you*!" Vandar shouted. "Hedge-magic is for children! Stand aside, and let *men* into the cellar."

Conan was glad to hear Vandar's faith in him, but facing magic was still no pleasure. A cold hand gripped his heart briefly as he faced the dark stairway, then passed as he plunged down it. Vandar followed, and after him four Damaos guards, two with torches.

They hardly needed the torches. The light in the cellar might be magical, but it was real enough. Rose and crimson, turquoise and emerald, it danced and flared from every metal object, even the hoops and barrels. It distorted objects and distances, but it also showed obstacles underfoot. Conan and his men left the stairs at a dead run.

"Where's an entry to the tunnels?" he whispered to the nearest Damaos man. The man clutched his sword with both hands, waved it in front of him as if to exorcise the lights, and said nothing.

The rearmost torchbearer called, "Never heard of one, not in this house."

"No," said the other torchbearer. "But I've heard of strange sounds and smells and sometimes a wind, near the northwest corner of the wine cellar."

Conan thanked the gods that someone had at least the wits of a flea, and led the way toward the wine cellar. They found it ankle-deep in wine from leaking casks and jars. Conan stopped on the threshold and thrust his sword into the wine.

As he did, he noticed that in a far corner of the chamber the surface of the wine was rippling. A breeze seemed to be blowing across it, growing stronger as Conan watched. A breeze, blowing from the corner of the cellar.

Conan urgently waved his men back. As they began their retreat, a rumble and the scream of metal on stone filled the cellar. As the scream rose to tear at the ears and seemed about to sunder the earth underfoot, the magic lights died.

So did every other light in the cellar, including the torches of Conan's party and the few surviving torches in sconces on the walls. Conan flattened himself against the nearest pillar.

Now he saw a section of the cellar wall turning slowly, until a narrow gap opened. One by one, men slipped through the gap. Men mostly ragged, some half naked, but all with serviceable steel in their grimy, callused hands.

By the time a dozen had come through, the Cimmerian's comrades had seen what was happening. Somehow they had the wits to remain silent. Prodding gently with his sword, Conan urged them all back toward the stairs. By the time the last of them departed, the cellar held a good score of invaders.

Conan felt at his belt for his flint and steel, then measured distances with his eyes. If his memory was not playing him false and these visitors spent even a little more time rallying after their journey through the tunnels beneath the city. . . .

The visitors began to move as Conan reached the barrel he sought. He gripped the rim, wheeled on one foot, and brought the other booted foot crashing into the bung. The bung not only started, the barrel itself was sprung in a dozen places.

The crash of the Cimmerian's kicks stopped the invaders in their tracks. They looked about them, trying to judge direction and distance. None of them had Conan's night sight, so none of them saw him turn, shielding his flint and steel with his massive body. A spark flared, tinder blazed, and the blazing tinder dropped into the firewine pouring from the breached barrel.

Firewine did not travel well. Few outside Argos had ever heard of it, let alone drunk it. After one cup, Conan was ready to leave it to the Argosseans. But while it might lack flavor, firewine had one virtue very useful to the Cimmerian at this moment. Exposed to an open flame, it would blaze up like liquid tar.

The firewine Conan had let loose was so mixed with common wine that it was slow to catch fire. For a long breath, Conan wondered if the common wine had drowned his flame.

Then a blue glow like a will-o'-the-wisp spread across the cellar floor. It began where Conan had cast in the timber, but crept steadily toward the men, rising higher as it went. By the time it reached them, the glow had become actual flames, rising as high as a man's knee.

The men did not stand and wait for the flames to reach them. They howled, screamed, and clawed their way toward the walls or the door. Without striking a blow, Conan judged he had taken the fighting heart out of half the men.

The other half were of stouter stuff, or perhaps feared something more than the flames of firewine. They swarmed forward, splashing through the wine and the flames, cursing and shouting as they came,

In a moment they were all around Conan. He set his

back to the nearest wall and laid about him with his broadsword. None of the men seemed particularly expert with their steel, or perhaps it was only that they were in one another's way. It certainly took Conan no great time to have three foes down and two more wounded past fighting.

The remaining five were enough to keep even a Cimmerian's sword fully at play. He wove a veil of steel before him, thinking that perhaps he had sent his comrades to the rear a trifle hastily.

He also heard at last the warcries the men were shouting. It was ''Onward, ever to battle,'' the cry of House Lokhri.

The House that was courting Lyvia, sending armed men against her? That made as little sense as anything Conan had ever encountered, and in his twenty-three years he had seen more of the world's madness than most men twice his age.

Unless they were planning an abduction? Perhaps. If so, best he finish off these men or at least confine them in the cellar, and see to matters elsewhere. Conan had no doubt there would be more than enough of such matters.

In the next moment it seemed that it might be the men who finished off Conan. A furious attack by the leader drove Conan hard against the wall. The man gripped the Cimmerian's sword arm with a mail-gloved hand and twisted.

Conan's arm snapped forward, and the leader flew backward, knocking down one of his comrades. His head met a pillar with a sodden crunch. He slid down to join the other man in the wine.

But the movement left Conan's grip on the sword's hilt weakened for a moment. In that moment a overhand cut with a tulwar struck sparks from the steel and the sword from the Cimmerian's hand.

In their next and last moments, Conan's opponents learned that a Cimmerian disarmed was not a Cimmerian helpless. A handy barrel stave crushed one man's knee. The other two gave way.

Now Conan had time to grip a wine barrel. Full, even his strength could not have lifted it. But feasting and battle had drained most of its contents. He heaved it aloft, then flung it. It was more than heavy enough to knock both remaining enemies off their feet into the wine and hold them under until they drowned.

Conan knelt in the wine, one hand on his dagger, and groped with the other hand until it met his sword hilt. After shaking the wine off the blade, he used the mace to stave in several more wine casks. Two were common wine, one was firewine.

The firewine fed the flames, and the common vintage raised the level in the cellar. Conan watched as the wine overflowed the sill of the secret door and began rushing down into the depths beyond. A moment later he heard a chorus of screams.

He had thought of closing the door, to bar the path of any further enemies waiting in the tunnels. Now it seemed that the flood of burning firewine would do the work as well.

Conan backed away from the wine-drowned cellar. The blue flames of the firewine now lit it clearly, showing the face of the fallen leader. There was something uncanny about that face, too. . . .

Conan could have sworn that the leader's face was pale and freckled, his hair light almost to fairness. A Bossonian, Aquilonian, or even Vanir, no doubt.

Yet now the face had darkened, the hair likewise, and

it was not from burning or smoke. The man seemed almost as dark as a Kushite, or one with kin in the Black Kingdoms.

Conan told himself that it was a trick of the light and his having other matters on his mind. But the chill knowledge that unknown sorcery lurked close at hand tightened his grip on his sword as he rejoined his comrades.

Vandar met Conan. "We locked the door to the rest of the cellar. If any had passed us, they would have gone nowhere."

"Aye," the second torchbearer said. "Not that any came, save one. He ran at us, the same moment a maid tumbled down the stairs. What she had been about, I can wager, for she was as bare as a babe."

Vandar put his arm around a slim figure hardly more than a girl, now clad in the shirt of a man twice her size. "Indeed. The son of a Stygian must not have ever seen a woman, for he goggled and gaped until Gebro came up behind him with a mace." He kicked a bound and gagged figure on the floor, and got a stifled grunt for reply.

"That's one prisoner, at least," Conan said. "Good work." He turned to the maid. "How go matters above?"

The girl drew herself up, which displayed to advantage her womanly figure in the wet shirt. "*I* had other things on my mind, until suddenly—ah, he had to run off to fight witches or wizards or swamp demons or whatever. I came straight down here, and since then I know only what these men do." She nestled back into Vandar's arms, and the lad grinned.

"Very well," Conan said. "I'd best go up and—"

This time they heard few screams in the din upstairs,

and much shouting. Also many cries of "Onward, ever to battle."

Conan sprang to the stairs, Vandar after him. "Watch the cellar," he shouted over his shoulder. "If a handful comes through, fight and call for help. If there's more, come up and close the door after you. The firewine may hold them back until we settle matters upstairs, anyway."

The Cimmerian was halfway up the stairs when he saw that the maid was following them.

"Crom, girl! It's safer down there!"

"I am seventeen, Captain. Do not call me a girl. And I must find Psiros. He—"

"Is probably too cursed busy staying alive to think about a wench," Vandar grumbled. Clearly he had thought the maid smitten with him, and was jealous of her seeking her lover.

Conan briefly considered knocking their empty heads together and leaving them on the stairs. Then someone at the head of the stairs flung the door open.

"The sorcerer!" he screamed, and started pushing the door shut. Conan covered the remaining steps in a single leap, gripped the man's arm, and heaved. It slid into the gap between door and jamb, as the man's comrades flung themselves against the door.

The man screamed like a score of demons at once. Conan, his shoulder already against the door, felt the man's comrades waver. He threw all his weight against the door, and felt it opening.

All at once resistance vanished. The massive iron-bound oak flew open, crashing against the wall, scything down several men in its path. A swordsman ran at Conan. The Cimmerian parried the downcut with his mace, saw that the man wore the white armband of House Damaos, and roared in his ear.

"Ho, you fool! Friend, friend, friend!"

Half dazed, the man stepped back, just in time to take a shortsword in his belly. The attacker had to turn half away from Conan to free his sword. The Cimmerian's broadsword split his skull from the crown to the bridge of his nose.

Then came another of those spaces when Conan had to weave a veil of steel before himself, against opponents too numerous to count and too skilled to be slighted. He was vaguely aware that Vandar had come up to stand beside him, and the girl—woman, if she insisted!—stood behind Vandar.

It took some time for even Conan's stout arm to turn his opponents into bleeding corpses or fleeing survivors. As he became aware of fewer foes before him, the Cimmerian also became aware of a vast figure looming up in the foes' rear.

This he needed even less than a bloodthirsty wench—an opponent nearly his own size, and to all eyes fresh, when he himself—

"Captain Conan!"

"Reza?"

"The gate is closed. I left enough men in the gatehouse to keep it that way, and came inside with the rest."

Conan got inside a final man's guard, laid his arm open to the bone, then drove him back against the wall and set the sword point at his throat. The broadsword was no thrusting weapon, but the point still sent blood trickling down to join the sweat on the man's lean body.

"Do you yield? Or do I push this in?"

"I—"

Reza reached over Conan's shoulder, clutched the man's hair, and slammed his head back against the wall. The shreds of bloody tapestry hanging there were no padding for such a blow. The man slumped bonelessly to the floor.

"There's another prisoner downstairs," Conan said. "And I saw something—"

Reza held up his hand for silence. Conan held his tongue, but heard nothing except the dying uproar of the battle in the house.

"That comes from the north staircase," Reza said. "Come on!"

Conan did not argue. As they set off, he asked, "What's up the north staircase?"

"A way to block the way to the roof, from the lady's chambers."

If the house was openly attacked, Lady Livia was to gather the women and the men unfit for battle in private chambers. The entrance to them could be guarded by two men against many. A spiral stairway led from the suite to the roof, where the archers were posted. But if the attackers made their way to the upper stairway quickly, they might yet snatch victory, or at least hostages for their own safety.

No doubt the Guardians would come to settle matters according to their notions in their own good time. But Conan now feared that their coming would not save even the lady of House Damaos, let alone a score of innocents who had trusted to her protection and his.

Fury and offended honor drove Conan ahead of Reza. He was still in the lead as they stormed up the north staircase. The big Iranistani drew level with the Cimmerian as they reached the top.

"I know the way better than you," Reza said. "And

95

I guard the honor of House Damaos.'' He sheathed his tulwar and unslung from his broad back a two-handed mace. It looked well used, and told Conan that Reza must have served in the very pick of the irregulars, the Band of Haruk. Alone in the hosts of Turan, they were trained to fight both mounted, with the bow and lance, and afoot, with the tulwar and mace. It would be no dishonor to let such a man be first into this fight.

"Leave a few for me, Reza."

"The lady would pluck me beardless if I did not, Cimmerian. Never fear!''

The two big men stormed up the stairs, drawing their followers up behind them like buckets from a well. At the top of the stairs, Reza sent four of the Damaos men to search the side chambers.

"Take prisoners if you can, but keep yourselves whole and save our own people before everything!''

The door to the second stairway to the roof was easy to pick out. Half a dozen armed men guarded it, looking in all directions at once. At their feet lay the two Damaos guards, in pools of their own blood.

A wildcat's screech tore at Conan's ears. The girl from the cellar leaped forward, snatching a dagger from inside her shirt. The invaders gaped at this apparent madwoman rushing upon them.

They were too busy gaping to notice Conan hard upon the madwoman's heels. All the gods forbid that a slip of a girl beat him into a battle!

His sword whined, reaching out over the girl's head like a deadly tongue. The tongue licked at a man's head, and suddenly the man was falling, with no face. The girl leaped on another man's back, clawing at his eyes with one hand, stabbing wildly with the dagger in the other.

The remaining men had the craft to give way before Conan. Doubtless they hoped to draw him forward, then close in behind. Their hopes were in vain, for as they began that maneuver Reza came up.

The Iranistani steward was not as fast on his feet as Conan, but made up for this when he finally reached his enemies. The great mace whirled, light blazing from its polished head. Then the polish vanished under clotting blood, as the mace crushed skulls and ribs, shattered knees and hips, and ruined limbs with awful speed.

Reza and his mace wrought such havoc, indeed, that Conan and the others found themselves short of opponents. From the sounds floating down the stairs, however, this could be cured on the roof.

"Follow me!"

Conan had been swift to close in the hall. Now he seemed to fly up the winding stairs. Halfway up an arrow cracked into the stone by his head and bounced off downward. A few steps farther up lay a body, an arrow between its ribs. Oozing blood made the stairs slippery, but Conan was still on his feet when two living men rolled down the stairs, locked in a death-grapple.

Conan waited until the man without the armband was uppermost. Then he gripped the man by one arm and his hair, heaved him off his opponent, and slammed him against the stone. The man went limp, but Conan thought he could see breathing.

He had no time to be sure, though, for the uproar from the roof was reaching a climax. As Conan reached the head of the stairs, he saw the archers backed into one corner against the chimneys, defending themselves as best they could with shortswords and knives. Several were already down, likewise several of their opponents.

As long as the archers were too busy at close quarters to shoot, the gardens were a free path for the enemy, in or out.

Conan ran to the edge of the roof, nearly tumbling over the edge into the branches of an apple tree. Everyone he could see in the garden was running frantically toward the walls. The invaders had the edge in numbers, but their pursuers of House Damaos were driving them like leaves in an autumn wind.

Conan whirled, ready to free the archers for long-range work. He found that Reza and the rest of their party had already come up to do that. A seething mass of bodies surrounded the chimneys, hacking, screaming, and clawing at one another.

As Conan closed, the mass spewed out a tall fair-haired man with a long mustache. He took one look at the blood-splattered Cimmerian and darted aside.

"Stop him!" came a shout from within the mêlée. "The one with the mustache, he's the leader!"

Conan's sword sliced air a hand's-breadth from the leader. Instead of riposting, he flung his weapon down. Then he sprang on to the coping stones and hurled himself into the air. When Conan looked down, the man lay sprawled on the garden stairs, his head at an impossible angle to his neck.

Desertion by their leader took the heart out of the remaining invaders. They could not cry for quarter loudly or quickly enough. It took much shouting and a few smart blows for Conan and Reza to persuade their men to grant that quarter.

The battle on the roof was the invaders' last gasp. While the archers were otherwise occupied, most of them still free and fit to run did so. The gatehouse being held by Reza's men, the one way to safety lay over the wall. Most of them took it.

It was not long before the only invaders in sight were the prisoners sitting bound by the chimney, and the bodies draped over the wall or sprawled in the garden. Reza returned to the main floor, to see to matters there, while Conan descended to Lady Livia's chambers to recount the victory.

He found the lady binding up a long gash in an elderly manservant's leg. Her arms were bare and red to the elbows, and her hair hung lank down either side of her sweaty face. But she had a smile for Conan as he bowed.

"You do that so well now that you might be an Argossean born."

"Thank you, my lady." He told the tale of the fight, as well as he and Reza knew it.

"You do not know who sent these men?"

Conan shrugged. "I heard the warcries. But they might have been as false as those faces."

Livia nodded. "The spell of the shadowface was one of the first to be banned in Argos. If I had used it for murder, I too would be careful to cover my tracks."

"I'm not so bad a tracker," Conan said. "With your ladyship's permission, I'd ask a few of the prisoners some questions."

"And if they refuse to answer?"

Conan shrugged again. "How long they refuse depends on what you let me do to them."

Livia swallowed and stared hard at Conan. After a moment she seemed to understand there would be no appeal from the judgment in the warrior's cold blue eyes. Her head jerked.

"The law is strict about torture. But it is also strict

about invading another's house, to rob and maim and murder! What must be done, you have my permission to do.''

"Thank you, my lady.''

The Cimmerian turned away, weary but satisfied. He was serving a mistress who knew that in war knowledge was half of victory.

CHAPTER 7

Lady Livia sat on her bed, holding a gold plate on her lap and sipping from a wine cup resting on the floor. Most of the furniture in her chambers had been pushed into barricades, save for her night table. That was now below in the kitchen, where Kyros the Healer used it to hold his medicines and instruments.

What Kyros needed from the Damaos palace, he would have. Snatched from his bed by Livia's messenger, he had come at once, himself and a discreet servant. He would know or guess what had happened, for few houses in Messantia had many secrets from Kyros. But what he knew would never pass his lips, for gold or torture or magic.

From the outer chamber came a long wall, followed by sobbing. Some wounds were beyond Kyros' healing. He could not raise the dead, nor make less grief-stricken those whose lovers lay beneath blankets in the wine cellar.

The voice of one of Livia's maids cut through the girl's wailing, with comforting words, firm and not falsely reassuring. Both lady's maids had weathered this second attack far better than the first, an example to all the women of the house and even some of the men.

She would have to see about good marriages for one or both of them before long. She had no illusions that many of her old servants would be welcomed by most husbands. One lady's maid, a cook or two, perhaps grooms and gardeners if her new house had short service—that would be the end of it. As for taking Reza—as well ask for an archonship—

The maid broke off, and Livia wrapped her robe more tightly over her shift, as someone knocked at the outer door. A moment later she heard a familiar deep voice, and then an almost equally familiar pantherlike tread.

"Good morning, Captain Conan."

The Cimmerian looked toward the window. The sky was paling for dawn. "Good morning, my lady. We have finished with the prisoners."

"Did you—was it hard to make them talk?" She found that the word "torture" would not come to her lips. She despised herself for such squeamishness, the more in that Conan would surely do so and she found she greatly wished his good opinion.

"Crom, no!" Conan said, genuinely astonished. "I didn't have my wits knocked out in the fighting last night, to go torturing Argossean citizens. Not that most of them do Argos much credit, my lady. But—"

Livia took a deep breath. "If you did not torture them—"

"What did we do? Simple enough. I told them that

if they wanted to die as whole men instead of eunuchs, they'd talk and talk fast. Then I led one of them to one room, and a man of mine who can imitate anything or anybody to another.

"I had my man scream like a man being gelded. Meanwhile, I visited one of the corpses and borrowed his—what he no longer needed. After my man had screamed himself hoarse, I went back to the prisoners with my little token. After that, they all wanted to talk at once."

Livia gripped the plate with both hands, but her fingers seemed to lack strength. The plate slid off her lap and spattered oil and bits of fish on the rug. Conan knelt gracefully and picked it up, then handed her the wine cup. For a moment their fingers touched. From that touch fire seemed to run up Livia's arm to her throat, so that for a moment she could not swallow.

When she could speak, she said, "So they talked. What did they tell you?"

Conan was brief but left out nothing she wished to know. As she saw his massive shoulders sagging and smelled the dried sweat and blood—surely that of other men!—on him, she realized that even this iron Cimmerian could be weary.

"Well, Conan, 'thank you' is only words and poor ones at that," Livia said at last. "When I have my wits about me a trifle more, I will find some better reward, for you and your men.

"Now we must see about preparing the house for the visit of Lady Doris and Lord Harphos—"

Conan interrupted her only by clearing his throat, but it was still an interruption. Livia frowned.

"Forgive me, Lady Livia, but I think you ought to send a messenger to the House of Lokhri and tell them to come another day. Tomorrow at least. The day after that would be even better.''

Livia sought to keep an ungracious chill from her voice. She knew that she had not succeeded, from the look on the Cimmerian's face. Like a badger in his hole, he was digging in for a fight.

''I know it will help, to make them think nothing can put us out. But our men need rest. *You* need rest. Then we need to search the palace and grounds. Somebody may have gone to earth, maybe by accident, maybe by design. Suppose he jumps up this afternoon and puts a knife in Harphos?''

Livia nodded, for all that her head wanted to settle on her chest and stay there. ''But—Lady Doris will use her knowledge of what happened to us.''

''Let her!'' Conan snapped. ''I'd like to show her the bodies! Maybe that'll scare her enough to loosen her tongue. Something about her made our enemy think we'd believe she'd try carrying you off. I'd like to learn what that something is.''

He was speaking sense, but it was from a great distance, as though she was at the bottom of a deep well and he at the top. She felt his eyes on her, then he stepped forward and his strong arms were around her. Not embracing her as man to woman, but lifting her onto the bed like a sick child, then stretching her out, covering her with her robe. . . .

Somewhere in the midst of this, he must have shouted for her maids, because they both came in. Their anxious faces were the last thing she remembered—that, and her murmuring. ''Send the messenger, Captain Conan. Lady Doris can wait. . . .''

* * *

As he watched the House Lokhri caravan pour through the Damaos gates, Conan would have gladly let Lady Doris wait a month. Her men would be all over the grounds like a tribe of monkeys. By the time they left, any remaining traces of the attack two night ago would be as hard to find as the bones of Atlantis.

Conan and Reza had done what they could. Any of the House Lokhri men who wandered in the garden would be followed, from a discreet distance but followed nonetheless. All would be entertained as royally as the palace's stocks of food and wine allowed, to keep them busy and perhaps loosen their tongues.

Nor would they find much to tell them that the palace had recently seen a desperate battle. Everything damaged in the battle had been either put to rights or removed. Every space large enough to hide a lurking daggerman had been searched and either guarded or sealed.

"We've done our best, the gods know," Conan told Reza, as they sat over watered wine and barley cakes before going to bed, just at dawn. "If the gods care, they may reward us by keeping Lady Doris's lips sealed. If they don't, we can still trust to this." He slapped the hilt of his sword.

Conan remembered the steward nodding heavily, but looking pained. The Cimmerian wondered if the steward could be jealous of the new man's strong position in the house where the Iranistani had reigned supreme for years. Conan had seen such things come to blood in noble households.

If that happened this time, some of the blood might be his. Certainly no one would gain but Lord Akimos. So he would keep his tongue between his teeth and his hand away from his sword hilt when Reza was about, and save both for the fight against the real enemies of House Damaos.

Now the Lokhri caravan was entirely within the gates. Conan watched one man dismounting from a mare laden with gilded harness weighing almost as much as her rider. The man's attempt at a graceful leap turned into a graceless sprawl into a freshly manured flowerbed. He rose with neither his dignity nor his clothes the better for the fall.

Lady Livia stepped forward to stand beside Conan. She wore a gown that could be called plain only in the way that a piece of pure gold is plain. White silk with a pale pink border and bound with a sash of the same color, it set off alike her height, her graceful figure, and her commanding carriage.

Livia, Conan decided, should have been born to some royal house and destined to reign over mighty realms. She was altogether wasted on this city of merchants and their inky-fingered clerks!

"Greetings, Lady Doris, Lord Harphos," Livia said. "Forgive our message of yesterday and our scant hospitality today. All has not been well with us."

Lady Doris opened her wide mouth, but could not command her full red lips to form words. It was a fine enough face, although a trifle too plump for Conan's taste, and the same could be said of the woman's figure.

It was only then that Conan noticed the gangling boy—no, man, for all his awkwardness—standing beside the woman. In spite of his fine blue tunic and gold-worked sandals, he seemed as much at her beck and call as any servant.

That was the Cimmerian's first notion. Then he saw that the eyes of the man—he must be Harphos—were roaming about the house and gardens. Not vacantly, like the idiot he seemed, but with purpose—the purpose of finding anything unusual or out of place. Conan had seen such eyes in the faces of accomplished thieves as they studied a house they intended to rob.

"I understand that all has not been well," Lady Doris said. Her voice set Conan on edge, like the sound of a good sword beating on rock. "But I do not understand why. Your message said little. Has the sorcerer struck again?"

The way she said "sorcerer" was in itself an insult. Conan saw Livia's nostrils flare. So did Harphos.

"Mother, she—ah, Lady Livia—she could hardly put all the story in a message. I mean—anybody might have seen it, and then—"

"Indeed," Doris interrupted. Harphos's mouth remained open for a silent moment before he closed it. Conan saw him flushing like a boy. It began to seem to Conan that Harphos had more sense than he let show—or that his mother let him show. It would be no bad idea to speak to the man alone, if one didn't have to burrow under Lady Doris's skirts to find him!

"That is quite true," Livia said. "Therefore, I would bid you enter my house. What we must say is not for everyone's ears."

"There is no one about, save the sun in the sky," Doris said.

"But the sun is hot," Livia said smoothly. "Our words may grow heated enough without that."

"Indeed?" the older woman said. Her heavy black brows twisted, as did her lips.

Conan thought he saw Livia nod slightly. "My lady, you insult this House," he said. "Do you fear for your safety within?"

107

Doris looked outraged. "Who is this hulking oaf of a—?"

"Captain Conan is a free lance, and he and his men are serving House Damaos," Livia said, slicing the outrage like a silver knife cutting an apple. "Without his aid, I doubt not that the plan of whoever sought to carry me off would have succeeded." Her voice left no doubt of her suspicions.

Once again Doris was speechless. Fortunately Harphos had the wits to see his opportunity—not that he could be without practice in that, Conan thought.

"Mother, I cannot imagine any danger to you from such an old and honorable House. If you wish to enter, I will see to the servants. Who would you take with you?"

Doris seemed to realize that standing there with her mouth open was handing victory to her opponent on a platter. She rattled out a half-dozen names. Harphos turned to go.

Conan did his best bow. "My lady, with your permission, I would accompany Lord Harphos, to see to the Lokhri servants' comfort."

Livia nodded. Doris looked as if she would have rather left her son at the mercy of a snake, but her hostess was holding out one slim arm. She had no choice but to take it, and vanish through the great doors into the shadows of the entryway.

Conan did not wait to see the women go. He was already on his way down the steps, striding so quickly that Lord Harphos nearly stumbled trying to keep up with the Cimmerian. After that, Conan slowed his pace. The young man had to be kept sweet-tempered if his tongue was to be loosened without the aid of wine.

Not that Conan would scruple to use the wine if

needed. But even a fool like Harphos would be wary of too many cups too swiftly poured.

The two noblewomen were alone together for the greater part of the afternoon. By the time Doris reappeared, Conan was certain of two things. One was that Lord Harphos had a very hard head or a very tight mouth or perhaps both. The other was that the young man was much less of a fool than he seemed—or *wished* to seem.

Why Harphos wished this, Conan did not know. His experience of noble houses told him that there might be a dozen different reasons. Picking which would be guessing—and Lady Livia was not paying him wages as a soothsayer.

The wine he had drunk to stay level with Harphos swirled in Conan's head as he mounted the stairs to Livia's chambers. As he reached the head, a man passed him at a brisk pace, a man in Guardian's armor with the badge of the Chief Archon on his breastplate and helmet.

A moment later, Conan heard the sounds of a woman sobbing from within the chambers. At that sound, the Guardian broke into a run. He was down the stairs and out the door before Conan could shout for the guards to halt him. Conan cursed the man, then knocked on the door.

One of the lady's maids answered it.

"Oh, Captain Conan. My mistress would be alone for now. She will send—"

"I send for you now, Captain," came a voice barely recognizable as Livia's. "And Sherma—send for Reza."

"My lady—"

"Now!"

Conan heard glass shatter, then more sobs. The maid hurried out the door, nearly as fast as the Guardian. Conan pushed the door open and entered Livia's chambers.

"My lady, you sent for me?"

Livia raised bloodshot eyes, blew her nose, and nodded. "Forgive me, Captain. I should not have been so weak, but . . ."

If Lady Doris was responsible for this, Conan vowed that he would visit the woman, turn her over his knee, and spank her until her hindquarters were as red as Livia's eyes. If that didn't improve her manners—

"Captain, Lady Doris denies that she had anything to do with the attack. I did not doubt her in that matter. But she also refuses to say a single word about who might wish to make trouble between our Houses!"

Conan frowned. Drunk or sober, Lordling Harphos also had said little. Some of that little, however, made Conan wonder if he was not more concerned with justice than his mother seemed to be. Perhaps it was only an act, one that he expected to deceive a great brute of a Cimmerian. But if it was not, if Harphos was seriously interested in courting Livia on his own terms and not his mother's—something might be made of that.

Meanwhile, Conan judged there was more troubling his mistress than the closed mouth of Lady Doris. He brought water and a clean towel, and by the time Reza appeared Livia had washed her face.

She sounded almost her usual self as she faced the two men. "I sent a petition to the archons, to ask for a questioning of our captives and an inquiry to Lord Akimos. I hoped that Lady Doris would join with me in that petition. It is even more to her profit than to mine, to clear her name.

"The archons have refused the petition. They claim that while our House was unlawfully invaded, we had no right to have Captain Conan and his men in our service."

"Crom!"

Reza muttered something longer but hardly kinder in Iranistani. Livia nodded.

"So because the two violations of the law balance each other out—"

"By Erlik's brass tool!" Conan thundered. "Are your archons men or eunuchs! And do the men of Argos have nothing better to do with their day, then pass laws to keep honest men from defending themselves?"

"It has been known to seem that way," Livia said. Her voice was steady, but Conan noticed that she bit her lip when she was finished.

"Well, then, let's pay Akimos a visit," Conan said. "We can make it a state visit, grand and gaudy as Lady Doris at her worst." Reza seemed torn between smiling and frowning.

"That might tell us something," Conan continued. "Or I can take a few of my likeliest lads and pay him a less formal visit. That might tell us even more."

Reza shook his head. "Conan, you propose folly. Invading Akimos's palace would break more laws than I could count on my two hands. For one, you have no authority to lead your men outside the Damaos palace. Not unless you are admitted to the ranks of the Guardians—"

Conan's fist slammed on the table, making the wine

cups dance. "Mitra drown the Guardians in dung! How long does it take to join them?"

"That does not matter, Conan," Reza said.

"Captain Conan," the Cimmerian growled. "And I asked you a question."

"One I can answer," Livia said smoothly. "One must be an Argossean citizen or nominated for citizenship. One must have no crimes to one's name, and be able to post a bond of fifteen drachmas."

Conan had for the moment exhausted his store of curses. He had not exhausted his wits. He drained half his wine cup, seeing Reza frown and Livia hold back a smile. Then he wiped his mouth with the cloth and grinned.

"Very well. My lady, have the archons or the Guardians or the gods or anyone else said what we are to do with our captives?"

"Not yet."

"Good. Then why not send them up to that lumber camp where a certain merchant prince found me? I'm sure the lumber merchants won't mind having a few new hands to haul logs. After a month of that, our captives may have less strength for climbing other people's walls."

"Akimos will surely buy them out," Reza pointed out.

Conan shrugged. "Let him. That's fewer drachmas he'll have for hiring more, or bribing the archons, or any other tricks."

"Cimmerian, you go far, questioning the archons!" Reza snapped.

"Not as far as the archons do, throwing our lady's honor into the chamberpot!" Conan replied, in a level voice. "I've never met or heard of a man who couldn't be bribed!"

"Peace," Livia said. "Reza, I want you to command our men, escorting the captives to the mountains. Take good men, but be sure that all who stay behind will obey Conan."

The Cimmerian decided that one man who would not obey him if matters went on this way might be the steward himself. If the big Iranistani was not jealous of the new captain's influence over his mistress, then Conan had never in his life seen jealousy.

It was no jealousy over a woman as bedmate, either. Reza knew his "place"—Argos had made him a good servant. Even the best servant could be jealous of anyone besides himself who might win his mistress's ear as Conan had done.

That sort of jealousy could lead to daggers in the dark as surely as any quarrel over a tavern trull. Quarrels over tavern trulls did not commonly have an Akimos waiting to play jackal, either.

"My lady," Conan said. "Sending the captives to the mountains was only an idea. If it means dividing our forces when we don't know what we're facing, perhaps it wasn't my best idea."

"That's as certain as—" Reza began.

Again Livia cut through her steward's grumblings. "Surely the timber merchant must have an agent in Messantia? And surely that agent must have the power to hire men and guards for them, if they need?"

Reza knew when he had been outflanked on both sides. He bowed. "Most certainly, my lady. I will make inquiries. Have I your permission—?"

"By all means. The sooner the better, before he who sent the captives decides to try rescuing them."

"The rescuers will only join their friends," Reza said. He was smiling at Conan as he bowed himself out, but the smile did not reach his eyes.

At Lady Livia's bidding, Conan sat down and poured himself more wine. No doubt about it—Argos's vintages were almost worth enduring Argos's laws!

CHAPTER 8

The foothills of the mountains had long since swallowed the grain fields of the plains. Now they were swallowing the road under the hooves of Lord Akimos's mount.

A league behind, the road was hard, dry, and broad enough for a troop of mounted Guardians to ride four abreast. Now the firm surface was barely wide enough for two horses to pass. On either side lay mud, marsh, thickets, orchards, rank second growth, or sometimes all of these at once.

It was perfect ground for the bandits reported in the area. Meanwhile, the hour was late and the last daylight was draining from the western sky.

"Are we going to ride all night?" Akimos grumbled. "If we are, best we see about lanterns while we can still find our flint and steel!"

In the fading light, Akimos could not be sure of Lord

Skiron's expression. It seemed to be a smile, but perhaps less tainted than usual with a sneer at Akimos's caution.

"We have less than a quarter league to travel," Skiron said. "I do not forget landmarks."

"Can you see them in the dark?"

"Those we need, yes. So do not light the lanterns. They may reveal the road to us. They may also reveal us to any bandit within a league."

From the grunts around him, Akimos knew that his guards were of Skiron's mind. None of them cared for this groping in the dark. None of them cared to fight bandits, either, not with only a dozen men.

To the west, the crimson was fading from the sky, the gold following it. Overhead the sky was already a rich purple, with early stars winking.

It seemed to Akimos that they might be mocking him for being so far from Messantia on a fool's errand. Or at least the errand of a man who would rather appear a fool than a coward.

He was also a man who would not let it seem that he trusted his tame sorcerer too much. Skiron was like a leopard on a chain. The chain might break, and even if it held, it gave the beast rather too much freedom for a leap at your throat.

Akimos had to see what Skiron had prepared, here in the hills, and that was an end to it. He could only pray to Mitra that it was worth the journey, and that neither gods nor men would throw his affairs in Messantia into chaos while he was away.

By now the leading guards were dismounting to lead their horses on foot. The sergeant of the guards had drawn his sword and was using it to tap the road ahead of him, like a blind beggar's cane.

Akimos thought of dismounting. He felt a painfully large and naked target on horseback, for all that he wore mail under his silk riding coat. He also knew that he could never hope to turn his mount and ride clear of any ambush. Not on a road that now seemed as narrow as any back alley in Aghrapur, and as close-pressed by foul stenches—

A faint slithering was Akimos's only warning. He had his sword drawn, ready to hack at the serpent, when the weighted net plummeted down to block the road. One of the weights struck the sergeant, smashing his skull like a melon flung from a temple roof.

As the sergeant's sword clattered to the road, Akimos opened his mouth to shout orders. His tongue seemed as stiff as a dead branch, and a sour-tasting dryness filled his mouth. Words welled up in his throat, but refused to pass his lips.

In a moment, Akimos knew that he would vomit. He was not only going to end his life here on this dark road, at the hands of bandits. He was going to end it with all men who saw him knowing that he was a coward.

That thought was blacker than the road. It so engulfed Akimos's mind that he did not see the dark shapes leaping down from the moss-hung trees to either side of the road.

He also did not see Lord Skiron strike sparks, or the sparks fall into tinder ready in a brazen bowl. The tinder caught, glowing with a sinister vermilion hue like a serpent's eye.

Skiron raised the staff, and the bowl rose with it on the end of a silver chain. Smoke curled from the bowl, and Skiron's free hand danced through the curls. The smoke danced in time to the sorcerer's hand. For a moment it seemed to those who watched with clear eyes and wits that the smoke formed runes. Runes higher than a man, stretching across the road and vanishing on either side into the trees.

Akimos's vision cleared in time to see the vermilion light flowing from the bowl as though it were a liquid. It streamed out on to the road, engulfing the legs of men and horses. A horse screamed, another reared, and its rider clung desperately to his saddle, his mouth working as he prayed frantically not to be cast down into that demon light.

The light flowed onward, reaching the bandits. They also seemed to be praying or cursing, but no sound reached Akimos's ears. Then he realized that the horse still had its mouth open, but its screams were also mute.

Akimos could not make a gesture of aversion without taking one hand off the reins. Instead he prayed as if by the sheer torrent of vows he could fling his words free of that awful light, up to the gods.

Except that tonight, on this road, in the presence of that light, it seemed that the gods might not exist.

The bandit leader was a brave man, who had fought well in all of the armies from which he had deserted. He held his ground as the demon light crept toward him. He saw one of his men thrust a spear down into it, and the spear shiver and remain fixed as if the light had been a crocodile's jaws.

Then the light reached him. He felt a burning that might have been from heat, or cold, or both together. It was not painful, and when he looked down he saw his feet in their muddy boots and his legs in their ragged trousers as they had always been.

He drew his sword and shouted a rallying cry. Only

the nearest man seemed to hear; he was turning, trying to unsling his mace, when a slimy gray mass plunged from above onto his shoulder.

It was a strand of moss from the trees above, but a strand animated with demonic life. It had already gathered itself into a clump the size of a man's head. Now it writhed like a nest of serpents, creeping over the man's face. He opened his mouth to scream—and the moss curled over lips and teeth to fill his mouth.

The bandit leader's eyes bulged as he watched, and his hand tightened convulsively on his sword hilt.

Dropping his mace, clawing at the moss with both hands, the man went mad. He accomplished nothing, for the moss suddenly seemed to have the strength of brass wire. He also did nothing to block the fresh moss that crept over his nose and into it, blocking off his last hope of breath. Face already darkening, his body arched and he fell on his back into the light. He kicked and writhed briefly, then lay still. With unearthly life, the moss flowed off the dead man's face and began creeping toward the bandit leader.

He had held onto his courage until that moment. Now it took flight, and so did he. If the light had held his feet motionless, he would have gone mad in the next moment. As it was, it was like pulling his feet out of knee-deep mud. He could move, but only just fast enough to keep ahead of the moss. If any more fell down he was doomed.

Yet the edge of the light crept closer and closer, faster than the moss, and no fresh moss fell. The mud-like suction eased, then vanished. The bandit leader lunged for the edge of the light, crossed it, and felt his boots strike wholesome ground.

He ran, not caring where he went nor looking even

for a moment behind him. He could not save any of his men caught in that demon light. As for his enemies, an arrow in the back might be merciful, compared with his fate if any more sorcery was abroad tonight.

Neither arrows nor spells pursued the bandit leader down the road. A hundred paces from the edge of the light, he stopped in the shadow of a tree, after making sure that no moss hung from it.

Those of his men who had followed him on to the road all seemed to be down. But they were not all who followed him. Another half score of men waited on either flank. He had given no orders, but if they had eyes in their heads they would see their comrades' fate and hold back. Hold back, beyond the limits of the spell—but not, perhaps, beyond bowshot.

Archery by night was always a chancy business, likely to skewer friend and foe alike. But the sorcerer's demon light had revealed him and all his company as plainly as daylight. The flankers had some good archers among them, and a sorcerer bristling with arrows was a poor spell-caster.

The bandit leader turned and headed uphill. Another fifty paces, and he rounded a bend in the road. Now he was out of sight of the sorcerer and his party. He stopped, looking for the young cedar that marked the beginning of a dry route back to his men.

With his night sight destroyed, he was some time finding it. At every moment, he expected to hear the rattle of hooves and the warcries of the sorcerer's comrades—or even some words that neither gods nor men should know, as the sorcerer cast another spell.

So it was no surprise that when the bandit leader found the cedar, he dashed toward it. It was also no surprise that he failed to notice the crack in the ground, a hand's-breadth wide and stretching entirely across the road.

He stumbled and caught his foot in the crack, bruising knees and hands as he fell. He cursed, raised himself, and felt something grip his feet. Something that burned, but not the mild burning of the demon light. Something that seemed to sear away his flesh to the bone in one moment, and dissolve the bones in the next.

When he felt the burning eating its way up his legs, he screamed. He screamed louder still when he felt himself being dragged into the crack. He went on screaming, until the burning ate its way up to his chest and dissolved his lungs.

Only the bandit leader's left hand remained whole when the ground shuddered. Smoke in colors for which there were no names billowed up from the crack in the ground. Then the two sides of the crack lurched toward each other, and the crack closed. Only the bandit leader's hand remained, lying palm upward on the blackened gravel, fingers curled into a claw and the nails a peculiarly foul shade of gray.

Akimos could not stop shuddering for some time after the scream died. Then it was even longer before he could shape words with his dry lips and tongue.

"What was *that*?"

Skiron shrugged. "The gods only know, and they send me no messengers."

"This is no time for jests!"

"Forgive me, my lord," the sorcerer said smoothly. *Too smoothly*, Akimos thought. *He knows more than he will tell me.*

"I doubt not that the bandits had men on either flank,

121

ready to move in once their comrades on the road had engaged us. Even a sorcerer can see the wisdom of such tactics.''

"Skiron—"

"Your pardon. I only wished to remind you that I am no soldier."

"No, and I am no temple image, to wait patiently for an age. *What screamed?*"

"I would wager on one of the flankers stepping into quicksand, or perhaps onto a snake. The marsh vipers here are deadly, and their poison not only slays but burns like fire while it does so."

This was the truth, as far as Akimos knew. So why was he sure that it was not the truth he sought?

No reason, except knowing Skiron too long and too well. Also, tonight, on this road, there might be no such thing as truth, as men commonly understood it.

Lord Akimos rallied his men, so that they slung the sergeant's body over his mount and moved on. While he was doing this, a curious weasel scrambled onto the road, scented the bandit leader's fallen hand, and lunged for it.

The weasel died in agony only moments later, but before it died it was clear of the road, along with its intended meal. Lord Akimos's courage was never tested by seeing the severed hand. Where the road had cracked, nothing remained except a softer patch of blackened gravel, hard to find unless one studied the road on hands and knees.

Akimos, Skiron, and the rest rode over it without noticing, although a pungent smell in the air did make some of the horses skittish for a few paces.

* * *

Far beneath the hills, the Great Watcher achieved awareness. It cannot be said that it awoke for many reasons, foremost being that it had no senses as men understand such.

But it had been unknowing, and now it had knowledge.

Knowledge that a part of itself far away and long apart from it had also achieved awareness. Indeed, it had reached farther than that, opening a path to the sky-world and its food supply. It had even found a morsel of the sky-food, and was now assimilating it.

Awareness of the isolated part's feeding and the contentment that came from that feeding rose in the Great Watcher. If one could use human terms for the Great Watcher, one might almost say that it felt envious of the isolated part.

In what for the Great Watcher did the work of a brain, an idea took form. It would reach out to the isolate and learn from it exactly what happened. It might even find other isolates, and tell them all that had happened. It would give pleasure, as the Great Watcher understood it, to learn that a time for feeding might be coming again.

To the Great Watcher, a century and a minute were not so very different. Yet it also remembered that it had never been so long between feedings. What had brought awareness to the isolate and allowed it to feed might be moving about. It might even reach the Great Watcher and its companion.

Then there would be a mighty feeding. After that neither would need any aid from the sky-world to be aware, to seek and ingest food, move where they might wish, and multiply as they pleased.

The Great Watcher rippled with pleasure, and the ripple passed into the rocks about it.

The damp rock of the cave floor quivered under Lord Skiron's feet. From a vast distance he heard the rumble of falling rock. From closer to hand, sand hissed from crevices and a stalactite crunched to the floor. The guard it had nearly impaled leaped back, hand on sword hilt, eyes showing only whites.

"Easy, you—everyone," Skiron said. "The rock of these hills has stood since before men lived on the earth. But there are underground springs in plenty. Those springs wear away the hardest rock, and sometimes it falls."

"If it falls on me, I don't care what pushed it!" someone muttered.

Skiron cursed under his breath, wishing that Akimos had half the wits and courage of his forebears. Then he would not leave calming his shaken men to a sorcerer who had more important matters at hand!

What Akimos finally said, Skiron did not remember clearly. He did remember that the merchant prince's voice began as high-pitched as a woman's, which did little to ease his men's minds.

Somehow, Akimos found the right words. He was not, after all, a fool. No one who had not only upheld but advanced the House of Peram so well could be such. The guards turned to with a will, unloading the pack animals and carrying the loads up winding tunnels to drier caves above.

"There is even a crack in the rock, to let out the smoke of a fire," Akimos said, pointing at the wall. He laughed. "A common fire, of wood or charcoal, at any rate. I do not know what it will do with the stenches of your magic.''

''I do not expect to need such spells once we are— ah, fortified here.''

Akimos frowned, and Skiron realized too late that his voice had betrayed him. The merchant prince looked at him long and hard.

''You will not need them? Or you will not dare cast them?''

''What is there to fear?''

''You have never heard of the Watchers, and you a sorcerer?''

Skiron laughed. Too late, he realized that his laughter was sending echoes rolling up and down the maze of tunnels and caves. He had to wait until the echoes died to speak, and by then Akimos's face was a thundercloud.

''There is some doubt that the Watchers were creatures of sorcery. Many of the tales say that they were only the creations of a remnant of the Atlanteans' wisdom about nature.''

''Perhaps they say that to you,'' Akimos said. ''To most of us, the Watchers reek of evil magic.''

''Wisdom or wizardry, they are certainly long dead,'' Skiron said. ''But I certainly do not mind it if men believe the tales. They may be more ready to keep their distance.''

''Men such as a certain Cimmerian?''

''Exactly.''

Skiron turned away, relieved to have the matter ended so easily. He did not wish Akimos to be too curious about the matter of the Watchers.

That scream in the night came from no common death. Nor did the stench that clung to the road come from the marsh or Skiron's own magic. Where it did come from, Skiron did not know.

He did know that Akimos had chosen to place his refuge in the very heart of the land where the Watchers once roamed and fed. If they were dead or at least as weak as the spells that bound them to this land, then no harm might come of it. Otherwise . . .

Yet that was a matter that Skiron must guard within his own heart. To speak of it would be to admit fear, fear that his own arts were less than he boasted. Akimos would not forgive or forget such a deception, and without Akimos what could Skiron do with the remainder of his life?

Granted, that is, that Akimos allowed him to survive their parting!

CHAPTER 9

The message from Lady Doris of Lokhri came by a hired messenger whom neither Lady Livia nor Reza had ever seen before. It could hardly have caused a greater uproar had it set the place on fire. Lady Livia read it first, then summoned Reza and Conan to hear her read it again.

"If Captain Conan comes to the seat of House Lokhri tonight after the fourth hour, he will learn of a matter vital to the safety of House Damaos."

That was all, except for Lady Doris's seal, pressed into perfumed wax. Livia and Reza vouched for the seal, and Conan remembered the perfume from the day of Lady Doris's visit to the Damaos palace.

"So it's real enough," the Cimmerian said. "She also didn't say anything about coming alone. So I think it best that I go."

Livia's mouth opened, but Reza spoke first. "By all

means, Conan. I will pick three or four of our best, and you can pick the same from yours. We had also best be ready to send messages. If it is a trap, you may send out what you learn even you cannot escape yourself.''

Conan grinned. ''I've been walking into traps set by better trappers than Lady Doris for a good many years. I'm here. Most of the trappers aren't. If she's set a trap for a fox, she'll find she's caught a bear.''

Livia finally got some words out. ''Conan—Captain— this is folly! Lady Doris can hardly trust you enough to tell you anything this House must know. If you go, the danger to you will be great, and the danger to this House no less.''

''That's always a chance when lords plot,'' Conan said. ''But I'd be a fool to ignore the other chance too, that we might learn something.'' He decided against mentioning the chance of a meeting with Harphos. In his home, the Lokhri heir might have his guard down.

''At the cost of you and the men who go with you, perhaps!'' Livia snapped. ''That is more than this House can pay, for a promise of the Chief Archonship itself!''

Reza frowned. ''As Conan said, he will be in little danger, at the head of eight or nine well-armed men.''

''But if Lady Doris refuses to admit the guards—'' Livia was clearly digging in her heels for a fight.

''*Then* we can suspect that Conan faces a trap,'' Reza said. ''We can also trust him to act wisely. My lady, forgive me for plain speaking. But if we cannot trust a man taught by High Captain Khadjar, we can trust no one under the sun.''

''I trust Conan, and I suppose I must trust your judgment of Khadjar.'' Livia sounded like a petulant small girl. ''But can I trust you, Reza?''

"What do you mean by that, my lady?" The steward's tone bordered on disrespect.

Conan held his breath and rested one hand on his sword hilt. If Livia was ready to accuse Reza openly of jealousy of the Cimmerian, it would make matters worse rather than better, for Reza would likely be more in fear for his position, rather than less. If Reza's jealousy got the better of him, the Lokhri palace might be safer than the Damaos one!

"My lady," Conan said, "I think I had best go. If nothing else, Lady Doris will be offended if I do not. We have enough enemies already."

Livia bit her lip but nodded. "The gods be with you, then, Captain Conan."

Conan grinned. "I don't know about the gods. But with Reza's help, good men and sharp steel will be! I trust in those more than the gods, by your leave."

The Cimmerian still felt Livia's eyes on him, until the door closed behind him.

Conan raised a hand, and the ten men behind him stopped. The water clock atop the fountain in the Square of the Cagemakers said that the sixth hour was not yet half gone.

"We've time enough to make the work of anyone following us a trifle harder," he said. He pointed toward one of the streets leading to the harbor. "Down that way, as far as the Street of Steps. Mekhas, you know this quarter best. Take the lead."

The Damaos man nodded and stepped forward. When he had passed out of earshot, Conan signaled to Jarenz.

"Join him in the lead. Keep your sword sheathed but ready. If he seems to be nervous, ask him why. If you have to draw on him, use the flat if you can."

129

"Yes, Captain." Jarenz hurried forward. He still favored the leg injured in the lumber camp, but could cover ground swiftly enough.

Conan fell back to bring up the rear as his men turned toward the waterfront. For some time his instincts had told him they were being followed. He had seen and heard nothing, but he had trusted his instincts too long and too successfully to ignore them.

For a few hundred paces, the street was as well lit and deserted as most in the wealthier quarters of Messantia. In those parts of the city few had lawful business after nightfall. Few of those whose business was unlawful cared to risk meeting a Guardian patrol. The life of a thief in Messantia, at least in any part of the city where there was something worth stealing, would be exciting and probably short.

As the street began to wind downhill toward the harbor, the Guardian patrols were no longer to be seen. The lights grew few and far between, until at last there was only the moon, the stars, and the glow from wineshop and brothel windows to show a man the way. Meanwhile, the smooth cobblestones grew rough and littered with filth, where they did not give way altogether to patches of reeking mud.

Conan shrugged broad shoulders under his mail coat. For all its light and air, its good food and clean beds, the wealthy quarters of Messantia did not feel like home to him. A man who had first seen cities as a slave, then as a thief, he was more used to the way of the poorer quarters.

When the waterfront hove in sight a hundred paces away, Conan called another halt. Then he signaled a turn west. This took the band sharply to the right. Making the turn, Conan was able to look down three streets at once without turning his head.

All were dimly lit, but in one of them a shadowy figure was creeping forward. Conan saw it flatten against a wall until it thought none saw it, then move forward again.

Hand signals sent Conan's message forward: "Prepare for an ambush." That would set the men in front and rear watching to the sides, the men in the middle watching for attack from above.

The street twisted like a drunken snake, then narrowed until Conan could touch the walls on either side. It also began to climb. They were on their way back uphill, toward the Lokhri palace.

They were also still being followed. No night sight less keen than the Cimmerian's could have kept watch on the band, but clearly the follower was Conan's match in that regard.

The street climbed four steps, then broadened. Ahead Conan saw a lantern. He also saw three massive wine barrels in a rack—and a thin arm reach from the shadows to snatch a wedge from the rack.

"The barrels!" Conan roared. He leaped forward reaching the head of the band as the barrels rumbled out of the rack. On the steep slope they rolled swiftly toward the men.

Conan saw a roughly trimmed log leaning against a door. He snatched it up, balanced it in both hands, then leaped into the path of the barrels. As he leaped, he thrust the log forward like a lance. Its trimmed end drove under the lead barrel, bringing it tottering to a stop. The second barrel crashed into the first, and the third into the second, so hard that it split open.

Wine poured down the street, scouring the filth from

the cobblestones. "Waste of good wine!" shouted Jarenz cheerfully.

Before Conan could curse him to silence, alleys to both right and left spewed men. So did the street behind the band.

Conan's hands gripped the log again. As he jerked it free, the two remaining barrels began to roll. They rolled straight downhill, to where the street turned into steps. Of the four men climbing the steps, the barrels knocked three down. They screamed as the barrels crushed the life out of them and Conan feinted with the log at the last man. That fellow leaped aside, but slipped on the wine-slick stones and cracked his skull as he fell.

By now Conan's band and their attackers were fully engaged and thoroughly entangled. Two men ran at Conan. Not wasting time getting rid of the log, he held it up to meet their downward slashes. Both swords stuck in the wood. Conan twirled the log, jerking the weapons out of their owner's hands, then flung log and swords straight into the men's faces.

They flew backward to smash into the walls. One went down and lay under the log; the second drew a knife. He barely had it raised before Conan's sword flickered out and took his arm off just below the elbow. His thin scream was lost in the uproar of the fight.

That uproar soon began to fade. The attackers must have been expecting the barrels to scatter Conan's men, perhaps hurt a few of them. Instead they had seen the Cimmerian's colossal strength take six of their number almost without drawing breath.

Whatever they had expected, it was not that. Most of the attackers who could still run did so.

Two ran into one of the houses and slammed the door behind them. Conan saw three of his men pick up the fallen log and start using it as a battering ram on the door. He gripped the log and heaved. It flew out of their hands and clattered on the stones as they turned to stare.

"We don't have time to chase those fatherless dogs! Besides, knocking down their door's sure to be against some law the Argosseans thought up when they'd drunk bad wine!"

The men, all Conan's free lances, grinned. The Cimmerian raised his voice. "Rally, and call out! Have we anyone hurt?"

Two men called out, then Jarenz did the same, feebly and from the ground. Conan knelt beside him, mouth setting in a grim line as he saw the young man's pale face and gaping thigh.

He said nothing; he did not need to. Jarenz's hands groped feebly for his belt pouch and tore it loose.

"For Vandar—a little—to help him with—that girl. First—first time he's courted on—his own." Jarenz smiled, although it was like a skull smiling.

"Sorry, Captain," he added. "Don't think I—did my share. Hope the gods. . . ."

What Jarenz hoped of the gods, Conan never knew. The young man's eyes drifted closed and a moment later his breathing stopped. The Cimmerian rose, wiping bloody hands on the tunic of a dead enemy.

It helped that the dead enemy had a deal of company—eight more bodies, to be exact. But that would not bring Jarenz back to life, ease his brother—or keep Conan from a red vengeance on those who had set this ambush.

"Make a litter," Conan snapped. "Jarenz comes with us."

* * *

133

The Lokhri palace was even larger than the Damaos one, although not as well kept up. One blind wall, dribbling stones and half overgrown, faced a small park.

Conan sent one man up to a stout branch of an oak in that park, a second man up to the top of the wall to perch where the iron spikes had rusted away. Both protested, the Damaos man as loudly as Conan's.

"I thought I was the captain here," the Cimmerian said mildly. "If you want to argue the point, shall we try it with swords?" Two heads nearly fell off their shoulders, so vigorously did the men deny such an ambition.

"Good. Then keep your ears and eyes open and your mouths shut. We need somebody outside the palace, to run with a message if there is one. We need somebody on the wall, to watch the grounds. We'll have a man on the roof once we're inside, to send the message. The last two can jump down and get themselves killed or not as they please, *after* they send the message.

"If they fall in that, they'd better run for Khitai. Anywhere closer, I may find them."

The Damaos man laughed. "And if the trap takes you along with the rest, Captain?"

The Cimmerian's smile held little mirth. "Do you want to wager on my leaving you unpunished just because I'm dead?"

Neither man seemed to have much enthusiasm for facing the Cimmerian's vengeful ghost. They were already in place when Conan led the remaining seven live men and one dead one toward the main gate.

The two gate guards were each about half Conan's size and old enough to be his father. If there was a trap planned, they were no part of it. They studied the seal on the message and the pass from the Guardians as though they might hold the secret of eternal youth. This gave Conan time to study them in turn.

The guards were not only ill-suited for fighting, they were ill-equipped. From their stained helmet straps to their mismatched sandals, they were men Conan would have thrown out of any company of his at one glance.

Crumbling, overgrown walls. Guards who looked as if they slept at their posts, if not in the streets. And Lady Doris eager to make a match for her son with Lady Livia, mistress of one of the great fortunes in Argos.

If Conan had doubted before what sort of intrigue was afoot here, he doubted no longer. He also swore that when he had avenged Jarenz, he would deal with Lady Doris's insult to the House of Damaos.

And if Lady Doris and not Akimos or a friend of his had sent those men tonight? Conan's hands gripped the rusty iron bars of the gate as if they were a throat. It was not in him to think lightly of harming a woman. But a woman whose treachery had taken a man sworn to him—he would find a way to repay her.

This vow turned his face into a mask even grimmer than before. The guards sprang hastily aside as the Cimmerian led his men through the open gate and up a weed-ridden path toward the house.

"Lady Doris will receive you in the Amber Chamber," the steward said.

Conan nodded. The steward was nearly as large as the Cimmerian, but old enough to be his grandfather, nearly bald, and paunchy. The only way he could take part in a war, Conan decided, was to be fired from a siege engine. He would doubtless smash through almost any roof from sheer weight alone!

"Did she say *when*?" Conan asked.

"Ah, young warriors are so impatient," the steward said, chuckling.

"That wasn't what I asked," Conan said. "If you don't know—or your mistress doesn't know—you won't shame the House by saying so." He frowned. "If you keep us waiting like beggars, though, it might do more than shame the House."

Conan left to the steward's imagination what that "more" might be. He wasn't disappointed. The steward's rheumy eyes widened and he turned ponderously. Then he vanished up the stairs faster than Conan would have imagined of him.

He returned shortly, wheezing and paler than ever. "My lady bids you to follow me."

"What of my men?"

"Your—oh, them. They will find hospitality in my quarters, wine and food. If they wish to bring that gift they bear to the kitchen on the way—"

"That gift is a dead body," Conan said.

"A—?" the steward began, then his mouth was gaping too wide for speech.

"The body of one of my men. Slain tonight, in a treacherous ambush, as we approached the house."

That stretched the truth a trifle, but Conan did not mind frightening the steward. It might frighten him into speaking the truth. Or it might frighten him away, which would be no bad thing either!

"I doubt it would be very welcome in the kitchen," the Cimmerian went on. "My men will keep their comrade with them. Now, I believe Lady Doris waits above?"

As Conan climbed, everything he saw told the same tale, of a once-mighty House now fallen far and still sinking. Stained, patched, or crumbling walls. Bare spots once covered by tapestries or rugs. The few rugs and tapestries remaining, faded, threadbare, mold-spotted, or all three at once. Holes gnawed by mice or rats in richly carved woodwork. The servants mostly either old or very young, thin-faced, and moving furtively, as though they feared the lash.

Conan remembered the tales of the display Lady Doris had made on her first visit to the Damaos palace. How many tapestries had been sold, how many servants had eaten thin porridge, to pay for the hire of all that splendor?

At least Conan began to see why Lady Doris had summoned him, rather than Reza or Lady Livia herself. A Cimmerian barbarian might not know what the raddled and battered house meant. If he showed that he knew, he might be bribed or worse to hold his tongue.

Conan swore to himself that if Lady Doris tried to seal his lips with gold, he would test his sword on some of her furniture. Did everyone in Argos think Cimmerians were dropped on their heads as babes, at least until the Cimmerian dropped them on *theirs* so that some sense entered?

The walls gave no answer. Nor did the steward. He only stopped at the head of the stairs and pointed to the left. "The door set with amber, at the far end of that hall."

"Very well." The steward obviously expected silver. Conan spread one broad hand over his purse and shook his head. If all went well with Lady Doris, *then* he would spend some of House Damaos's silver to loosen tongues among her servants.

The door was not only set with amber, it was of rich wine-hued wood, lovingly carved and polished to a high sheen. Conan knocked, and the sound of his knocking told him that the door could have resisted a battering ram.

"Who is it?"

"Captain Conan, at Lady Doris's summons."

"Enter."

The door gave to a push, opening soundlessly on well-oiled hinges. Within, Conan's boots sank into rich carpeting, dark blue with dolphins woven in silver. He smelled incense, and also a familiar perfume. He raised his eyes, to meet the gaze of the one who wore the perfume.

Lady Doris wore more than the perfume, but not as much as Conan had expected. Her gown ended at mid-calf and left her shoulders bare. It was also slit down the front almost to the waist, but closed decently by a massive clasp of gold set with amber and tiny emeralds.

"My lady," Conan said, giving his best Argossean upper servant's bow. He did not much care for these rites, but to ignore them *would* brand him a barbarian. To perform them as though he were an Argossean born, on the other hand, surprised people and put them off guard.

"Rise, Captain Conan, and be seated."

Conan looked about the richly paneled room. The only places to sit besides the floor were the lady's own couch, ebony with purple cushions, and the great bed canopied in what seemed to be cloth of silver. Not wishing to have to shout across the room, Conan took his place on one end of the bench.

"So, Captain Conan. All is well at House Damaos?"

"As well as can be expected," the Cimmerian said curtly.

"You still do not know who struck at you, with magic and then with men?"

"We are seeking the truth, my lady. It would not be my place to say more. Not until Lady Livia gives me leave, at any rate, and she will do that only when she is ready to strike."

Lady Doris took a deep breath. This brought her gown tight against her breasts, which were not only full but looked remarkably firm. The woman had a son of twenty, but she could have claimed no more than thirty years herself and been believed. Certainly the olive skin of her shoulders was unwrinkled, and the blue-black hair without a strand of gray.

"You make Lady Livia sound like a serpent, lying in wait for prey."

For the first time that evening, Conan's laugh held no grimness or mockery. "Lady Livia is someone I wouldn't care to have as an enemy. I've been a soldier a good part of my life, Lady Doris, and I've seen few captains more cunning."

"Yet even the best captain needs to know who her enemies are. Is that not so?"

"Quite true. But as I said, that's something we are all hard at work to learn. House Damaos is of one mind on that. And when we know, and can prove it to the archons—whoever has been hiring hedge-wizards and knifemen will be hiring a ship to take him far from Argos."

"Him?"

"My lady, we don't suspect you. At least, we don't suspect you in the attacks on the palace."

Lady Doris licked her full lips. Conan could sense anticipation, interest, and something more—something very like fear.

139

"Captain Conan, if you wish my help, you will speak plainly. What do you suspect I did against House Damaos?"

Conan turned toward the woman. "Tonight we took a long road to your house, fearing spies. We were still followed. In a street—I don't know the name, but it goes up four steps—"

"The Street of Dithambres the Sot," the lady said, just above a whisper.

"A good name," Conan said. "In that street, a score of sots attacked us. Even a sot can be dangerous, with steel in his hand. We killed half of them at least. But they wounded two of my men and killed one. Men oathsworn to me as their captain, and to House Damaos as guards.

"Somebody used silver to buy those men's steel. House Damaos and I have a blood-debt to pay that somebody—"

He broke off, because Lady Doris had turned as pale as her complexion would allow. Her eyes had turned into vast dark pools, and one cheek was quivering uncontrollably.

The quivering spread to her lips. She put both beringed hands over her mouth, to hide it. Then she closed her eyes, and all the breath went out of her in a sigh.

So did all the strength. She swayed and toppled. She would have toppled off the couch if Conan had not caught her, one long arm around her shoulders. As gently as if she had been a child, he drew Lady Doris against his massive chest and listened for her breathing.

He heard nothing, because wild cries at once split the air.

"Dog!"

"Take your foul hands off our mistress!"

A hidden door crashed open, and three men leaped through it. Two more sprang out from under the bed, and a final pair swung in through the window.

Conan dropped Lady Doris unceremoniously on the couch as he leaped to his feet. He saw her breasts rising and falling, but her eyes remained closed. Then he had no more time for her, as the seven men formed a ragged circle around him.

At least he knew now that young and robust manservants were not unknown to House Lokhri. They also bore steel, shortswords, long daggers, and one spear, and well-used steel at that. Yet they did not have the air of men who knew what they were doing, let alone whom they faced. The spearman appeared to be the leader. He also had his eyes wholly fixed on Lady Doris, as though Conan had been armed with no more than a willow wand.

His longer weapon made the leader the most dangerous to the Cimmerian, and therefore the first opponent. Rather, say "victim," for one sword stroke chopped the spear in two. A second was a feinting cut at his legs. He crouched, while comrades on either side closed.

They closed a little too much, offering Conan a target a blind man could not have missed. His sword leaped from his right hand to his left. It weighted his left fist as he drove the hilt into the face of one man. Conan let the blow wheel him half around, and his booted foot flew up into the other man's crotch. The man tried to sit down on the empty air, failed, then collapsed to the carpet, fighting for the breath to scream.

The leader thrust at Conan with the broken end of his spear and drew a knife. Conan shifted his sword back to his right hand and brought the flat of the blade down on the leader's knife hand. He screamed and dropped the knife. One of the men lunged for it, at the same time slashing at Conan's legs with his own long dagger.

Conan let the dagger's edge graze his skin, then whirled again, faster than the eye could follow. Somehow his foot ended up tangled in the daggerman's legs. The man lost his balance but did not fall. His frantically scrabbling feet hurled him forward into one of his comrades. Both men flew backward into the wall.

The tapestry on the wall was an immaculate hunting scene, archers surrounding a tiger. It did not cushion the wall for the two men. Both sprawled senseless, and the tapestry parted its moorings and slithered down to cover them like a rag flung over a heap of garbage.

Conan tossed his sword from hand to hand, again faster than the eye could follow, and laughed. Which act froze the last two men into statues, he never knew. They were still gaping at him when Lady Doris gasped and began waving her arms.

Conan honored the lady's appeal. Carefully gripping only her wrists, he pulled her gently up to a sitting position. Then he turned back to face the seven men he had disabled in about the time it took to drink half a cup of Argossean wine.

"Conan—Captain—are they—?" Lady Doris began. Her eyes widened more than ever as she looked around the chamber.

"If any of those—men—has lost a drop of blood, I'll personally tend his wounds," Conan said. "I'm not saying that they'll all be fighting fit before morning. If they ever were," he added, glaring at the two statues.

The insult made both men quiver. Then they stepped apart and raised shortswords.

"Hold!" the lady commanded. "I forbid the raising of any steel to Captain Conan. Or his men."

The leader had recovered his senses and his voice. "My lady, you said—"

"I spoke without full knowledge. Captain Conan has told me—what alters matters. Be off, all of you. And take this message with you. The men with Captain Conan are to receive the hospitality of House Lokhri."

"My lady—?"

"Did Conan's fist make you more of a witling then you already were?" the lady snapped. "Perhaps I should have him strike you again, to knock your wits back into place!"

The idea of facing the Cimmerian again seemed to give winged feet to five of the seven men. They lifted their senseless comrades and fled, so quickly that they jammed in the door and had a deal of trouble untangling themselves.

By the time they had, Lady Doris was laughing so hard that the clasp of her gown threatened to snap. At last she lay back down on the couch, her gown hoisted almost to her knees, and trailed one bare arm over the edge of the couch as her laughter died.

Conan stood silently until Lady Doris gave a deep sigh and sat up.

"Forgive me, Captain Conan. I do not suppose this is so amusing to you."

"No, it isn't," he said. "It's never funny to see fighting men humiliated, carrying out witless orders. And since they were your orders—"

"My orders?"

"My lady, I can tell a trap when I see it. I can even tell the kind of trap. They were supposed to avenge your virtue."

The dark eyes were half closed now, and would not meet the Cimmerian's ice-blue ones. But Lady Doris nodded.

"I thought as much. Then something didn't go as you'd planned it, true?"

Another nod.

"Do you want to tell me, or do I have to force it out of you?"

Lady Doris smiled. "In my own house? And with what weapon?" She fingered the clasp of her gown. Conan noticed that it had slipped farther down one shoulder, so that the upper curve of one breast stood bare. It was as fine a curve as all the others he had seen on the lady of Lokhri.

"If I can meet seven men without bloodshed, I'm sure I can do as well with one woman."

"Even in hand to hand combat?"

Conan felt his blood beginning to seethe. If he had mistaken the meaning of those last words, he knew nothing about women.

"Even that?"

Lady Doris rose, and her hand went to the clasp of her gown. Nimble fingers danced, the clasp opened, and the gown opened to her waist. A quick shrug, and it slithered from her shoulders to the floor.

Everything was as splendid as Conan had imagined, beginning with breasts that cried out for a man's hand. His blood now felt like molten rock in his veins.

"I challenged you to hand to hand combat, Cimmerian," the lady said, and lay back on the couch. "Do you refuse the challenge?"

"Do I look that big a fool?" Conan said, and stopped her mouth with his before she could answer the question.

CHAPTER 10

The knocking was slower than usual to awaken Conan. He slept as lightly as any wild animal when in danger. But he could not hear the knocking until it grew louder than Lady Doris's snores.

When it did, the Cimmerian was awake in an instant. Sword in hand, he padded over to the door.

"Who is there?"

"Captain Conan, I want to talk to you." Conan recognized Harphos's voice.

"In a moment." Conan returned to the bed, pulled the quilts over the nude Lady Doris, pulled the bed curtains shut, and drew on his clothes and dagger.

Harphos looked impatient at being kept waiting when Conan finally drew the bolt. He also looked red-eyed, but Conan smelled no wine on his breath.

The heir of House Lokhri contented himself with one

look at the curtained bed and another at Conan. Then he turned toward the door.

Conan's hand descended on the lordling's shoulder. "Stop right now. Where are we going?"

"To where what we say remains between the two of us."

Conan looked around the room. There were no obvious places for eavesdroppers, but that only meant cunning enemies instead of careless ones. Also, Lady Doris might not be so soundly asleep as her snores said.

"Lead on, but not into another brawl, thank you."

Harphos laughed, a short harsh bark. "There's few enough men in the house fit to face you, and none of them willing. I couldn't lay a trap if I wanted to."

Conan knew that pitfalls, traps, set crossbows, and other such devices required no hands on them to be deadly. He was prepared to trust to his instincts, his sword arm, and his mail coat against these, and otherwise leave it to the gods as he tried to learn the secrets of House Lokhri.

If there are any, he thought, *besides Lady Doris feeling even better in the dark than she looked in the light, and knowing everything a woman can do to please a man.*

Harphos moved swiftly down dim halls to a door opening on a spiral staircase. He led the way down these two at a time, moving with an assurance Conan had never seen or expected in him.

At last they came to a door of what seemed to be solid stone, with a lock set in it large enough to anchor a castle's gate. Harphos took from his pouch an absurdly small key and turned it three times, in three different holes in the lock.

At the last turn, the lock sang a high-pitched note,

like a vase of fine glass. The slab of rock turned on a bronze shaft, leaving a gap on either side. Both men had to stoop to pass within, and Conan's mail scraped rock.

Conan did not know what he had expected in the chamber beyond, but certainly it was not what he found. Worn but comfortable rugs softened the floor, while shelves of sweet-smelling pale wood carved with flowers and leaves lined three walls. By the fourth wall stood a long table, good ebony, but plain as a post save for a design set in silver in one corner of the top. A closer look told Conan that the design was ancient Vanir runes.

The shelves themselves were filled with dozens of jars, porcelain, glass, stoneware, even earthenware, with silver or brass stoppers. At intervals Conan saw piles of scrolls, some of them brown with age, mortars and pestles, flagons of firewine, and other things he did not recognize.

Nor did he really wish to. Had someone told him that the secret of House Lokhri was that Lord Harphos was a sorcerer, Conan would have called the man mad.

Harphos sat on the table, long legs dangling, and grinned. "You look uneasy, Captain. Does the odor of my herbs and potions make you sick?"

"It's a poor host who insults a guest with his first breath," Conan growled. "That's the law in more lands than Argos.

"It's also the law in Argos that no one may practice sorcery. Do you expect me to keep my tongue between my teeth, now that I've seen this?"

"Yes."

"Why?"

"For two reasons. One is that it's no secret, save to my mother and her trusted servants. The second is that there's no sorcery to it. It's matters for healing. Nothing great, like bleeding from within or a belly wound, but common wounds and sickness.''

''Like what I dealt out to your mother's pack of prize fools?''

Harphos laughed. It was a much heartier laugh than one would have expected from the almost gaunt young man.

''Conan, it's hard to hide anything from you, is it not?''

''If it's something that can save me or my men, yes. So you're a healer. Is that the secret of House Lokhri?''

''No.'' Suddenly Harphos looked about fifteen, and as awkward and callow as Conan had once thought him. ''Captain Conan. I want Livia for my wife. I want to court her as a man courts a woman he loves. Not as my mother wants me to court her, as a way of patching up our rat-gnawed fortunes. But how can I make her understand that I love her? How?''

Conan had never been in love as Harphos seemed to be, but he had seen it often enough in others to recognize the ailment. He bit back the suggestion that Harphos take one of his own potions to kill his desire—or perhaps feed Livia one that would increase hers!

Harphos had probably been laughed at often enough by his mother and her servants. It would be a pleasure for the young man to be taken seriously.

''I've heard that some women can read a man's thoughts,'' the Cimmerian said, grinning. ''But I don't know that Livia's one of them. So why not tell her yourself?''

Harphos looked as horror-struck as if Conan had proposed he leap from the walls of Messantia. ''My mother!''

"You're not telling your mother—"

"She would learn. Then she would end the suit. She wants to rule me as much as she wants to grasp Livia's money. If she thought I was slipping from her power, I would have no peace. She might even search the house and find my hiding place!"

"What's more important? Livia or this storeroom?"

Harphos stood up, with considerable dignity. "Captain Conan. If I had not used my skills and materials for healing, you might have the Guardians to reckon with. As it is, none of my mother's men will suffer permanent harm."

"You might thank me a trifle for that," Conan said. "I'm not usually that kind to men who come at me with drawn steel."

"I don't expect you are," Harphos said. "That is another reason I would have you for a friend, Captain. Or at least someone I can trust. It is not an easy situation, guarding one's back from one's own mother."

Conan couldn't dispute that, so was ready to drink the toast Harphos proposed. It was not the best wine he'd tasted in Argos and the cups were wooden, but Harphos was careful to drink first, lest Conan think the wine was poisoned.

"And now, Captain, I think it best you be on your way, you and your men. As the last part of my healing them, I gave my mother's men a sleeping draught. The sun will be high in the sky before they waken. With luck, it will be tomorrow before they even remember how they came by their wounds or who healed them."

Harphos's tone made the request an order. An order that Conan decided he would do well to obey. He had hopes of seeing Lady Doris again. He did not care much whether they had another bout in bed, pleasant as the thought was. He was reluctant to leave the house without a few words with its mistress, lest there was really a secret she alone knew that might help Livia.

No matter. Battles seldom went as captains would have them, and Conan knew now that the battles of Argos went by that rule even when no one laid a hand on steel!

Lady Livia's eyes were the color of an ice cave in Vanaheim as they studied Conan. They also seemed to make the lady's chamber as cold as that cave.

"So, Captain Conan. You lost a man and endangered the rest. You yourself barely escaped a trap. Yet you say you have no notion of this 'secret' of House Lokhri?"

"Only a guess, my lady." Since he left the Lokhri palace before dawn, Conan had found scant time to consider what Lady Doris might be about. Bringing his men home, finding a place for Jarenz's body, and speaking a few words to the prisoners Reza was leading out had taken much of the morning. Then posting the men Reza left behind to cover every point of danger took much of the afternoon. By the time Lady Livia's demand for his presence became dangerous to ignore, twilight's shadows were embracing the garden.

"Guesses are of small use in war," Livia said. "My father and keeper-father both told me this. You yourself have said as much."

"I don't deny it, my lady."

"Then why do you offer a guess as the best you can do?"

"My lady, sometimes it *is* the best a captain can do. At least when he can't just sit and wait for his enemy to make the next move. If you think we're that lucky—"

The blue eyes narrowed, and Livia licked her full lips. It seemed to Conan that those lips were redder than before, and the perfume clinging to her stronger and more subtle at the same time. Livia also seemed to have her breasts thrust out a trifle farther than before.

Conan shook his head. "I think we've used up about all the luck the gods or anybody else is going to give us. We need to decide what *we'll* do as soon as Reza and his men return."

"I agree. Very well, Captain. I will listen to your guess, if you will tell me why you have nothing better. You did have a chance to speak to Lady Doris after the fight, did you not?"

Conan's tongue would not obey his command. Silence filled the room, a silence like water. It flowed around Conan and made his breath come hard. In that silence, he heard from the garden the sound of a lyre played softly.

The blue eyes went in an instant from ice to fire.

"So! You spent the night with Lady Doris, but had no chance to speak to her?"

Conan could no more have lied to Livia than he could have to a goddess. Indeed, he suspected that Livia's vengeance for a lie would be much swifter and surer.

"Yes. I'm afraid that when a man and a woman—"

"Are wallowing in bed until they lose all sense—"

"My lady—"

"Well, I can't see what else you could have done. And don't call me unmaidenly. I never want to hear that word again. A woman doesn't have to be a high-born trull like Doris to know a few truths about bedsport!"

Unmaidenly was the last thing Conan would have called Livia, if only because he did not wish his head broken with a perfume jar. Indeed, it seemed best to let his tongue lie still, until Livia's rage abated.

That took some time, and during that time Conan heard himself called names that few women of any land had ever flung at him. Half of what Lydia called him would have earned most women a brisk spanking or a plunge into the nearest midden.

Neither being wise with Livia—at least, not right now—Conan held his peace, barely, until she exhausted both her stock of names and her breath. When she finally collapsed into a chair, he even ventured to pick up a fan and wield it. She did not protest, only raising a hand to wipe the sweat from her face.

Another long silence followed, until Livia could command her tongue.

"Conan—I will not ask forgiveness. If you thought Doris would cast off all her secrets along with her robe— no, I already called you that, didn't I?"

"Yes, my lady."

"While we are alone, you need not call me that."

"As you wish, my—Livia."

She sat up, her robe falling away from one arm, and rang for a maid. When the maid had left with a message for wine and cakes, she motioned Conan to draw up a chair beside her.

"Now, your guess?"

"My guess is that Doris is no friend of Akimos. She told you the truth when you last met, but you doubted her. True?"

Livia had the grace to flush. "I more than doubted her. I called her—well, not as many names as I called you. But enough."

"Too many, you mean. That woman's frightened, and

152

frightened people are like frightened animals. They'll claw you without meaning to.''

"Conan, you were born a hundred years old.''

"Livia, I was born a Cimmerian. It's a harsh land, and its first and last law is: fools don't grow old.''

"We could use a law like that in Argos. Except that we already have too many laws, you said.''

Conan shrugged. "Perhaps you could do with that one. But as for Lady Doris—she wanted to disgrace or perhaps wound me, not kill. She thought I was a bad influence on you.

"When I told her that someone had tried to kill me and my men on the way, she was horrified. I can't be mistaken about that.''

"You know so much of women?''

"I know when somebody's stepped off a cliff and learned there's no bottom to the fall. That was Doris. She thought I was going to butcher her men, because I suspected her of having a hand in the attempt.''

"I wouldn't have thought she'd care about her servants. She has an evil reputation for casting them off when they displease her or grow old.''

"Livia, maybe that happens sometimes. But I'd wager all the wine in your cellars that it's mostly a tale she puts about. That way her servants shrink without anyone learning that she's too scant of silver to keep them.''

"Poor Doris.'' Then the blue eyes widened, and Livia stared wildly about the room. "Poor Doris! What am I saying? Conan, have you infected me with madness?''

"Livia, I—''

"You will address me as 'Lady Livia,' or lose your place and your men along with me. Go, and may the gods teach you manners if I cannot!''

153

Conan went, and not unwillingly. He had indeed been hoping for dismissal for some time, as the farewell to Jarenz would soon be starting. His "place" now was much more beside the lad's bier than here in this lavish chamber listening to his second madwoman of the day.

No, not a madwoman, Conan realized as the door closed behind him. A jealous woman. Which often enough led a woman to the same end.

As long as it wasn't *his* end. Reza's jealousy was enough to have behind his back; with Livia's added to it he'd be safer in Stygia! Thank the gods it was a night for drinking good wine with his fighting men, and not worrying more about women and their ways!

The spy crept catfooted away from where he had been eavesdropping on the lady's meeting with Captain Conan. He felt more like dancing, singing, and emptying jugs of wine.

It had not been easy, having to stand aside the night Akimos sent his men against the House. He had seen friends among the dead, more among those sent to slave in the mountains. It had been harder still, when he had not yet found a safe way to listen to what was said in the lady's chambers.

But the gods smiled, his luck turned, the way opened, and now he had not only heard but seen what happened there. If there was no desire in Lady Livia for Captain Conan, he could not tell desire in a woman when he saw it. Since he had once practiced the profession of pleasing women with more desire than beauty, he thought himself well-versed in the matter.

This was knowledge that Akimos must have. It could give him a weapon worth all the men he had lost, and ten more besides. It might even avenge on Captain

Conan the friends of his that great-thewed oaf had slain or taken!

The spy hurried back to the kitchen. The hours would crawl, before he could leave the palace to deliver his message. He could not sing or drink until he did, and indeed even a smile would not be prudent. Not when Reza or someone who would tell him might see it, and wonder whence it came.

CHAPTER 11

"Conan is in our path. This must not be."

Akimos looked at his tame sorcerer, knowing that bewilderment and weariness mingled on his face. To learn what had come of his effort to abduct Lady Livia was no pleasure. To endure yet one more outburst from Lord Skiron was even less so.

"Why?" Akimos said. He did not glare, but his voice did as well to show his impatience. "Have you learned that he is truly a sorcerer, a rival to you?'

If that was by some miracle so, then Akimos intended to win Conan over, if it cost him a thousand drachmas and half the tavern wenches in Messantia. Skiron needed a rival to keep him honest—or at least no more dishonest than the gods had made him.

"Conan has not the magic to heat a bowl of soup," Skiron sneered. "But—I cannot speak the whole truth about this, for it is an arcane matter—"

"Arcane or not, can you at least speak plainly? Or must I listen to riddles? I have little patience for the latter, I warn you."

"How little patience has the great master of intrigue, Lord Akimos!"

Akimos drew back, so that he would not be tempted to strike the sorcerer with his open hand. He hooked his thumbs into the belt of his riding leathers and grunted.

"I have enough to listen to what you fear about Conan. That is all you can expect for now."

"Very well. There is a darkness in Conan. A darkness and a destiny. To have such a man anywhere near our affairs—all our resources might not be equal to meeting him."

Akimos nodded, more in politeness than in agreement. Skiron certainly seemed truly frightened. But the merchant prince suspected it was more fear of Conan's solid sword than of anything so arcane as a dark Cimmerian destiny.

Akimos would not say it aloud, for Skiron would not tamely endure the charge of cowardice. Indeed, it might not be wholly just. Conan was a vastly formidable warrior, and leaving such an enemy free *was* dangerous.

Also costly. Akimos had not yet added up the cost of silencing the kin of his slain men and ransoming the captives from the lumber camp. It would be more drachmas than he cared to lay out when matters were coming so swiftly to a head.

"I will seek ways of removing Conan from our path. It is possible that he may serve us better remaining where he is. But even if that is so, I will see that he does not halt your work. Is that within reason?"

Skiron's nod was grudging, and he left without a further word. Akimos ignored the rudeness, sipped his wine, and considered choices.

The spy was trustworthy. Therefore Conan and Lady Livia could not be many days from making a scandal of themselves. If Conan was locked deep within the Watchhouse of the Guardians, that could not happen so swiftly, if it happened at all.

Yet did it matter if the Cimmerian truly bedded Livia? A tale to that effect, spread about the streets, would make enough scandal. If the girl then received a chance to redeem her reputation by a suitable marriage—to the son of a woman Akimos was about to wed—would she not leap at the opportunity?

Unless she was a fool or a wanton, she must. Then the matter would be settled, except for Conan himself. He would offer no great trouble, as the Guardians in the Watchhouse could be paid to look the other way. Then poison or a dagger in the night would end the Cimmerian's mischief.

Akimos poured himself more wine. Indeed he had not lost his gift for intrigue, if he could think so far ahead. He would need Lady Doris's goodwill, of course, but his plans for winning that could hardly fail.

Now it was time to think of his friends among the Guardians. Who would do the best work against Conan, and for the least gold?

Conan was inspecting the gate guards when the band of Guardians marched up. He could tell at once that this was no ordinary visit.

The Guardians numbered close to two score, with two captains over them, one mounted. The mounted captain remained in his saddle, and Conan recognized Helgios, from the Great Bridge.

"The Guardians of Argos, on a matter nearly concerning the Lady Livia and House Damaos," the sergeant of the band shouted.

Conan assumed his most formal Argossean manner. "The Lady Livia is within, but at her music. What may I tell her of the matter?"

"It concerns Captain Conan, of her guards."

"*I* am Captain Conan," the Cimmerian said, baring all his teeth. "If it concerns me, there is no need to disturb the Lady Livia."

"Is your name really Conan of Cimmeria?" the sergeant said, peering with near-sighted eyes at the head of a parchment scroll.

"It's the name on my—what's that pox-ridden paper?—oh, my bond warrant. Is that good enough?"

"Insolence to the Guardians!" the captain on foot shouted. "Note that down, Sergeant."

"What about the insolence of telling a man he lies about his own name?" Conan asked, more politely than he felt. His eyes met Helgios's.

Conan decided in favor of caution. With Helgios present, he had small chance of either surprising or deceiving these Guardians. Without surprise or deception, thirty to one was long odds even when the one was a hill-bred Cimmerian warrior and the thirty city-bred Argossean Guardians. To say nothing of the problems that a battle royal at her gate would make for Livia.

Helgios nodded to the sergeant. "Conan of Cimmeria, you are arrested for unlawfully assuming the rights belonging only to Captains of the Guardians. Further charges are under investigation and may be laid against you. You are warned that anything you say may be made the base of a fresh charge, and that resisting

159

the Guardians in such a matter as this is an enslavement offense. You are warned—''

"Oh, bog-trolls carry off your warnings," Conan said. He thought he had spoken quietly, but the entire band drew back two paces, except for a few who drew back four. No one actually raised a weapon, but many hands were closer than they had been to sword hilts and quivers.

Ignoring the Guardians as if they had sunk into the cobblestones, Conan turned to the gate guards. "One messenger to Lady Livia, concerning what is happening here. Another to Sergeant Talouf. He is to consider himself Captain over Conan's Company until my return."

Some of the Guardians could not keep from smiling at that. As if it had been written on the air, Conan knew then that he was not intended to emerge alive from wherever the Guardians were taking him.

So there would be a battle royal after all. But it still would not be at Livia's gate, or anywhere else that would bring blame to her. She would have enough problems if the Guardians could be bought so easily.

Conan considered that perhaps he should have told Livia of Harphos's passion for her. Then she might consider him friend rather than foe. To be sure, she would need a way of reaching him that his mother could not overhear. If Harphos could not find such a way, though, it would hardly be beyond Livia to do so.

Conan looked at Helgios. "May I visit my chambers, for food and clothing?"

"Only if four of my men go with you and search everything you bring," the captain said.

Conan bowed. "I will not presume to ask the Lady Livia to tolerate such a invasion. If she values my comfort more highly than the honor of her House, she will no doubt—''

"What will I no doubt do, Conan?" came a voice from behind the Cimmerian.

He turned slowly when he wanted to spin, and saw Livia in a cloak, hastily thrown on over a house robe. Her feet were not bare, as he thought, but clad only in light silken slippers embroidered with roses.

"My lady," Conan said, emphasizing the title. "I'm going to have to leave your service for a while, until a certain matter is done."

He explained, standing so that he could watch both her and Helgios at the same time. At first Livia's lips trembled, and she gripped the hem of her cloak. Then she sensed that Helgios was watching her like a cat studying a bird, seeking any signs of unease. Conan saw her straighten, tighten her mouth, and fold her hands in front of her. Again he thought that he had seen queens of twice Livia's age show half her dignity.

When he had finished, Livia nodded. "Captain Conan, I suspect that someone has taken—false information." She looked hard at Helgios, who suddenly could not meet her eyes. Conan almost laughed.

"I will send food and clothing and everything else necessary for your comfort," she continued. "Sergeant Talouf will rank equal to Steward Reza—unless he is suspected of pissing in the Chief Archon's roses or some such crime?"

Even the sergeant laughed at that, and Helgios's mouth opened soundlessly before he shook his head.

"Very well. Then—the gods be with you, Captain Conan." She gripped both his hands, but stopped her fingers from reaching higher than the Cimmerian's elbows. On his part, it took a heroic effort not to embrace her hard enough to lift her feet off the gravel!

Then Conan stepped out the gate, laughed as the Guardians drew back still farther, and with his own hands pulled the gate shut behind him.

"Well, my friends? Do I have a nice cool dungeon waiting for me, as you promised? Or do we stand here all day in the sun?"

Akimos did not drink or shout for joy when word came from the Watchhouse.

"Conan the Cimmerian is safely within, locked in the House of Charof."

The House of Charof was the lowest level of the Watchhouse, named after the ancient Argossean god of death. It was normally reserved for criminals condemned to death, but enough gold had changed hands to secure Conan a place there.

Which was not altogether inappropriate, Akimos decided. The Cimmerian was doomed, even if his fate would be less public than that of a murderer or traitor. But it would be no less certain. Not even his thews— yes, and his wits—could let him pass the gates, the guards, and the other traps waiting in the path from the House of Charof.

Argos had seen the last of Conan of Cimmeria, save as a body to be found on a suitable midden-pit. *After* the rumor of his scandalous bedding of Lady Livia was spread about the streets like the dung of stray dogs.

Instead of drinking or shouting, Akimos went quietly downstairs to Skiron's chambers in the cellar. He did not approach the door, let alone knock, for the sounds from within were unmistakable.

A man and a woman, grappling in frenzied lust. Or

at least frenzied in the woman. It was hard to tell from the sounds how Skiron was going about this coupling. Clearly he was not one of those sorcerers who required celibacy to work—and indeed, such were most commonly women.

Akimos turned away, smiling. Another time would do for speaking with Skiron. The merchant prince had told the sorcerer many times over how important it was that the Flowers of Desire potion should do its work. His whole plan for Lady Doris hung upon it. So who could blame the sorcerer for testing the potion?

Fireflies glowed in the twilight-hued garden, and beyond the garden wall the lamplighters were at work. The western sky was turning purple, and from the waterfront the songs and music of wineshop revelry floated up on a soft breeze.

The evening would have been perfect for Lady Livia had she not been alone on the roof of the Damaos palace. She would not say, even to herself, "If Conan was here beside me." But he was not as absent from her thoughts as he was from the house.

Tears blurred her eyes as she thought of all that splendid strength and shrewdness locked in a Watchhouse cell. A cell in the House of Charof, too—old family friends among the Guardians had been able to tell her that much at least.

She had asked more, but learned nothing. Nothing, that is, save that it would not be wise to be too curious about Captain Conan. One man had told her this in plain words. Others had merely looked away, but she needed no words to know what they had to be thinking.

She did not care if all of Argos whispered that she and Conan were lovers. Nay, if they shouted it from the rooftops and to the ships at sea! She would not let Conan languish, let alone die, if there was anything she could do to save him.

But what? She could not force from her mind the notion that Reza might have something to do with Conan's arrest. His jealousy of her favor toward the Cimmerian was as plain as his nose. Had that jealousy led him to treason?

And if it had, what hope did she have of bringing him to punishment? Sergeant Talouf and the others of Conan's men had sworn to follow Reza. Perhaps they trusted him. Perhaps they only refused to divide the forces of House Damaos in the face of an enemy.

If so, they were wise. She would be wise, too, if she followed their lead. But then, anything she did to save Conan, Reza could turn aside!

She gripped the stone until her knuckles were white. She bit her lip until it bled, and finally let the tears that blurred her eyes overflow onto her cheeks.

When her eyes at last were dry, she rang for a servant. The maid Gisela appeared.

"Wine, Gisela."

"A jug or a cup?"

"Who are you, to tell me how much I shall drink?"

"My lady. A cup often sharpens the wits. A jug always blunts them. Do not all of us need our wits about us now?"

Livia had to smile. Had Livia's mother not died when she was born, she might have a sister just Gisela's age.

"You sound as if you have said this before."

"I have been arguing with Vandar."

"Only arguing?"

Gisela did not blush. "When we have nothing else at hand." She lowered her eyes. "That is not as often as

I could wish. But I understand. He will be slow, healing from his brother's death. They were not only born at one birth, they have never been apart until now.''

Livia's eyes threatened to overflow again. ''He will have vengeance for his brother's death. We will all have vengeance.'' She struck the tile underfoot. ''By this House and all the years it has stood, I swear it!''

''The gods grant it,'' Gisela said. ''And—a jug or a cup?''

''A jug, but bring two cups and stay with me. Perhaps if we both sharpen our wits, we can begin that vengeance.''

The spy hurried toward the door of the wine cellar. One hand was pressed to his stomach, as if it ached. In truth, the bag of Akimos's gold inside his tunic would cure many aches, if he lived to spend it.

To do that, he had to be free of House Damaos. That might have been written in letters of fire. It certainly was written on Reza's face. The big Iranistani had been asking too many questions. When he began to find answers he would not be long in finding the spy.

Some seemed to doubt Reza's loyalty. Jealous of the Cimmerian, they said. He might not want House Damaos overthrown, but if he could have the Cimmerian out of the way and save it by himself—?

The spy would have laughed, if his throat had not been too dry and his breath too scant. Reza would shed the last drop of his blood in defense of his mistress, though Conan made her Queen of Cimmeria! Indeed, he would be all the more ready to shed the blood of anyone he suspected, to prove that loyalty.

The wine cellar door opened easily to the spy's key. He scurried from shadow to shadow, hiding behind the largest barrels when he could find no shadow. A few paces at a time, the wall he sought grew closer. The floor underfoot grew sticky, where the blood and fire-wine from the battle had not yet been scoured from the stones. One more dash of a dozen paces, and he would be at the door to the caves. He fumbled in his pocket for the key that opened the inner lock.

As his hand closed on the key, an iron grip closed on his wrist. The grip tightened, and now two hands held him, one by the wrist, one by the neck of his tunic.

The hands spun him around, so savagely that his tunic ripped. That did not matter. Reza shifted his grip to the spy's hair and held him for a moment, their noses almost touching. The spy's feet dangled in the air, and he felt an awful urge to foul himself.

Before that urge mastered him, he felt Reza shifting his grip again. One giant hand held his neck, as if he had been a kitten. The other gripped his belt. Then two powerful arms whipped the spy in a half-circle, driving his head against a stone pillar.

He was dead before he could feel more fear. Reza dropped the corpse and wiped his hands on its clothing. He really wanted to take a complete bath, scrubbing his skin until it was red. Nothing else would take the memory of touching such filth from him.

But that could wait. Only he and the gods knew it, but House Damaos had just taken its first vengeance against its enemies.

CHAPTER 12

In the night, sorcery stalked House Lokhri and its mistress.

It was not mighty sorcery. In some lands, even so poverty-stricken a House as House Lokhri would have a sorcerer, to whom besting Skiron's spells would have been child's play.

But this was Argos, where any kind of sorcery was barely a memory and great sorcery not even that. Had Lady Doris searched the land, from the Rabirian Mountains to the Western Sea, she could not have found anyone fit to meet Skiron.

It was a small achievement, but a real one. Skiron had made himself the greatest sorcerer Argos had known in generations. Now his talents, such as they were, turned upon House Lokhri.

Lady Doris awoke in an empty bed from a dream in which she had been reliving her bed-sharing with Captain Conan. Now there was a man worth any ten others she had known!

No, make that any three. Doubtless the Cimmerian was not made of iron, but of flesh and blood, which could be pressed only so far. But his could be pressed farther than most—and she would give much to have his flesh pressing hers again, his weight spreading her while she wrapped arms and legs about him and tried to make that weight still heavier—

A scream shrilled from the outer chambers. Doris sprang from the bed, her bed robe slipping from her shoulders as she did. Ignoring her nudity, she padded to the door.

She had no time or need to open the door. It flew open, the lock bursting like a rotten fruit, the hinges twisting like snakes. It struck her, flinging her to the floor, half dazed, aching, and frightened. Then anger came to join the other sensations and in part drive them out.

"Guards! To your mistress!"

She thanked the gods for Conan's shrewdness in defeating her men without crippling or killing them. If she knew who had healed them so skilfully, she would also thank the gods for that man's skills. Between Conan and the healer, her House was still fit to defend itself.

The reply was another scream, then laughter. Deep, mocking laughter—if a great shark could laugh, it might sound like this. Doris tried to stand, but her legs and wind betrayed her. Writhing on the floor, she sought to cover herself with her hands.

A third scream. It came from the outer chamber, where the maid on night duty was writhing in the grip of something vast and invisible. She was also losing her garments, a shred at a time, and beginning to twist in unmistakable desire.

By the time the maid was nude, her head was thrown back, her eyes were closed, and her mouth open. She seemed to be embracing the empty air. Doris stared, desire beginning to boil up in her so hot and quick that it drove out the fear. If that invisible presence was fit—

The maid let out a final shriek and collapsed on the floor. Doris now found the strength to rise, then held herself upright by gripping the door frame. The metal of the lock was hot to the touch, and she smelled smoke as well as the musk of the maid's ecstasy.

Then her eyes fell on the maid's face. Where the skin had been young and fresh, now it was wrinkled. Even as Doris watched, the wrinkles deepened. Youth and freshness fled, and the dry wrinkled grayness of age took its place. As blood trickled from her mouth, age spread over the maid's face, then crawled steadily down her body. Doris wanted to turn away, but her eyes had a will of their own. They remained fixed on the maid's body until it was the gaunt remnant of the fair young woman she had been.

Then Doris tried to scream and spew at once, for the nightmare was not done. Now the maid's body went past age into the grave, and from the grave to a mouldering *thing* that was half dust, half hideous blood-hued ichor. The dust blew into Doris's face, reeking of the grave, an she knelt while her stomach rebelled. The dreadful miasma of the ichor rode in on the heels of the dust, and Doris felt all her senses reeling.

She knelt by the door, trying to empty a stomach already empty, clawing at the rug, whimpering like a small trapped animal. She did not see two vast yellow eyes open in mid-air, and a black mist flow and dance around the eyes. She did not see the mist flow forward, until its foremost wisps were playing over her bare skin.

Then she felt their touch, cold as death itself and smelling worse than anything that had gone before. She did not feel the touch long, for her mind could bear only so much. As Lady Doris plunged down into the refuge of senselessness, the terrible mocking laugh echoed around the chambers again.

Conan sat on the bench that was one-third of the furnishings of his cell. The other two-thirds were a straw pallet and a large bucket that did duty as a jakes.

The Cimmerian had been in worse prisons, and indeed he had hardly expected one as good as this. It was his experience that men who had only days before they met the executioner seldom enjoyed lavish hospitality.

The food and drink were also adequate. The drink was only water, but it was clean enough and almost fresh, not half solid with living green scum. The food was a porridge of barley and beans, with a few thumb-sized bits of meat hiding in it. The meat was at least good enough for dogs.

Conan had eaten his noon meal of the prison fare, but some time later the promised basket from House Damaos came. Lady Livia must have turned out her larder, for the guard could barely lift the basket. Wine, cheese, sausage, flat bread and long bread, raisins and apples, even a jug of ale—if he was here for less than five days, he would hardly need the prison fare again.

Bread and cheese were all he'd wanted at first, but he knew that he had to keep his strength up. Lady Livia might have ways of bringing him out of here peacefully, but he would not wager much on that, certainly not his life. So he pulled out one of the sausages and cut off a piece.

As he did, he saw two things. One was a rat peering out from a crack at the base of the rear wall. The other was a thin slit in the other end of the sausage.

Conan had no love for rats, but this one was a sorry creature indeed, gray, slow-moving, and gaunt. It would have run from a mouse, let alone a cat.

"Very well," the Cimmerian said. "Never let it be said that I turned away a beggar when I had food to spare." He cut off a small slice from the slit end of the sausage and tossed it to the rat.

The rat could move fast when it saw food. It seemed to snatch the sausage out of the air. Three bites and it was gone. The rat sniffed at the floor, as if hoping for more. Conan started cutting another piece.

Then the rat squealed as if it were being roasted alive. It rolled over on its side, then on its back, drawing its thin legs up to its matted belly. It writhed and twisted, while foam flecked with green drooled from its mouth. Its eyes seemed to glare with knowledge no mortal creature should have, then closed. A moment later it went limp.

"The gods rot them!"

The trail of that basket led through so many hands that now the gods only knew whose had poisoned the sausage. Nor did Conan expect to learn, if the poisoner lay within this prison.

But if the poisoner was under Livia's roof, then Conan vowed to ferret out his secret and end his life.

Most folk in Messantia would have been surprised that Lord Harphos did not run screaming from his mother's house at the first whiff of sorcery. Even those who knew there was more to Harphos than met the eye would not have expected his night's work.

Harphos was fortunate to be awake and in his private chamber. He was a long way from the heart of Skiron's attack, and ready to meet it when it spread through the house.

His knowledge as a healer included no spell-working. Old Kyros who had taught him made it clear that he would teach Harphos no such thing. "Not without your mother's consent, and maybe not even with it."

"No fear, Master. She would throw a fit, and perhaps more."

"In some matters your mother may be wiser than she realizes."

Now, wise or not, his mother was in danger, and it was Harphos's place to use the knowledge she had forbidden him to defend her. If he could not defend her, he could at least defend House Lokhri and avenge his mother.

So Harphos made two plugs of herbs that would trap wind-born or spell-cast poisons and thrust them into his nostrils. He made an infusion of more herbs and soaked a scarf in them, then drew it across his mouth. He drew on an iron-studded belt and a purse with an iron lock, and in the purse put two stoppered vials. One would fight off any drowsiness the magic might send. The second would give him strength perhaps matching Conan's for half an hour or so.

As an afterthought, Harphos thrust a shortsword into his belt. He did not expect to face human enemies tonight. But if by chance he did and they were not in too great strength, they would have a disagreeable surprise.

So girded for battle, Harphos ascended the stairs to his mother's chamber. On the way he saw no one who was not senseless, and some who were surely dead, dying, or mad. He could only hope that the wits of the mad could be restored once the spells left the house.

As he climbed the stairs, fear gnawed in his belly like a wolf at a rabbit. At his mother's broken door, the fear turned into something solid, cold as ice, and so large that it seemed to press outward in all directions. He subdued his bowels and his stomach and stepped within.

It was not, he thought afterward, the fear-binding spell Skiron had left behind that finally broke him. It was the sight of what was left of the maid, the reek of her death—and the image Skiron left floating in the doorway to Lady Doris's bedchamber.

Harphos took one look at the spike-studded black arms wrapping themselves around his mother and cried out. Then he turned and ran.

He did not remember leaving the house, or plunging through the streets faster than he had ever run before. He could not indeed have run faster if he had taken both vials. His hands writhed, his eyes stared, and those who prowled and preyed by night gave way before him, because they thought him a madman.

Indeed, he did not remember anything until he found himself clawing at the gate of the Damaos palace. A moment later he found himself facing Conan's Sergeant Talouf.

"What in the name of Erlik—?"

"This—this isn't—gods'—work," Harphos gasped. He gripped the bars of the gate as if loosening his grip for a moment would cast him down into the mouth of a volcano. "Sorcery. Sorcery at—our house."

Talouf had his wits about him. The gate slid open— Harphos noticed how silently it moved, compared with the rusty monster at the Lokhri palace—and guards surrounded Harphos. Some gave him water, others gave him shoulders to lean on. All in time led him up to the house, where Lady Livia waited.

She sat on silk cushions in a chair of carved ivory, and her face was the same hue as the ivory. So was her night shift. It revealed more of her fair body than Harphos had ever dreamed of seeing, but otherwise might have been armor. Certainly her eyes were as cold as steel—and they grew no warmer as Harphos finished his tale.

"You fled, then?" she said. A judge condemning a man to the impaling stake might have spoken more kindly.

"My—Livia . . ." Harphos said, trailing off as his legs began to weave of their own will. "I—the sorcerer left a spell behind, to make anyone afraid. He left more, too." He described the image of his mother—or began to describe it, because Livia raised one hand to silence him and put the other over her mouth.

When she had command of herself again, the blue eyes seemed less cold. "What do you think has become of your mother?"

"I do not know," Harphos said. "But it seemed to me that your enemies might have become mine. I thought you might know at least whether she is alive or dead."

"We do not," Livia said. "But I think we may know who does."

"Lord Akimos?"

For the first time she smiled, then nodded. "I would be surprised if he knew nothing."

"Then let us call—"

"I do not think he will answer any questions put to

him by lawful means. As for other means—before we can use those, we must free Captain Conan.''

Did something pass over the big Iranistani steward's face at those words? Harphos reminded himself to find some Truth-Teller, or make it if he could find none ready to hand.

''Where is he held?''

Now it was Livia's turn to tell a tale. Harphos listened, his legs growing weak again until Reza pushed a stool under him. When Lydia was finished, Harphos was staring at the floor, so she would not see the look on his face.

He would rather have bones broken than return to that house where sorcery's horrors now reigned. But he would rather be flayed alive than have Livia think him a coward.

''Then—if some of your men can return with me to the house—''

''What about the sorcery?'' Reza growled.

''There is a way into the cellar that does not go through the rest of the house. All we need is in the cellar, and most of it one man can carry. I will be that man, since I have protected myself a trifle.''

The sun came out in Livia's face, and if Harphos had not been sitting down he would have fallen in a heap. To keep that look on his beloved's face, flaying alive would be a small price!

CHAPTER 13

The guard at the door to the House of Charof was alone, as indeed he was expected to be. The devices for keeping those within from escaping were so numerous and so cunning that a single guard was considered sufficient. His duty was to stay awake (and if wise, sober) and mark those entering and leaving on a wax tablet hung by the door.

He stretched his legs halfway across the tunnel, and his arms halfway to the ceiling. Then he stiffened, as light footsteps sounded from just out of sight up the stairs.

He rose and drew his shortsword.

"Who is there?"

"Only a friend." The voice was female, and more a girl's than a woman's. A moment later the source of the voice came into view.

She could hardly be more than seventeen, but was

well-formed for all that. Her tunic was threadbare, patched, and stained, and the guard would have wagered a month's pay that she wore nothing under it. Certainly she wore nothing on her feet, or on her head to conceal a mass of dark brown hair.

"A friend, you say?" The guard didn't sheathe his sword, but he let the point drop.

"Well, one who may be a friend, in time."

"I haven't seen you above."

"When was your last time above Himgos's Door?"

The guard laughed and shook his head. The girl smiled.

"That long? Then I don't wonder you haven't seen me. I came to the kitchen only five days ago."

The guard nodded. That explained her being a stranger, and also clad like an escaped prisoner. The cooks and scullions in the Watchhouse had starvation wages and took their revenge by offering only starvation fare. The guard remembered better meals aboard ships a month at sea!

"Well, if you have nothing better to do, shall we see if we can be friends?" The guard hoped his cloak would be all the padding she needed, because if she needed more between her and the floor a fine chance might slip past. . . .

"Surely." She sidled past him, brushing her hip against his and trailing long fingers across his arm. Then she sat down and thrust a hand into the bosom of her tunic. It came out with a small bottle. Clear glass, it plainly revealed what it held—vintage firewine.

The girl held the bottle out. As she did, her tunic slipped off first one shoulder, then off the other. Slowly it crept down toward her breasts, then past them, to her waist.

177

He had been right. She wore nothing under the tunic. He took a step forward—then thunder crashed and lightning blazed in his head. His next step forward was a boneless stumble, and after that he crashed face-down onto the floor.

The girl pulled her dress up, pulled the cork from the bottle, and sprinkled a few drops over the guard. Sergeant Talouf leaped down the last three steps and knelt beside the guard. Practiced fingers retrieved the keys from the guard's belt and his own dagger from the corner. Thrown to strike hilt-first, the dagger had laid the guard out as neatly as anyone could ask.

"That's a waste of good firewine, you know," Talouf said.

"The worse he smells, the less they'll suspect," Gisela said. "I'd like him deep in dung, for the way he looked at me—"

"Gisela," came a voice from the stairs. "Men will look at you whether you will or no, unless you hide yourself in a cell."

Gisela flashed a mocking grin as Lady Livia descended the stairs. Flanking her were two of Conan's men and two of her own, all wearing the tunics and sandals of Guardians. Bringing up the rear was Harphos, wearing the same garb but with a captain's badge on his belt and the badge of a healer on the shoulder of his tunic. A bulging leather bag was slung over one shoulder.

"I bow to my lady's vast experience in such matters, of course," Gisela said.

"Vandar, best you thrash this impudent wench at least once a week until she can keep a civil tongue," Livia said.

Vandar grunted. "Like as not, she'd serve me as Talouf served the guard."

"No, the dagger would go point-first," Gisela said.

"Enough chatter," Talouf said. He picked a key nearly the length of a child's arm, thrust it into the lock, and turned it. Metal screamed and stone grated against stone, chains clanked, and a distant hissing floated up from somewhere far below.

When silence reigned again, the door to the House of Charof stood open. A narrow drawbridge had swung down, spanning a gap that ran from wall to wall. Looking down, Talouf saw rock plunging down into darkness. As he stepped onto the drawbridge, he thought he saw something moving in the darkness far below. He knew he heard the hissing again.

He could barely breathe until he felt solid rock under his feet again, and the others were no slower. All except Harphos, who stopped and peered down into the darkness with his near-sighted eyes.

"Curse you, Har—Captain. What are you looking for, the Treasure of Gilmi?"

"I'm trying to discover what sort of beast is down there. If I know, I may have something to quiet it."

Talouf forced his mouth closed. If Harphos wanted permission to try sleeping draughts on serpents, he could ask it of Captain Conan. The sergeant was a great believer in either cold steel or a fleet pair of heels as the solution to most problems, and not at all a believer in encouraging madmen!

Conan's stomach had reached the point of rumbling peevishly, but it took more than that to sap his strength or slow him. So he was off his pallet and ready for any aid or menace the moment he heard voices outside.

179

Then he heard the unmistakable sound of picks in the lock.

"Talouf?"

"Captain?"

"Here."

"Are you shackled?"

"Free as a bird."

"The gods be thanked."

That voice made Conan miss a breath. Livia, here? Was she a prisoner too, or had she insisted on coming with this rescue party? Knowing Livia, Conan suspected the second, and doubted that anyone would have dared stand against her.

The clinking and clicking of well-wielded picks went on. Then it stopped, and curses took its place.

"That fatherless last lock—" Talouf growled.

"How big is it?"

"Finger-thick—"

"We don't have much time. Stand back." Conan took a deep breath, found purchase for his feet on the rough stone floor, then set his shoulder against the door and pushed.

He pushed until the veins started from forehead and neck and sweat sluiced from him like water in a mill-race. But he could feel *something* giving, and from outside he heard shouts.

He drew back, caught his breath, set his back against the door, and pushed again. Metal groaned, then squealed, then yielded with a ghastly scream.

Conan felt a chill on his spine as he thought of all who might have died here, with just such screams on their lips. Neither gods nor priests could help much with ghosts, if a man could not stay away from their haunts.

The door grated open. Conan stepped out, to see Livia throw the hood of her cloak back from her face and take a step forward. At that, Harphos's face twisted.

With a deep bow, Conan caught Livia's hands in his own, lifted them to his lips, and kissed both of them.

"My lady, I rejoice in returning to your service."

Harphos's face visibly eased. Livia looked ready to either scream or weep.

Vandar, however, had a warrior's wits. "Your sword, Captain."

Conan belted on the steel. "Have any of you thought of a story to get us all out of here?"

Harphos showed a pass with more seals than Conan had thought such a small piece of leather could hold. "I doubt that I will have many friends left, when they learn what I did with their gifts. But that's for the gods to settle."

They turned and retraced their steps, Conan in the rear. He was looking back for any signs of pursuit when he heard Talouf curse.

"The pig-spawned door's closed, and the drawbridge is up!"

So it was. Conan looked down into the dark depths, and a long hiss answered him. He looked across the gap, and judged that there was no hope of pulling the drawbridge back down. Even if they could reach the hook, the hinges most likely locked solid when the door was closed.

Meanwhile, whoever had closed the door must be waiting outside, most likely with more men than the rescue party could face. There would also be all the other doors on the way out, each one guarded.

In the end, defeat and death waited for the Cimmerian and his men, defeat and disgrace for Livia. Unless they could find another way out. . . .

Conan peered over the rim of the gap. He could dimly make out coils the thickness of a man's body writhing at the bottom. More clearly, he saw bronze rungs set in niches on the far side of the gap.

He sat and began pulling off his boots, then drew his tunic over his head. Conscious of the women's glances toward him, he belted his sword on over his loinguard.

"I'm going to see if there's a way out from the bottom of this pit. I've fought bigger serpents than the Guardians' pet down there, and it's their hides that have made my shields."

Livia opened her mouth. Harphos spoke first.

"Wait. I have something here." He fumbled the bag off his shoulder and rummaged in it until his hand came out with a bottle in the style of Khitai.

"What's that?" Gisela asked. "A love potion?"

Harphos flushed. "A sleeping powder. There's enough in the bottle to lay six men senseless. Perhaps that will be enough for one serpent."

"Serpents are sluggish beasts," Conan said. "Steel works faster."

"Yes, but if the Guardians only find the snake asleep, they'll not be sure we escaped past it," Livia put in. "Let him try it. At worst, it may make your work easier."

Conan began a sharp reply, that he needed no help in any work with a good sword. Then he remembered that he was captain over some six or seven people, two of them women, one no warrior, and none fit for serpent-wrestling even had they the time.

"Give me the bottle. If the snake comes close enough, I'll give him a good dose."

"I'll go—" Harphos began.

"No, Harphos," Livia interrupted. "The ladder is on the far side. You are no leaper, like Captain Conan. Nor could he catch you."

"Not without us both going down to make snake fodder," Conan added. "Unless you're thinking to just leap down and make it easier for me to kill the snake while it's feeding on you."

Harphos turned pale, then flushed as Livia put a hand on his arm. With that settled, Conan gathered himself for a leap, soared over the pit, and caught the topmost rung of the ladder.

The darkness below instantly came alive with hisses, and now he could make out a monstrous fanged head rising toward him. Nostrils and mouth both gaped wide, and two red eyes the size of melons glared at him over a horned black snout.

Conan pulled the stopper from the bottle, waited until the snake reared as high as it could, then flung the bottle straight into the gaping maw. The hissing rose to a deafening pitch, and scales grated and squealed on rock as the snake flung itself about.

Conan drew up his legs as far as they would go and rather hoped that Harphos's potion would work. That he was the best serpent-fighter in the band did not mean that he did it for his own amusement. Besides, Livia was right about leaving fewer traces of their escape.

It struck Conan that Livia and Harphos might not make a bad match. At least they could try, if Lady Doris could be silenced by something short of strangling her, and if Harphos did not care that his wife had twice his wits.

Time seemed to stretch toward the end of the world as Conan waited for the potion to take effect. He also drew his sword, as the snake was striking to within an arm's length of his feet. If the potion had no effect, or was slow—

Sparks flew as the fangs scraped rock. Then the snake reared back until its gaping maw was pointing straight up. Green foam bubbled up in its gullet, and its tongue thrashed frantically. Then with a sound like an iron gate closing, the jaws slammed shut. A moment later the whole immense length of the serpents seemed to lose all its bones. It slumped down into the shadows and lay still.

Balancing haste against prudence, Conan counted to ten, then pried a chunk of mortar loose from the wall and dropped it on the snake's head. He might as well have dropped it into a well.

"Well done, Harphos. I'm climbing down to make sure. Talouf, did I see a rope under your tunic?"

"Would I go out without a rope, or Lady Livia without a tunic?"

"Mind your tongue—" Harphos began, before Livia said something Conan did not hear but which certainly silenced the man.

Conan scrambled down the ladder, landing in ankle-deep black ooze, foul to the nose and still fouler to the touch. But a glance told him that his efforts had not been wasted. A tunnel led away into darkness, a tunnel that rose slightly.

Conan stepped over the motionless serpent. "Talouf, the rope!" The Cimmerian raised his arms, but as he did he took one final look down the tunnel.

It was as well that he did. A hiss like all the geysers of Vanaheim erupting together echoed from the stone, and the darkness came alive. Conan leaped backward, his sword slashing at the monstrous scaled head that thrust itself out of the tunnel at him.

"There's two of them!" Harphos squalled.

"Tell Conan something he doesn't know," came Livia's voice, then the Cimmerian was too busy with his opponent to hear what went on above. The serpent's surprise at finding its mate still gave Conan a heartbeat's worth of time, which he put to good use. He sprang backward over the sleeping serpent, crouched with his sword over his head, then slashed two-handed at the exposed neck of the other monster.

Palm-sized scales tinted in cinnamon and rose parted, and the pale flesh under them. But the snake had taken no vital hurt, and now it knew that its opponent was not to be despised. Serpents, Conan knew, were mostly sluggish of wits, but they did not live to grow this large without knowing how to fight.

Man and serpent settled into a deadly duel. The pit was too narrow to let the serpent throw its coils around Conan. So it struck at the Cimmerian time after time, with a speed that would have been deadly against any lesser opponent, seeking a grip with its teeth.

Each time it struck, Conan's steel was there, slicing scales and flesh. Sometimes the strike carried it past the Cimmerian, to lunge with the force of a battering ram against the stones. Conan saw mortar and even whole stones start from the walls under those blows. It began to look like a race between the serpent's knocking itself senseless and its bringing the whole pit down on top of them both!

With a rumble and a crash, a stone plunged from the top of the pit. It bounced off the snake, then off the wall, nearly took off Conan's sword arm, then buried

185

itself in the muck. Before he could curse, a second stone followed.

This one struck the snake on its horned nose. It uncoiled and struck upward, hissing in a greater frenzy than ever. It also exposed its throat to Conan.

With all the strength of his iron arms and all the speed in his legs, the Cimmerian struck. His sword slashed through scales and flesh to reach the serpent's life. Blood fountained for a moment as the creature seemed to rear higher still, then like its mate it seemed to lose all strength. Conan was barely able to leap aside in time, as the serpent came crashing down on its sleeping mate.

"Did one of you throw those stones?" he shouted.

A small voice broke the silence. "Yes," Gisela said. "I thought—"

"If that's what you do when you think, Crom spare me when you don't!" Conan snapped. "Talouf, let's be down and out of here."

The pile of serpents made a slippery landing place, but everyone made their way down the rope without mishap, except for Gisela. She slipped, caught her tunic on one of the nose horns, and landed in the muck bare as a babe.

Vandar stripped off his own tunic to clothe her, as she tried vainly to wipe the muck from her legs and buttocks.

"Pheugh!" Livia said, wrinkling her nose. "What did those beasts—Conan, what are you doing?"

Conan was carving chunks out of the sleeping serpent. As a final measure, he drove his dagger through one eye, deep into the brain. The serpent passed from sleep into death with only a faint shudder.

"Your own advice, my lady," Conan said, wiping

his sword on the scales and sheathing it. "With both slashed as they are, it will seem—I hope—that they killed each other. Also, the first one won't be waking up, to hunt us through the tunnels."

Livia shuddered and put out one hand to Harphos, the other to Conan. For a moment both men needed to hold her, to keep her from falling into the muck. Then she took a deep breath.

"Let us be on our way."

"As you wish, my lady," Talouf said. "But best I lead. I have learned these tunnels rather better than the rest of you, I think."

Conan glared at the sergeant. "Talouf, have you been lying about your not being in Messantia before?"

"Captain, you only asked if I was known to the Guardians. I said that I was not, and that was the truth."

"Because you spent all your time out of the light of day, no doubt," Livia said, with a faint smile.

"It's not only thieves who have business best done in the dark," Talouf said, and turned down the tunnel.

They were not long in learning what the serpents ate. Thrust out from the muck were bones, the greater part of them shattered by the serpents' teeth or coils but recognizable as human.

They were mercifully not much longer in finding a way to the streets, with fresh air and dry stone underfoot. They emerged into twilight, and by the time they were approaching the Damaos palace darkness had fallen.

They had also settled one matter among them. Before they could move against the enemy without, the enemy within must be foiled. A spy there was, without a doubt, and if his name was not Reza, then Reza would help them hunt that spy or suffer the same fate.

CHAPTER 14

Reza awoke swiftly at the noise in his room. Those who did not wake swiftly on the Iranistani frontier did not serve long with Khadjar's Irregulars. If Khadjar did not send them away, the Iranistanis took their heads and sometimes other parts.

Swiftly awake, Reza rolled even more swiftly to the side of the bed away from the door. As he rolled, his hand darted under his pillow. It came out holding a shortsword.

But as he rolled off the bed, the flat of a broadsword came down across his wrist. His fingers opened and his blade clattered to the floor. He saw a vast looming shape move with the speed of a striking adder, and a booted foot slam down on the sword.

Then something hard smashed across his temple. He fell face-down on the floor, vaguely aware of cold stone against his cheek. Not so vaguely he felt iron hands binding his feet and hands. He wanted to curse, but he lacked the strength.

He could see clearly, though. Looking under the bed gave him a view of the door, and the people standing by it. When he saw them, Reza was quite sure he was dreaming. The Lady Livia here, watching him trussed like a pig for slaughter? And Harphos of Lokhri, standing so close to Livia that his breath might have ruffled her hair and wearing a bulging leather bag slung over his shoulder?

Reza had just decided that he had struck his head and addled his wits, when he felt a giant's strength pulling him to a sitting position. He found himself staring into icy blue eyes in a dark face that might have been carved from the stone of its native Cimmerian hills.

"He's awake," Conan said.

"I—" Reza began.

"The less you say now, the sooner we'll be done with this," Conan said. His voice sounded less harsh than his face. "Harphos, are you ready?"

"Yes, although I would urge that we have some olive oil ready to hand."

"Olive oil?" Livia and Conan asked together.

"Yes. A dose of the herb as strong as we may need will make him spew his guts all over the room after a while. If we feed him some olive oil when we are done with the questioning, this may not happen."

Livia nodded. "Gisela, you can move about with the fewest questions asked. To the kitchen with you."

"Yes, my lady." Reza saw the maid slip out the door, and Harphos put down the bag and begin setting out bottles and vials.

"Now, Reza," Lady Livia said. "It appears that there is a spy in our house. He has betrayed too many of our secrets. In spite of your long service, you have ample reason to be that spy. Lord Harphos has devised a potion that will make you tell the truth in the matter. If you refuse to take it, we shall have to judge you guilty. Then we must use harsher—''

Reza began to laugh, and could not stop. He saw the others looking at one another. No doubt they thought he was mad.

When he had his breath back, Reza smiled again. ''My lady, forgive me for leaving you in doubt so long. I—the reasons you suspect I have are real enough, but I am neither spy nor traitor nor breaker of the oaths I swore to both your blood father and your keeper-father! Bring on your potions, and when I am done with them I will show you where I left the real spy.''

Livia looked at the others. ''If he is so fearless—''

Conan shook his head. ''He might be telling us all this to put us off our guard. It does no harm that he is willing, though.''

''Conan, will you stop talking of me as though I were a brute beast without speech? And Harphos, you may dose me with what you please. But if I spew until I am too weak to fight the real enemies of House Damaos, be out of here before I regain my strength. Otherwise I shall kick you down the stairs, throw you out the door, and drown you in the fish pond.''

Harphos laughed nervously, then returned to measuring out the potion. That gave Reza time to watch his mistress as she looked at her two companions.

Conan had touched her heart. This was past denying. But he had no power over her wits, to lead her astray. Unless Livia cast aside all the wisdom she had gained in the years Reza had known her, the Cimmerian could do no harm to House Damaos.

Now all that remained was to persuade the Cimmerian that he, Reza son of Shiram, was quite as innocent!

Lady Doris of Lokhri awoke to pains that had nothing to do with unsatisfied desire. They were more like what she remembered from the time she had fled from an attacker straight into a quickset hedge. Tiny prickles and stings ran up and down her limbs and body, from shoulders to knees.

The swaying and rattling told her that she was in a light cart, moving fast on one of the High Roads. It was covered as snugly as a bird's cage at night with a cover of canvas as heavy as sailcloth.

Secure against prying eyes, she stripped off the robe that was her only garment. The prickles and stings were not imagination. Red spots like insect bites covered her everywhere she felt pain.

A moment later she felt the wagon stopping. As silence descended, she heard bird songs and horses blowing, then men's voices. She began to look about the cart, seeking food or at least water, and more than either a chamberpot!

She had just concluded that the cart held no such thing when a flap of canvas flew back. Into the gap thrust a square face, with a pointed gray beard and a bald head.

Doris decided not to give the man the pleasure of seeing her snatch for the robe. She rested one hand in her lap and covered her breasts with the other arm.

"Lord Akimos. To what do I owe the pleasure of this visit?"

"It seems, my lady, that it is you who have chosen to avail yourself of my hospitality. I would be a poor host if I took no thought for your comforts."

"The one comfort I would like is an explanation. If you cannot give me that, what of a horse to return to Messantia?"

"Alas, my lady. Pressing matters prevent me from extending either courtesy. But anything else within my power will be yours on the instant."

Doris thought of refusing any favors from the man who had clearly abducted her, for reasons which she would learn at his pleasure if at all. Certainly that chit of a Livia would think it a fine way to display courage.

Doris knew better. She had started poor enough to be hungry and cold much of the time. She knew that thirst, hunger, and living like a pig in your own filth all sapped strength and wits she would need.

"A chamberpot. Food and water. Some decent clothes. And salve for my—insect bites."

"Of course."

Akimos's face vanished and as she drew on her robe she heard his voice calling his men. The open flap now showed a triangle of purple twilit sky over dark hills. Closer to hand was a gnarled olive tree, and sitting by it a thin young man in a travel-worn blue robe.

At first glance Doris felt a thrill of horror. The man looked much like her son Harphos. Could he be part of this plot, seeking to free himself from her at the price of slavery to Akimos?

Then she saw that the man was old enough to be Harphos's father, and his eyes were dark and deep within knowledge. Knowledge of a kind not meant for men, and knowledge that she knew would surely be used against her before she left Akimos's hands.

The man raised his eyes and stared at her. Doris shivered, although the night was warm. Those eyes seemed to pierce the robe and the skin under it, to study her bones, her internal organs, even her soul.

She drew the robe more tightly about her and turned her back on the man. She no longer wondered when she would be free. It was now a question of *would* she be free?

"How close are we?"

Talouf put a finger to his lips and whispered, "Too close for your Cimmerian bellowings, Captain."

Reza grinned, but he was sweating and pale. "Are you well?" Conan asked.

"It's not the potion that lingers, Conan. It's the taste of the olive oil."

"If there was rancid olive oil in the kitchen, Reza, it was your fault—" Harphos began. A large Cimmerian hand clamped over his mouth.

They moved on in silence, Conan, Reza, Talouf, Harphos, and eight picked men, half from House Damaos and half from Conan's Company. Four of the men and Talouf were garbed as Secret Guardians.

The Secret Guardians were not so secret that Harphos had not learned how they were garbed. They were a band of men skilled at slipping into houses to obtain evidence that was lacking by other means. By the strictest notions of Argossean law, they were criminals, but those notions had not bound them nor their masters for centuries.

Conan laughed when he heard that. "Argos begins to seem more like other places I've been. It has ten laws where they have one, but the laws are still what the men who rule say they are."

"Wait until you rule, Conan, before you laugh at that," Harphos said.

"Only a god's going to wait that long," the Cimmerian said, laughing again.

Whatever the laws said about them, the Secret Guardians were going to be a handy weapon. Lords like Akimos seldom had much to fear from them, but the lords' servants were another matter.

Another hundred paces brought the band to a narrow tunnel sloping upward. Talouf went to hands and knees and crept up it. A moment later Conan heard the serpent's hiss that told him all was well.

Reza and Conan scrambled up the tunnel to join Talouf. The passage was low but wide, so both men had room to grip the bronze grating that sealed off the tunnel. With their combined strength at work, even cold-forged bronze could not resist.

"One of those serpents would go through this like parchment," Reza said as they lowered the grating to the floor.

"It could hardly squeeze into this passage," Conan pointed out, flexing his shoulders. "And I'd wager there's some barrier we did not find, to keep the Guardians' pets out of noblemen's cellars. A servant or two might be no loss, but if one of them ate the venison for the chief Archon's banquet—" The Cimmerian feigned a shudder of horror.

He and Reza drew black masks from their purses and pulled them over their heads. Behind them four of the men did the same.

"Ready, lads?" Reza said. The men nodded.

"Very well." Conan added, "Remember, no bloodshed if we can avoid it. At worst, take a prisoner for Harphos to dose."

"I didn't bring any olive oil," the young man said plaintively.

"I don't care if Akimos's people spew their guts all over his pretty marble floors," Reza said. "Just you be sure that you're alive to feed them the potion."

Harphos looked resentful at being banned from the fight. His look only struck the big men's backs as they climbed through the opening. A drop the height of a man faced them, but both leaped down noiseless as cats, raising only a puff of dust. Behind them came the other masked men.

Conan said afterward that the part of the whole matter where he was most uneasy came next. They roamed the cellar of Akimos's palace without meeting anything larger than a rat for some time. Then a scout to the servants' quarters reported *them* deserted, save for old women and young boys.

Conan refused to trouble either one. He began to wonder if Akimos had decided to guard his secrets by taking with him every servant who might know them. If so, the raiders faced the bleak choice: question women and children, or search the palace from roof to cellar and pray that they found something revealing.

They had been in the palace for long enough to eat dinner at a good wineshop when their luck turned.

"I hear singing," the scout said.

Conan nodded. He heard it too, along with drumming. They climbed the stairs from the servants' quarters and advanced down the hall toward Akimos's private chambers. One man remained behind, to pass signals to Talouf's party.

The tapestries in the hall were as splendid as those of House Lokhri were shabby, even the one that covered a man and a woman asleep on the floor. They had no other covering, and what they had been about was as plain as the winestains on the marble.

195

From inside the half-open door, the singing rose louder than before. It did not drown out the clang of cups, the gurgle of wine, or the thud as someone with too much wine in him toppled to the floor.

Someone began beating a drum, or at least something that made a drumlike sound. Conan nodded. In this uproar, a band of Kozaki could have ridden up the hall without being heard.

He drew his sword, flung the door all the way open, and charged into the room beyond.

In the next moment, Conan's greatest fear was that Akimos's servants would slaughter one another trying to get away from him. If any of them was fit to hold a weapon, he could not see him. It was no easy matter to seem a thief out for blood as well as loot without actually harming any of Akimos's wine-witted servants.

Conan gave a Hyrkanian war cry, the signal for Talouf and his "Guardians" to close up. Then he faced a man who had altogether forgotten the sword at his belt, and was wielding a stool with more fury than skill.

A lucky swing of the stool met Conan's sword. The blade jammed in the tough wood. Conan twisted, wrenching the sword free and at the same time kicking the chair as hard as he could. It slammed back into the man's stomach. In turn he flew backward against a table laden with wine jars and plates of delicacies. The table went over with a crash of falling plates and the gurgle of spilling vintages.

Several servants, men and women both, were so witless that they went down on all fours like dogs and began lapping up the wine. Conan's foot itched to kick them like those same dogs.

A Hyrkanian war cry rose over the din.

"Mitra be praised!" Conan said under his breath, but

aloud he cursed sulphurously. Then Talouf and his Guardians rushed into the room, swords drawn.

Conan had fought for his life with less care than he fought the mock battle now. His men and Talouf's had to appear blood foes, without actually shedding blood. Not theirs, and not that of any of the gaping or prostrate servants. That, indeed, was Conan's greatest problem—not slipping in the puddles of wine and food or stumbling over any of the servants too far gone to crawl out from under the ramping boots of the fighters!

One by one, Conan's men "lost their courage" and fled up the stairs to the roof. The Cimmerian brought up the rear, fencing so furiously with Talouf that their swords struck sparks from the walls. Conan reminded himself to have a smith look to his sword before he rode out on Lady Doris's trail.

At last Conan and his thieves were assembled on the roof. There two tasks remained to them. One was to listen to Talouf's speaking to the servants, to guard against something happening to Talouf and his men.

The other was to keep any servants from rushing up on to the roof and in desperation flinging themselves off. If they did not land on their heads, they might do themselves no serious harm. But the noise would doubtless reach beyond the walls of the palace. If it did not in time bring real Guardians, it would certainly bring Akimos's neighbors asking questions that Conan had no wish to answer.

Conan's plan reaped its reward. He heard the servants speak of the Caves of Zimgas, of picked men and horses provisioned for a long journey, of a covered traveling cart furnished as if for the comfort of a lady. He heard of servants being asked if they knew anything of House Lokhri, and much else.

If what Conan heard was rope, then there was enough of it to hang Akimos ten times over.

He waited until Talouf told the servants that they had served their master well and that he would be warned at once. He added that they should cleanse the house of all traces of their feasting, or not even their service to the Guardians would protect them from their master's wrath.

Then Conan and his men departed, as stealthily as the thieves they pretended to be. When they reached the planned meeting place in the tunnels, they found Talouf already there, and his men carrying two chests.

"One's scrolls from Akimos's desk," the sergeant said. "I said we needed to study them, to perhaps learn more about what the thieves sought."

"And the other?" Conan asked, prodding it with a toe. The weight told its own tale, so he was not surprised when Talouf opened the lid and showed it filled with silver coins, mixed with a few gold pieces and jeweled chains.

"That goes back," Conan said.

"To Akimos?" Talouf gaped like the drunken servants.

"No, to the servants. Call it a reward for their good service to the Guardians."

"By Erlik's tool!" Talouf said. "I was almost afraid you'd turned into a honest man, Captain."

"I don't know what Conan is," Reza said. "But I'll tell you this, Sergeant Talouf. If you've notions of turning thief, *don't* air them while I'm in hearing."

Lady Doris lay on her belly, lifted the edges of the tent, and peered out. She could doubtless have seen more from the tent door, but then the guards would notice her—and that she was not as witless with fear as she pretended to be.

So far, the guards had been easy to deceive. She did not imagine that Akimos or Skiron would be so easy, but the guards were at least a beginning. *Anything* was better than weeping herself into a lump of mindless flesh.

Also, the guards were the only men within reach of her a great part of the time. If they were at ease around her—well, it was no more than a slim hope. But the slimmest of hopes was more than she had had when that—*creation*—came to her chambers.

Uphill, she saw the red flames of a campfire. They seemed to be lighting up the mouth of a cave. A thin figure was dancing in that cave mouth, silhouetted by the flames. She thought it was Skiron, and he seemed to be unclothed.

Fear surged through her, making her bite her hand to keep from whimpering like a starved puppy. She was lying to herself when she thought that deceiving the guards would make any difference. She would not deceive them enough to escape before Skiron wielded his spells against her once more. Even if she did escape, Skiron might send his creatures after her.

After a time the fear ebbed enough so that she could breathe again. Now she saw other shapes silhouetted against the flames. Men carrying burdens—quilts, logs, jars, other articles she could not recognize. They seemed to be carrying them into the cave.

Now fear gave way to laughter. Had she nearly frightened herself into a fit, over Skiron's casting a preservative spell on Akimos's supplies?

The laughter eased her, so that she was able to eat sausage, drink ale, and fall into natural sleep.

* * *

It had taken several days, as men reckon time, for the isolate under the road to join the Great Watcher. Now it took only hours for the isolate in the Caves of Zimgas to rejoin the Lesser Watcher. The two principal Watchers had been feeding strength to the isolates— feeding strength, and carving passages in the rocks that divided them into scattered entities.

The Great and Lesser Watchers had also revived their ancient mind-bond, as the men who created the Watchers called it. The Watchers themselves did not use names, having no need of such aids to memory.

They, were, after all, nearly immortal. Certainly the centuries since they had gone into the rocks beneath the hills were as days to a man. They had forgotten nothing of what they knew then. Part of this knowledge was how to regain the strength they had lost.

Feeding was part of it. But living flesh could not satisfy all their hungers. Sorcery was part of finding new strength.

So it was precious knowledge, when the isolate came to the principal Watchers with word of sorcery being done in the Caves of Zimgas. Sorcery, moreover, of the kind on which the Watchers could feed.

If it had been in them to imitate humankind so, the Watchers would have rejoiced at the news.

CHAPTER 15

Lady Doris dreamed.

She dreamed of a lover handsomer, stronger, more civilized than Conan. He had the Cimmerian's magnificent strength and yet murmured charming love vows in her ear while they were locked together.

She wrapped arms and legs more tightly around the man, inhaling the odor of his sweat as if it were the finest perfumed incense. She threw her head back and cried out, heard him cry out, smelled his breath—

His breath? His breath had been as sweet as her garden, in those years long ago when it was properly tended. How had his breath turned foul between one gasp and the next?

How—?

She awoke, and the body entangled with hers, crushing her into the pallet, was neither handsome nor strong. As to whether Lord Akimos was civilized—

Roland Green

It did not matter. He would not leave off, and because he would not leave off she knew that she was helpless. Desire rose in her like a tide, swept her away, sent her limbs thrashing and her face twisting and her mouth crying out in ways both more and less than human.

With a grunt, Akimos exhausted himself and rolled off her. Lady Doris lay sprawled, clad only in tangled hair and dripping sweat, her mouth slack, her wits hardly more composed.

"Was that not splendid, Doris?"

One of Conan's virtues, Doris realized, was that he did not expect praise for his prowess. Of course, when a woman fell asleep afterward as if she were stunned, it was hard for a man to doubt—or to ask, if he did doubt. Yet Doris had not realized until now how she loathed men who expected praise.

"I am sure for a man of your age—"

His open palm struck before she saw his arm move. Three times, and hard. She felt her eyes water but refused to blink. She would *not* let the son of a street sweeper believe that he could make her weep. Or believe that he could frighten her, either.

"A man of your age does well to please a woman at all. I am content enough."

This time the slaps turned into blows. Doris rolled over on to her stomach. Then she realized where this might lead to if the need to give pain gripped Akimos. She rolled over on her back again, helped by two sweaty hands tugging painfully at her hair.

Akimos fell on her again, driving the breath from her body and making all her unhealed wounds throb. Desire had never before come with pain, in spite of the gossip spread about her.

Now it did. She knew that if Akimos began gnawing

202

her flesh like a wolf with a lamb, the ecstasy would rise higher. Horror swept like an icy wind through her mind, but nothing chilled her body. It had a will of its own, and its will was to ride the waves of desire like a ship in a gale.

A whimper forced its way into Doris's throat, grew louder, and turned into a full-fledged scream.

Skiron heard the scream and smiled. Then he cast a sidelong glance at the men by the campfire, and the smile faded.

The spell that left Lady Doris ready to become Akimos's love-slave was both powerful and complex. Still, it seemed to be working well enough. A few more days of its work, and Lady Doris would be a slave to Akimos, as much as any Vendhyan could be a slave to poppy syrup.

Meanwhile, though, the spell was reminding all the other men in the camp that they had no share in their lord's pleasures. Or was it merely the cries from the tent that had all the men looking sour or lust-ridden or both at once?

It did not matter. To let the men quench their desire was becoming important for the peace of the camp and the success of Lord Akimos. If Skiron could contrive the way to that quenching and let the men know what they owed him, they would listen with more respect.

Akimos's uneasy friendship and open purse had been sufficient until now. A time was coming, though, when Skiron's plans would need more hands and even more friends. Slaves spelled into witlessness and used up like sacrificial animals would no longer be sufficient.

And if those friends came from the ranks of Akimos's men—well, it would put a halter on any dreams the merchant prince might have of dispensing with Skiron's services.

Skiron walked beyond the circle of firelight, then out into the deeper night beyond the camp altogether. In the distance, he heard the bugling of a stag.

Deer in the forest, only a little downhill from the camp. Skiron knew the spells to turn does and other female animals into what would pass for women, at least in bed and by night. They were powerful spells, even for lands older and wiser in sorcery than Argos. No one would doubt the greatness of a sorcerer who cast them.

The sorcerer would also weary himself, and use much of the irreplaceable powders and herbs he had brought so far with so much labor. If he needed all his strength at some later time—no, there must be an easier way.

There was. It lay a little farther downhill, in the form of the villages they had passed climbing toward the cave. In every one of those villages there were girls and young wives. A few of them, bound with the same spell as Lady Doris, would keep the men smiling for a month.

Skiron walked back into the firelight.

"Partab!"

"Lord Skiron?" The big Vendhyan rose, the light shining on his bald pate and on the blade of the tulwar thrust through his sash. He rose with a negligent ease, as if to say that he would not defy Skiron but would not obey any more swiftly than he chose.

"A matter has arisen, concerning the health of the men."

Partab was slow to follow Skiron, but not slow to understand once the sorcerer began to explain. "Ah, you are wiser than I had dared hope," Partab said. "Indeed, I have lamented that when I feel like a boy again there are no women for my use.''

''That can be changed, if you and a half score of good men come with me.''

''I will pick them at once.''

''Good. Remind them that we must be as stealthy as weasels raiding a henhouse when all the farmer's dogs are awake. Akimos will not thank us for bringing the countryside about his ears, searching for lost wives and daughters.''

''They will find nothing,'' Partab said. He drew the tulwar and swung it so that the air hissed before its sharp blade.

''With only a little care, they will not,'' Skiron said. It would need more than a little care, as well as several minor spells to cause loss of memory. If he had no time for that, Partab's solution might be the only one.

Conan sat on his bed, oiling the sleeveless mailcoat he would wear tomorrow under his riding leathers. The leathers, together with the rest of his equipment from loinguard to broadsword, lay on top of the chest at the end of the bed.

Livia had offered him a servant to prepare his arms and clothes, but he had refused and Reza explained why.

''We'll be traveling light and fast, my lady. No servants for anyone but you. Some of the men will slack off on work they should do, if they don't see the captains doing it also.''

Livia nodded politely. She had heard in Reza's voice, as had Conan, the hint that they could travel faster and farther if she were not with them.

But Harphos insisted, and no one either could or would say him nay. Once Harphos had joined the rescue

party, Livia also insisted. Both Conan and Reza did try
to say her nay, as strongly as their place allowed. She
ignored them both as thoroughly as *her* place allowed.

It seemed to Conan that the two young folk had challenged each other to a contest—who could show the
more courage? Having seen such contests end mostly
with all the contestants ending as vulture's fare, Conan
was not easy in his mind about seeing Harphos and
Livia in one.

Well, they were hardly four years younger than he,
although the old head Livia wore on young shoulders
made that easy to forget. If they would not listen and
be careful, then they would have to ride and fight. With
as much help from the picked men he and Reza were
leading as the gods would allow, and more if possible—

Conan heard a hand touch the outside of the unlocked
door before he saw the door move. He froze where he
sat, making his breathing shallow and narrowing his
eyes to slits. He was as immobile as a boulder and
apparently as insensible when the door opened just wide
enough to let Gisela slip inside.

She took one look at Conan, seemed to think him
asleep, then tiptoed toward the bed. Standing beside it,
she slipped off first one sandal, then the other. She
reached down for the hem of her tunic—

—and Conan flung the oil pot across the room. It
struck the door, slamming it shut. In one leap Conan
reached the door, throwing the bolt. In another leap, he
was at the bed, scooping up Gisela in his massive arms.

Instead of protesting, she lay back and wriggled
her hips, not caring that her tunic had slid well above
her knees when Conan lifted her.

Conan laughed, lifted the maid higher, then flung her
on to the bed. She bounced three times before coming

to rest. By then she was laughing so hard that she had to catch her breath before she could sit up and finish removing her tunic.

She now wore only an undertunic that began just above her breasts and ended just below mid-thigh. The thin silk was embroidered with flowers, which did nothing to make the garment more concealing.

Conan laughed. "Since I threw you into the bed instead of out of it, I hope you know what you're here for."

She drew herself up. "Conan, I am no green girl." Indeed, seventeen was a woman's years in Argos, and those were surely women's breasts thrusting out the tunic.

"As well. They're not much to my taste. But I've seen you and Vandar—"

There was no doubting it. A shadow passed over her face at those words. Conan frowned.

"Have you and Vandar quarreled?"

"Captain Conan, is it your affair?"

"Yes, by Crom!" the Cimmerian growled. "If you've quarreled, I ought to know. It concerns one of my best men. If you haven't, what are you doing here?"

"Sitting on your bed—"

"Next to naked, and looking ready to leap on me like a tiger on a goat! Now, you're your own mistress, and if you have some good reason for being here, I'll not fight you off. But either you tell me that good reason, or you go out of here with a red arse and Vandar stays behind tomorrow morning."

Gisela turned pale and looked away. When she spoke, it was barely more than a whisper. "If Reza learns that I told you—"

"I'll swear any kind of oath you care for not to tell Reza. Just tell me, and be quick about it."

"Reza sent me. He does not—not want you to think about Lady Livia—as a woman."

"Trolls carry off Reza and demons push Livia into a midden!" Gisela cringed and buried her face in the pillow at Conan's snarl. She only lifted her head when he noticed that her undertunic now left her round buttocks exposed, and began to laugh.

It was so simple that he should have seen it without frightening this poor girl. Any man old enough to bed a woman should have seen it! Reza had one thought in his mind—guard Livia's reputation. How to do it? Play pander, of course.

Conan laughed again. He hoped Reza had room in his head for more than one thought, beginning tomorrow. Otherwise the Cimmerian was going to have to do the thinking for both of them. He would ask for extra pay if that came to pass!

"Livia has nothing to fear from me. I know she has her eye on Harphos."

"He's not worthy of her!"

"Don't let her hear you say that, if you want to keep the skin on your back. I've never been much for understanding women, but I've learned one thing. If a woman thinks a man's right for her, gods and demons together won't keep them apart."

"That's the truth," Gisela exclaimed. She snatched the shift off over her head and held out her arms to Conan. Her skin was fairer than Conan's, fair enough to freckle for all that her hair was black, and she had oiled it so that it seemed to glow in the lamplight. She slid off the bed and came toward him, breasts swaying gently, until he reached out and drew her the rest of the way to him.

It did not take long after that for him to remove his own clothes, carry Gisela back to the bed, and learn that she had a woman's arts in that woman's body of hers.

The Watchers surged towards each other, finding gaps in the rock where they existed, making them where they did not. As they moved, they drew in the last isolates, absorbed them, fed on all their strength and their memories, and grew greater almost by the minute.

By the time the two Watchers thrust tendrils through the last gap, they were almost the same size. As men reckon such matters, each was the size of half a dozen elephants. They could not stand or run like the elephants, but no herd of elephants could have come alive out of their grip.

They touched one another, exchanged all that they had learned in the time since the Awakening, and began to rest. It was not easy, with the spells still pulsing through the rock to agitate them, but ancient memories told them that this was wisdom.

They each had enough matter in them to make another pair of Watchers, fit to grow swiftly to full size if properly fed. But they would have to rest, and command their own substance to form into those Watchers while they rested. Then it would be time to forage in the mountains, and even to risk the surface under the open sky, for the more abundant food supply there.

Livia slipped barefoot away from the door to Conan's room. She did not fear those within hearing her. They were much too pleasantly occupied, and much too noisy in their pleasure.

She did fear meeting Reza. What she would have to say to him might shatter the fragile peace between them. In the daylight, without the memory of the sounds from that room burning in her mind, she could hold her tongue. Tonight, though—

Tonight was one night. It would be the last night she was under her own roof, in her own chambers, surrounded by women who might tell tales. *Would* tell tales, if Reza put them in fear.

Tomorrow night, and for many nights to come, she would be sleeping in inns, tents, or open fields. Where she went, and who went with her, and what they did when they came to where they were going—these could be her secrets.

CHAPTER 16

From the sky above the treetops Conan heard a woman screaming. He raised a hand to halt the party on the trail behind him.

"Vandar, come with me. Reza, I want men out to the flanks."

"I know these matters, Conan."

"As does Conan, and he commands here," Livia said.

If he commanded, Conan thought, he wished he could command the lady to be silent. Her goading of Reza chipped away at the peace between her two captains. Doubt of each other's loyalty was gone; Reza's jealousy of the Cimmerian's influence over his mistress remained.

Conan dismounted, not a great step from this horse. Argos was not horse country, and most of the party was mounted on scrubby little geldings or even mules. Yet they seemed sure-footed and enduring enough, and they were not to be called on to press home a charge or carry horse archers swiftly to an enemy's flank.

"Come along."

The thick canopy of pine branches hid most of the sky, shutting the ground around the man-thick trunks away from the sun. The sparse undergrowth and the downhill slope made easy going for the Cimmerian. He had to hold back at times, to let Vandar keep up with him.

They came out of the trees on the banks of a mountain stream. On the far side of the stream a sullen cliff of gray rock rose halfway to the sky. On the edge of that cliff stood a woman, head thrown back, arms raised, and screaming.

As Conan studied the cliff for ways up, a second woman appeared at the top. She seemed to be gesturing to the first woman. But each time the newcomer came within twenty paces, the first woman took a step backward.

"Ten more steps and she'll be over the edge," Conan growled.

"Perhaps that's what she wants," Vandar said. "Is saving the village witling our work for today?" Then he flinched at the look in the Cimmerian's eyes.

"Yes," Conan said. He drew sword and dagger to hold them clear of the water, then stepped into the stream. In three paces the water was up to his chest. Vandar took a deep breath and followed, flinching at the cold.

Vandar was as blue as Conan's eyes when they finally climbed out of the water. Conan had cast along the face of the cliff, looking for a way up, and finally found one.

Indeed, it looked as if someone had once carved a flight of steps in the face of the cliff.

Conan scrambled on to the bottommost of the crumbling steps and shook himself like a dog. Vandar followed, with a dubious look at the way up.

"That looks more fit for goats than men, Captain. Where are your beard and horns?"

Conan tapped the man's bare chin. "For that matter, where's yours? Grow one, *then* argue with your captain. Follow me." He began climbing, using arms for balance as well as for gripping vines and gnarled saplings that had somehow found niches in the rock.

By the time they were halfway up the cliff, the first woman had stopped screaming. The second was now speaking, in a low, urgent voice. Conan could not make out her words, but neither could he mistake the note of pleading in her voice.

Vandar climbed up beside the Cimmerian and took a deep breath. "Captain, what *are* we doing up here?"

"A madwoman wandering in this sort of country, far from her village—to me that smells of sorcery.

"Not all madness comes from sorcery, Captain."

"Enough does. Even if this doesn't, we may save her. If we do, her village and kin will thank us. They may have seen something that will help us, if they talk of it freely."

"Forgive me, Captain. I should have thought of that myself."

"When you've been living by your wits and your sword as long as I have, you will. Or you won't have lived that long!"

They went on climbing. At the next halt for breath, Conan set his back to the rock and looked out across the river. They were now above the level of the treetops, and he had a clear view across the mountain valley to the slopes beyond. They were not far enough north for the peaks to wear snow caps at this time of year, but they lacked nothing else to make them formidable.

An army could hide in this country, and seeking one merchant prince and his tame sorcerer would be a fool's game without what they had learned at Akimos's house. It could still turn back into such a game, if Akimos got wind of their coming. If the folk of the woman's village could do nothing else, Conan would ask them to keep their mouths shut about his band's presence in the mountains.

Conan and Vandar covered the last few score paces of the climb trying to be as silent as mice when the cat prowls. Whether ensorceled or mad, the woman could too easily fly into a panic. Then the rescuers would bring about the leap they sought to prevent.

The two men stopped just below the edge of the cliff. Conan saw the madwoman, standing with her arms crossed on her breast, less than five paces from the edge. Worse still, she was no more than two paces from a ravine leading to the edge of the cliff. If she leaped or fell into that, she would slide like mash in a pig trough, down and out into empty air.

Conan drew Vandar close and whispered. "We'll take the last steps at a rush. You run between her and the edge. I'll guard the ravine. Whatever you do, bare hands only."

"Very well. If she claws out an eye, Akimos's sorcerer can ransom himself by putting it back."

The Cimmerian took a deep breath, tapped his companion on the shoulder, then all but flew up the last few steps. Vandar was only a pace behind him, but one foot struck a loose stone that the Cimmerian had missed. It turned under Vandar and sent him sprawling, by the gods' favor on the level ground.

Even flat on his stomach, he still blocked the woman's path to the edge. She howled like a wolf and leaped for the ravine. Looking back to see that Vandar had not fallen, Conan was a heartbeat too late to catch her.

He was not too late to follow her into the ravine, clutching her ankles in an iron grip. He spread his legs, trying to jam his feet into the sides of the ravine and hold both of them. But the ravine was too steep, and although he used elbows and knees as well as feet he felt himself sliding. Another ten paces and there would be nothing left for either of them but the long fall to death in the river, and perhaps saving the woman *had* been a fool's errand after all—

Something soft fell on his ankle. Then sinewy fingers were tightening it around the ankle. He heard Vandar's voice behind and above him, shouting, "Hurry, you witless bitch!" Then another piece of cloth was looping around his other ankle.

He felt the knots tighten. At first they did no more than stop his slide toward death. Then he could let go of one of the woman's ankles and use his free hand to push them both backward. Finally he could use feet and knees and elbows all at once, creeping up on to level ground like a drunken caterpillar but *safe*.

Conan took a deep breath and stood up. The woman had fainted, and from the looks of her that was just as well. Conan saw fresh bruises, cuts, what looked like whip marks, and even burns.

"Captain, are you safe?"

Vandar and the second woman were standing side by side. Both were bare to the waist, and the woman looked rather the better for being so unclad.

Roland Green

"You've learned to think faster than I'd expected," Conan said. "If you'd gone down into the ravine yourself, it might have just been three bodies in the river."

"I had trouble talking Shilka here into using her tunic, but when it was her sister—"

"Her sister?" Conan began. Then Vandar raised a hand and pointed. Behind boulders, Conan also made out movement.

The two men were flat on the ground in a moment. Shilka stood, then cupped her hands and shouted.

"Ho! If you are of Stag's Leap village, these men are friends. They saved Komara."

"So you say," came a rough voice. "But when magic walks the hills as it has these past four nights—"

"Magic?" Vandar exclaimed, and Conan cupped his own hands.

"What kind of magic?"

"You should know, you—" someone else began.

"Wait," the first voice commanded. "Who are you?"

"Captain Conan, serving the Guardians."

"I've never seen you at the valley fort."

"I've never been there. I'm straight out from Messantia, maybe on the trail of the magic you fear. Tell me about it."

"Yes, tell him," Shilka shouted. "And while you're telling him, Oris, the rest of you see to my sister. We didn't snatch her back from death to let her bleed on the rocks."

Shame or hope or both together brought the four villagers out from behind the boulders. Conan noted that all four had crossbows and either spears or shortswords. He walked to the edge of the cliff, ready to signal to Reza to send up more men. He trusted the villagers

216

somewhat; he would trust them more when they knew they were outnumbered.

As Conan reached the edge of the cliff, a familiar head of fair hair thrust itself into view. Conan took a step backward and mentioned several gods not commonly invoked among polite Argosseans.

Livia's laugh was like the river rippling over rocks. "Forgive me for surprising you, Captain. But I thought I might be needed, to persuade the hillfolk that we are friends. Hillfolk can sometimes be as stubborn as the rock of their own hills, as I'm sure you know."

Before Conan could think of a reply to that, she turned to the villagers. "Has this poor woman kin?"

"She has a husband," the one called Oris said. "But if he'll have her back after this—"

"After she suffered from foul magic, he'll call her unchaste?" Livia snapped. Conan heard the ice crackle in her voice. So did the villagers. They took a step backward.

"Well," Oris said, "I'll not wager one way or the other. She'll have my voice, for sure, and—"

"Very well. Do your best. If that is not good enough, the woman will have a place in my house for as long as she needs one."

"And just who are you, Messantian trull?" the man who'd spoken second growled.

Conan took three quick steps and lifted the man by his belt and the collar of his tunic. "She is—one who can make good that promise. And I can make good a promise to break you in pieces if your tongue wags like that again."

"I am the Lady Livia of House Damaos," Livia said. For the first time, she appeared to realize that her riding clothes were soaked and clinging. The mannish appearance she'd worn on the trail was now altogether gone.

"She is that, and more," Conan said. He set the villager on his feet and carefully wiped his hands on his breeches. "But if word of it reaches our common enemies—"

"I will see to that," Oris said. "Now, my lady, Captain Conan, are you alone?"

Conan signaled Livia to let him speak. Somewhat to his surprise, she nodded.

"What of it?"

"If you are here in strength, I beg you to come to Stag's Leap and guard us from the women-stealers. If you are not in strength, please go away. You will only draw the women-stealers' wrath without being able to meet it."

It was plain that the man was not as sure of Conan's virtue as he pretended. Conan decided that picking up villagers like unruly children and waving them about like battle flags would not work a second time.

"How many villages have suffered?"

"Four. A different one each night."

"Then why not guide us to a place where we can reach all four villages swiftly? If the women-stealers come again, we'll catch them on the way home. If they attack us, they'll get bloody noses and the villagers can sleep in peace."

"That is wisdom, Captain."

"Trolls take the wisdom! Is there such a place?" He decided to gamble. "We've heard of a place called the Caves of Zimgas, in these—"

Oris had turned pale and looked ready to fall on his knees, in fear or supplication. "What's wrong with the Caves?"

"They—Captain, you do not know what you ask."

"Then tell me! Or does everyone in these hills speak in riddles?"

"The . . . the Watchers dwell in the Caves of Zimgas, Captain."

"Watchers? Well, speak, man!"

Oris swallowed. "The Watchers were creatures of magic, created centuries ago to guard the borders of Argos. When magic fled the land, they slept, but it is said that they did not die. If they live, the magic at work may wake them."

"All the worse for the sorcerer, then," Conan said. "Waking other people's pets has killed more sorcerers than anything else except good steel."

Oris shuddered. "If you really wish to guard against the Watchers, there is Castle Tebroth. It is not far from any of the villages. Only—you must know—"

"Yes, I must know, or you must go back to your village and seek leechcraft to restore your wits," Conan growled.

"It is said that the castle rose in a single night, its stones lifted into place by the Watchers themselves."

Conan did not shudder, but his old hatred of sorcery made him pause for a moment. Then he nodded.

"Oris. A bargain. We have—a good company—below, and food, wine, and leechcraft for your men and Komara. Guide us to Castle Tebroth and take your share. Then take Komara home, and warn the chief men of each village of our presence. Then they can use torches or messengers if the women-stealers come again."

"I must come too," Shilka said. She had not pulled on her tunic, and the look she gave Conan was hard to mistake. "My sister will need a woman's care."

Livia's reply to that died silently at Conan's look. But her face was just as eloquent as the village girl's. After a moment, the girl put her tunic back on.

Conan wished all women some place a long way from him until this matter of Akimos and the women-stealers was done. Then he looked at Oris.

"Well?"

"As you wish, Captain."

"Good." Conan turned his back on the others, walked to the edge of the cliff, and this time finished signaling to Reza's sentry watching below.

Conan was well prepared to believe that Castle Tebroth was built as a fortress. It perched high on a crag overlooking a narrow valley. The only way up to it was a twisting path that half a dozen archers could have held against an army.

Oris spun tales of the castle and how the Watchers had dragged the stones up the crag all the way up the path. As they drew closer, Conan began to wonder if there might be truth in the tales. Certainly many of the stones were the size of small houses. He could imagine no human power able to pull them up the slope. For the sake of the courage of his men, though, he spoke otherwise.

"I'll believe in Watchers when I find one watching me," he told Talouf. "Those stones are big, I give you that. But with enough slaves, you can move anything anywhere."

"Were you ever a slave overseer, Conan?" Livia asked. She was walking almost close enough to press her thigh against his—only because the path was so narrow, she told him.

"No," Conan said shortly. "I was a slave."

That silenced the lady until they reached the castle gate. The iron parts were long gone, but Conan saw enough loose stones lying about for an ample barricade. Once inside, they would be guarded well enough from any human attack. As for other kinds—Conan proposed to find the sorcerer before he found them, and then show any Watchers a clean pair of heels.

The castle had a courtyard, not much larger than a kitchen garden. They assembled there, listening to the wind pipe eerily about the sun-bleached and weather-scored towers.

"You know your way about this pile of mason's mistakes?" Conan asked Oris.

"As few men do," the man replied. He lowered his voice. "If I were you—"

"You are not. Go on. I need advice, not Argossean manners."

"I would advise posting sentries at the cellar entrance, as well as on the walls." Oris now spoke in a whisper, almost lost in the wind.

"The tales run that there are tunnels running right down through the mountains to the Caves of Zimgas. The Watchers were sent down those tunnels to sleep when their work was done."

"So if they're awake, they might come back up to call on us?"

Oris shrugged. "I would not jest about the Watchers, if I were—pardon. But I also remember that the Watchers were monstrous. A tunnel big enough for one would take a cart and horse. It could also take a good company of men."

"I follow you. I'll have sentries and a pile of stones before the cellar door."

The posting of sentries and piling of stones outlasted

daylight. By the time the work was done to Conan's and Reza's satisfaction, only a faint ruddiness in the west remained of the day. The wind had died to a faint whisper, which Conan realized was just as well. Had it been moaning as weirdly as when they arrived, he would have been walking with one hand on his sword, looking behind him with every other breath.

Oris's tales of the Watchers had made them seem a trifle too real. And there were the women-stealers roaming among the villages like mad wolves, and they and their magic were altogether real. What was abroad in these hills was more than the simple schemes of a merchant prince.

The thought of the women-stealers reminded Conan of Komara, lying on her pallet in the closest thing to a warm room the ancient castle could muster. He descended the winding stairs from the tower roof and rapped on the side of the doorway with the hilt of his dagger.

"Who is it?" It was Livia's voice.

"Captain Conan."

Conan entered, to see Livia kneeling beside the pallet, sponging the woman's cuts with vinegar and water from a pot heated over the cookfire. Reza sat in the window seat, looking tired and sullen.

"Where's Shilka?"

"I sent her off to get some sleep. She was chasing her sister up hill and down dale for two days with little rest and less food."

"How does Komara?"

"I think the spell is wearing off. She cries out, but from pain or as in nightmares. She seems to know she is among friends."

"She's also in an empty castle that may be facing the

gods know what attacks within days," Reza said. "I've urged my lady to send the woman back down with the other villagers at dawn."

"Well, Reza, if she won't listen to you I'll not waste breath I may need for fighting," Conan said. "Best you remember what Shilka said, too. Komara might not be among friends in the village."

"Indeed, Conan, she might not," Livia added. "Also, Harphos left me with some of his herbs and simples. The village would have nothing like them, and some have already done her good."

"Where is Harphos, by the way?"

"He also has gone to find a pallet," Livia said, but was Conan only imagining a catch in her voice and a faint flush on her face? "He said he wanted to take the watch from midnight to dawn, so he should sleep now."

"I had not heard Harphos was a soldier," Conan said, carefully polite.

"He said that this is the only chance he will have to learn those skills," Reza put in. "He wishes to go with us to the Caves, when the time comes to rescue his mother."

Conan's reply was a wordless grunt and a nod. More would have betrayed his suspicions. Harphos and Shilka gone off together, and Livia uneasy about it? Was she jealous, or had she played matchmaker for reasons of her own?

Conan doubted he would ever know, women being what they were and Livia worse than that! Certainly the answer would not be worth losing sleep to find.

He likewise doubted that Harphos would ever be much of a fighting man. Not enough to be more help than danger to the men rescuing his mother, certainly, but how to keep him safe if he wanted to run into danger? That also was a question not to be answered tonight.

"My thanks," Conan said. "I will be sleeping on top of the east tower, if anyone needs me."

The first sensation to creep through the deep veil of sleep around Conan was warmth. Had those blankets finally done their duty, or had these hills somehow brought a warm breeze to the castle's crag?

Then Conan's wits awoke, enough for him to realize that the warmth came from one place. A brazier or fire, perhaps—but there had been neither on the tower roof with him when he lay down.

He threw off the blankets and sat up, reaching for his sword as he did. He found himself staring into two wide blue eyes. Those eyes held laughter, and so did the wide red-lipped mouth below them.

"I could not sleep in the miasma of those chambers below," Livia said. "So I came up to sleep where I would be safe and the air fresh."

Conan noted that her shoulders were bare above the blankets wrapped around her. The brazier gave enough light to show a light dusting of freckles on those shoulders. It did not reveal what she wore under the blankets.

"You may find the air fresher than you like, before morning," Conan said. He stretched. If the wench was going to chatter, he would not be sleeping for a while, so best be comfortable. "Did you bring any wine?"

"No, but I brought a pot of one of Harphos's ointments. I saw that you were all bruised and grazed.

"Hardly that. I had my riding leathers on when I climbed the cliff. Try climbing rocks in your bare skin some time, and you'll know what bruising and grazing is really like. Or try a friendly bout of wrestling."

"What is a friendly bout?"

"When you're with a friend, to see who's the best, or just practice. I've been in bouts where owners were matching their slaves against each other. The loser had a flogging coming, or worse."

"Would you teach me a trifle of wrestling?" The catch in Livia's voice was there again, but he could not see a flush.

"Why?"

"I have my dagger, but if we are attacked and the fight is long . . ."

"I see. You and Harphos both want to be soldiers overnight."

"Do not insult us, Conan. We only want to learn what we can, to help defeat Lord Akimos. And I think I am fit to learn wrestling."

Livia must have practiced the gesture, because she threw off all the blankets in one movement. Under them she was clad as Conan had begun to suspect. Her own skin, lightly freckled in more places than her shoulders, and nothing else.

"Well, Conan?"

"For serious bouts, Livia, one normally wears a loinguard."

"Women are made differently from men, as I'm sure you know. Besides, I see no guard on your loins."

"No, but I see that the brazier has fallen over and the blankets will take fire in another minute."

Livia whirled, and the flow of muscle and sinew and the easy lift of her firm breasts held Conan's eye. His blood was alight already, and only the sternest command to his arms kept them from reaching for her.

Only a few coals had fallen, and the brass pot of

unguent sufficed to crush them out. When she was done, Livia turned back to Conan.

"If we need no loinguards, is there anything else lacking?"

"Wrestling is best done on something soft."

"Like blankets?"

"Yes."

She spread out her blankets, and as Conan spread out his their hands met. His hands took on a life of their own, leaping up her arms to grip her shoulders and pulling her close.

She resisted for a heartbeat. Then she flew forward, so that Conan fell over backward with Livia on top. Since all they intended could be done lying down, it was some time before they rose again, and then it was only briefly.

They were not still until the moon rose and found them both asleep, wrapped in each other's arms and the tangled blankets.

CHAPTER 17

"**C**onan. Conan, wake up!"

Conan was awake but busy admiring Livia through half-closed eyes. She was worthy of admiration, not having bothered to dress before walking to the parapet. By good fortune, it was high enough to conceal all but her neck and head from anyone below.

"I'm awake. What is it?"

"I see two score men on the path up to the castle."

Conan leaped up and likewise hurried to the parapet without concern for his garb. He shaded his eyes against the sunrise and studied the approaching men. Then he laughed.

"There's mostly women and children. I see a few lads with clubs and bows, but nothing more. I think one of the villages has sent their folk up to safety here."

"I'm sorry I didn't recognize them."

"No harm in your not being a soldier. You've other talents in plenty."

Livia blushed, turning fair skin made rosy by the dawn rosier still. Then she laughed and bent gracefully to don her clothes.

Conan hurried down the tower stairs as soon as he'd pulled on breeches and weapons. By then Reza and Harphos were both on duty, and swordsmen were drawn up, ready to help the archers if the newcomers proved hostile. Reza seemed as like solid granite as ever, but Harphos had the look of a man who had spent much of the night in bed but little of it asleep.

Oris offered to go out and meet the villagers, and quickly returned with their message.

"They are from Three Wolves. The headmen have sent them up here, to be safe from the women-stealers."

"Do they have their own food, water, and bedding?"

"I could see none."

Conan wished that trolls might carry off the village headmen, then took a deep breath.

"I'll not send them back, not when they've doubtless walked all night. But I want some of the lads to carry this message to the villages.

"No one comes to the castle without bringing their own food and bedding. We've plenty of water, but we're not fit to shelter half the countryside."

"Would it not also be wise, to ask them to send some armed men?" Harphos put in. "We shall have to divide our men when we march to rescue my mother from—"

"Harphos, be silent until we are alone," Reza snapped. The young man lost half his years and looked like a boy just threatened with a beating. Conan stepped into the quarrel.

228

"We will indeed be sending men out," he said. "But ten men could hold this fort against an army."

"True, if it were wholly intact," Harphos said. "But I—during the night, when I looked for a quiet place to—sleep—I saw weak spots. Also, the village fighters need not come into the castle. They can camp in the valley, ready to warn us of attacks. Then they can wait and strike the attackers in the rear, while we fight them in front."

Conan looked at Harphos with new respect. After a moment and with reluctance, so did Reza. "You're thinking like a soldier," the steward said, and gripped Harphos by both shoulders. "Your mother may finally thank you for learning something she didn't teach you, if this goes on!"

"Reza, you've a touching faith in human kindness, if you think that," Harphos said. "Captain Conan, may I show you the weak spots?"

Most of the weak spots Harphos showed Conan were nothing of the kind. Some would have daunted trained apes, and only two offered any hope for even the nimblest of human climbers.

Harphos looked rather cast down, but Conan reassured him. "My lord, I'd been captain in the hosts of Turan for a year before I learned much of fortress-building."

"Turan's not a great land for castles, is it?"

"Only in the mountains, where they can bar the roads. Otherwise Turan has too many open borders, and too many foes beyond each one, to spend gold on defenses that can't move."

"I see." Harphos turned away, looked out over the valley, and appeared to be struggling for words.

"Captain Conan, may I ask a favor of you?"

"To come with us?" Harphos nodded. "We could use your healing skills. But can you march and fight?"

"I kept up all the way from Messantia, did I not?"

"Yes. But we didn't have to fight. Harphos, I can't spare four men to—to—"

"Nurse the boy?"

"That's not quite the way I'd put it."

"No, I suppose not, and I'm grateful for your trying to be kind." Harphos rested a hand on the hilt of his shortsword. "Captain, shall we go a few passes with this against a weapon of your choice? If I show you that I will not be helpless, may I come?"

"Yes."

"Your word on it?"

"By Mitra and Erlik, show that you know steel and you may go wherever this journey leads us."

Conan drew his dagger, wrapped his cloak about his left arm, and stepped back. Added to his longer reach, his broadsword would have made the match pitifully one-sided. But with his dagger against Harphos's shortsword, reach was about equal. Other qualities would decide the match.

In the space of ten deep breaths, Conan decided that Harphos had a fair measure of those qualities. He was alert, as quick as necessary, and a fair judge of openings in his opponent's guard. Above all, he moved about the rough ground with a deftness that suggested much of his clumsiness was an act.

Conan still had the edge, but he had to work to keep it. The first pass ended as Harphos thrust hard, nicked Conan's ribs, then found Conan's dagger locking his sword in place as he tried to draw it back. A long Cim-

merian leg struck like a serpent, and Harphos's feet
went out from under him.

He struck hard but held on to his sword and had it
pointing at Conan's belly before the Cimmerian could
step back. Then he laughed.

"I reckon it takes more practice than I've had, to mix
sword-fighting and wrestling."

"So it does. But a good fighter never forgets the
weapons the gods gave him, just because the smiths
gave him more. Another pass?"

"Gladly." Harphos rose, brushed himself off, and
took position.

They went four more passes, and Conan won each
one of them but none without trying. He quickly fore-
swore any effort to let Harphos win. The young man
would surely know if this happened and be angry. Also,
he might give the Cimmerian a wound that would slow
him in days to come—and Conan knew he would need
a full measure of strength, speed, and wits for the battle.

Akimos and his guards were no weaklings, but also
nothing a good fighting man need fear. Akimos's tame
sorcerer was another matter, even more so when the
fighting man had to guard not only his back but a village's worth of wenches and babes!

There was something to be said, Conan decided, for
the old days as a thief in Zingara. Then he had to answer to no one, save at times the Thieves' Guild, and
for no skin save his own!

Harphos tried to end the last round with a close grapple. He contrived to launch it without warning Conan,
and in a real flight might have opened the Cimmerian's
belly before he died.

Conan tossed Harphos on to his back again and this

time stepped back. The head of House Lokhri caught his breath, then accepted Conan's offered arm.

"Well, Captain?"

"Well enough. I'll still put you in the center of the party. Not to shame you, but because we'll need your healing skills more than your sword arm. I've a dozen swords better than yours, but no one else who knows a purgative from a pisspot."

"As you wish, Captain. As long as I go. And—if I do fall—can you see that Shilka receives what I promised her?"

Conan did not say that if Harphos died it was likely enough that the rest of the party would do the same. He did promise to do his best, and see that Livia would help too.

Conan wasted no time seeking an underground way to the Caves of Zimgas. Even if it existed outside of legend, it might take a month to discover it. Also, below ground the foe would have the same advantage Conan had around the castle, with a handful of men able to halt ten times their number.

Surprise would come from speed more than stealth, and they would need surprise. Even if Skiron had no spells fit to fend them off, Akimos would hardly scruple to fling Lady Doris off the nearest cliff rather than let her live to bear witness against him.

So Conan led forty picked men, guards and villagers both, into the trees on the far side of the ridge from both the castle and the Caves. They left at twilight, intending to move as far as they could before dawn, then to go to ground for the day. After that, a march of less than half the night should bring them to the Caves.

The first night and much of the next day, Livia had

too much work to think about what Conan and Harphos might be facing. The women and children had to be bedded down, with families at feud with one another kept as far apart as the castle would allow. The lines at the well had to be kept from turning into brawling mobs. Children had to be kept from wandering off, lest their mothers make the night hideous with screams of terror at losing them.

From managing the Damaos palace, Livia knew most of what was needed. Reza knew the rest. So it was not until the evening after the rescue party's departure that Livia felt her wits and strength deserting her. She climbed the stairs to the tower where she had given Conan her maidenhood, and sat where their pallets had lain.

She was still sitting there when the sun sank below the mountains and Reza climbed the stairs.

"My lady, are you well?"

"Only weary, both in mind and body."

"This is hardly the best place to sleep."

"No, but it is the quietest. I think I will ask you to have a pallet and water brought up here."

Reza bowed, but also frowned. "My lady, it will still be no very comfortable place."

"The men seeking Lady Doris will be even less comfortable tonight. For some, it may be the last night of their lives. Should I wallow in luxury then?"

"I hardly think a pallet in a warmer room is luxury," Reza said with a smile. "But I see that you have the soul of a captain of war in the body of a woman. Indeed, I have seen that for some time. So I should not have been surprised at—what passed between you and Captain Conan."

Livia stiffened as if she had been slapped. Then she

quenched the first blaze of anger with the thought that Reza did not seem to disapprove. Moreover, if he was the only one who had guessed, her secret was safe.

As if he had read her thoughts, Reza smiled again. "I have told no one, nor will I. I doubt not that Conan will be as discreet."

"As do I. He has known many women, I am sure, but left none with a worse name unless they have ill-used him."

"Yes." Reza now seemed more sober. "My lady, have any promises passed between him and you?"

"Of marriage?" It seemed beyond belief, but she saw Reza nod. The anger burned again. "Reza, you have not called me a wanton. So why call me a fool?"

"Have you been one?"

"No. What passed between me and Conan—it may be over and done. Certainly it will not lead us to the wedding altar."

She could not mistake Reza's shoulders slumping in relief. "The gods be praised. I had to be sure. My lady, it is not unknown for men to use the chances of battle to rid themselves of rivals. Had you promised anything to Conan, he might have been tempted."

Livia's nails stopped a hair short of Reza's face. "Never insult Conan again like that! His honor is as strong as his manhood!" Reza's face was unreadable, but she sensed something unspoken but deadly lying between them. "Reza, you will tell me what you have done, or you will leave my service tonight and the castle in the morning!"

"I sent two men with orders to watch over Harphos like hens with a single chick. They were to strike Conan down if he seemed careless of Harphos's life."

Livia decided that screaming, weeping, or clawing

Reza's eyes out would accomplish nothing and waste time into the bargain. She gripped her dagger.

"You will send a messenger to those men. You will tell them that if they lay a finger on Conan I will personally flay them alive. The messenger will have his orders now, in my hearing, and leave the castle before I leave you."

Reza's jaw set. "My lady, there would be no time for anyone to reach the rescue party before they struck the Caves. Even if there was, Akimos's men might find the messenger on the way. Then he would die, but not before exposing our secrets to Akimos. Akimos would be ready, and our men and your reputation alike would perish."

Reza's words and calm determination cut through Livia's rage. "I suppose there is something in what you say. Very well. I will ask only that you speak to the two men when they return, and give them the same warning. I suppose Conan can guard his own back until then."

"At least from my men," Reza said. "As for the other foes he faces—let us pray for the favor of the gods. And then, my lady, wherever you wish to sleep, will you lie down and do so? You will be a rag in the morning if you do not."

Livia tried to answer, but her words vanished in a prodigious yawn. She put an arm around his massive shoulders.

"I will go down, Reza, if you will guide my feet now as you have done so often in the past."

"With pleasure, my lady."

Skiron no longer turned his back on Lord Akimos when he wiped the sweat from his face. Nor was it only the heat of the cave that was making him sweat.

The last three times he had cast the spell to keep Doris of Lokhri in bondage, he had sensed what he would have called an echo if it had reached his ears. As he apprehended it in ways that no sorcerer could explain to ordinary folk, he had held his tongue.

Now, though, Akimos was asking him for advice. If the merchant prince did not receive it, he might yet cast away their victory. If he won without Skiron's advice, it would be hardly better. Skiron would be lucky to escape with going back to the life of a hedge-wizard. Akimos might yet think of giving him to the Guardians, to prove how clean his hands—

"Lord Skiron. I have asked a question. Is there danger, that needs all of our men here?"

Skiron swallowed. A question in return could at least buy time.

"Where else would they go?"

"To take Conan's camp."

"I am no soldier, but—"

"For once you speak the truth. Continue."

"Is not that castle proof against any strength we could bring against it?"

"Any natural strength, yes. It was built by the Watchers, or so the tales run. But it was my thought that you might well accompany us."

Skiron swallowed again. He hoped Akimos had not noticed his shudder at the word "Watchers." To be sure, they might not be what replied to his spells, louder each time. Much magic had been wrought in these mountains over the centuries. Some of it besides the Watchers might linger.

He told himself this while his tongue shaped words that made no sense to him but seemed to soothe Akimos. Finally the merchant prince rose.

"Very well. If you are sure that you can cast spells against the castle as well from here as from before its gate—"

"No sorcerer can cast his best spells while arrows are whistling about his ears. Also, if I do not remain here to renew the bondage of Lady Doris, you might not find her so complaisant upon your return."

From Akimos's expression, Skiron knew that he had struck home. To have Doris bathing his feet in her tears as she begged him to violate her had become a source of great pride for Akimos. He would not give that up lightly.

So Skiron would stay, and do what he could to aid Akimos. But he would do even more to learn what he might have awakened in the bowels of these mountains, and what all gods lawful or otherwise might let him do about them!

Doris of Lokhri lay in on a pallet sodden with sweat from her last bout with Akimos and with the tears she had shed when he left her. She hated herself for those tears, but in a corner of her mind not twisted by Skiron's spells she knew that she had no cause for shame.

Skiron had made her need Akimos, as one enslaved to the poppy syrup needed it daily. Bound to him by this need, she would gladly wed him, then see her son wed Livia—and after that see Akimos rule both Houses.

Or would she be alive to see Akimos's rise? One thing was certain—if Skiron's spells were ever flawed, she might become mistress of her own will and her own hands again. Then not the gods themselves could keep her from driving a dagger into Akimos's heart.

Agony surged through her at the thought, mixed with

desire. She was a monster, to think thus of the man who so cherished her!

She rolled over, burying her face in the sodden pallet to muffle her cries. When she had command of herself again, she heard the tramp of marching feet, the clink of armor and weapons, and that big Vendhyan Partab's voice bellowing like a drill instructor of the Guardians.

Akimos was marching out, to deal with Conan. Conan, who had sullied her body with his barbarian's touch! Conan, who had almost made her unworthy of Akimos's love!

"Aiyyyyeeeee!" It was half a scream, half a moan. It brought two servants at the run, and behind them Skiron.

From a rocky perch better suited to hawks than men, Conan studied the column of armed men marching downhill. It was too far for even his keen sight to recognize men, let alone badges, but he could count easily enough.

When he'd counted forty men, he knew that they had found their quarry where they expected. Had anyone else besides Akimos brought such a band into these mountains, surely the villagers would have heard of it.

Conan was looking at the merchant prince's men. Moreover, he'd wager that he was looking at most of them marching off to attack Castle Tebroth, leaving the Caves of Zimgas scantily guarded.

The Cimmerian scrambled down to rejoin his men, and found that Talouf and Harphos were posting sentries.

"No need for that," Conan said.

"But, Captain Conan, you always—"

"There's no such thing as 'always' in war, my lord," Conan said. "This is one of the times we don't need sentries." He described what he'd seen.

"Can we be sure that Akimos has truly stripped the cave?" Talouf asked.

It was Harphos who answered. "I don't see how he could have more than fifty or sixty men. Unless he hired some free lances of his own, and would he do that if they might talk?"

"Never be sure that your enemy thinks the way you do," Conan said. Then he added, as Harphos looked sulky, "But that's likely enough the way Akimos thinks. We'll move down at once."

Leading the two men to the crest, Conan made his plans. They would move downhill to the upper end of a ravine. From there the archers could command the approaches to the cave. Their task: to keep Akimos from returning if he caught wind of the attack.

"We'll also signal our friends from the villages," Conan added. "If they put one or two stout bands across Akimos's line of retreat, I'll not wager on our seeing him again tonight."

The Cimmerian would lead the rest of his men himself, down the ravine, across the boulders at its lower end, and straight to the cave. They would have a litter and medicine for Lady Doris, and no plan or purpose save snatching her away.

Outnumbered and surprised, the defenders of the cave should not stand in Conan's way. Unless their number included Lord Skiron, and the Cimmerian knew that he had to gamble there. If he were Akimos, marching against Castle Tebroth with a tenth of the men needed to take it, he would bring every weapon and every spell at his command.

But as he had just told Harphos, it was not well to reckon that your enemy thought as you did.

CHAPTER 18

Conan's men were slower into the attack than he had planned. Akimos had left only a handful of men on watch, but these seemed alert. Also, the last stretch of hillside to the head of the ravine was open, offering barely enough cover to hide cats, let alone armed men. So they went to ground in the bushes and waited for the last of daylight to die.

Talouf grumbled a trifle at this. "We'll not do our best in the dark. I could go down now, unseen, and draw the guards off."

"Treachery!" growled one of Reza's men.

Conan had hasty work to keep Talouf from spilling the other's blood on the rock. Then he growled in the thief's ear:

"I thought you worked best by night."

"I do, but what about the rest of the lads? No cause to risk their necks."

"Nor my mother's, either," Harphos put in. "Even if Talouf drew off the guards, their going might warn Skiron and any men left inside the cave."

Conan grinned. He'd made no mistake, thinking that Talouf was now more captain than thief and that Harphos was fast learning war. "Enough," he said. "Or the guards will hear us arguing. I've no mind to chase Lady Doris all across these hills by night, with spells *and* arrows whistling about my ears."

The Great Watcher had rested, so its strength was almost restored. What it needed to finish that task was food—the precious sky-food that was so easy to catch yet gave so much strength.

It no longer needed spells cast by men to awaken or strengthen it. But as such spells were being cast, and in a cave no great distance above it, they could well be used for guidance.

The Great Watcher assumed a shape that would allow it to flow through cracks in the rock too small for a dog, then began its climb toward the sky.

In whispers, Conan pointed out the aiming marks for the archers.

"And if any of you puts one arrow short of those, I'll ram his quiver up his arse sideways," the Cimmerian added. "I want you dangerous to Akimos, not us."

The archers nodded. It was no small task they were facing, but they were the pick of the archers of both House Damaos and Conan's Company. Both had come to take pride in carrying out Captain Conan's orders, for they only *seemed* impossible and were always more dangerous to the enemy than to the men carrying them out.

Conan sat and pulled off his boots. On uneven ground in the dark, he could move faster with his leather-tough soles to guide him. Then he sheathed his sword, took the iron-shod staff Talouf handed him, and began his slow descent of the ravine.

He had just reached the top of the loose boulders when the ground quivered underfoot. It was only a faint quivering, like a bowl of gruel lightly tapped by a child's hand. But even in the dark, Conan could make out boulders shifting.

Go back or wait? The shock might be the only one, but if it was not, the next might send all the boulders roaring down the ravine. All the boulders, and anyone crossing them, to give the guards all the warning they could need.

He needed surprise, and that might vanish with the next shock. So what else to do, but be among the guards before it came?

Conan abandoned caution and silence, leaping from boulder to boulder like a lion launched upon its prey. He felt some shift under his feet, but the earth itself remained quiet.

At least it remained quiet until he was more than halfway down the ravine. He could see the guards' torches moving about briskly, as though they sensed danger but not its nature. Then the ground heaved underfoot, and all the boulders were moving at once.

Any man but the Cimmerian would have gone down then and there, to be ground to bloody pulp by the tumbling boulders. Even Conan's speed and agility was barely enough to take him clear of the boulders. If he had been ten paces farther from the solid rock at one side of the ravine even these gifts would not have saved him.

The solid rock was still quivering as he felt it underfoot, but he did not let that slow him. Using his staff over the rough patches, he slipped along the edge of the ravine until the ground began to level out. Then he broke into a run. The boulders were making such a din and raising so much dust that a company of Guardians could have marched behind them without discovery. Instead of killing him, the earthquake had given Conan back the surprise he needed.

Conan came up to a man-high drop at a run and took it without breaking stride. He landed, rolled to break his fall, felt stones gouge and even tear skin, but came up with staff in both hands. It whirled about him like a windmill in a gale, and the iron-shod ends broke shoulders and arms, smashed faces, and cracked skulls in fine fashion.

Conan put three men down and two more to flight before he even heard anyone coming down the ravine. He did not dare turn to see who it might be, since half a dozen more guards were swarming out of the cave. He also did not dare give ground, even against odds of six to one.

Two quakes might not be all. The third one could be enough to tumble the cave down on top of Lady Doris, unless someone was close enough to snatch her free.

For now, Conan was the only friend so close. A dozen stout companions would have been welcome, but not waiting until they came downhill if that meant losing surprise. He shifted his staff to his left hand, for parrying as well as striking, and drew his broadsword.

"Come on, you mewling milksops!" he roared, as loud as the rockslide. "Come on and try my steel. Or I'll hunt you down and then go tell your master that he pissed away his silver on cowards!"

Stung, the men came on. Steel met steel with a clanging that rose into the night like the din of a blacksmith hard at work.

Livia awoke from a pleasurable dream of Conan to find Reza shaking her by both shoulders. She threw her head back and tried to pull away. The iron hands let her go, and she fell back on the pallet.

Then a skyful of cold water seemed to descend on her. She screamed and jumped up, forgetting that she was clad as usual when she slept. Reza put down the bucket and instead of politely offering a blanket, threw her a towel and a tunic.

"And pick up your dagger before it takes rust, my lady," he said severely. "We're being attacked."

Now with waking senses, Livia saw men running, heard a trumpet sounding from beyond the wall, and smelled burning pine tar. She snatched up her dagger and ran down the stairs, tunic and towel under her arm.

Her appearance in the courtyard, bare as the day of her birth, nearly turned the tide of battle—against Castle Tebroth's defenders. So many eyes fixed themselves upon her that few watched the gate or the path to it. It was at that very moment that Akimos's men launched their attempt to carry the gate by storm.

Conan had not counted as well as he commonly did. Akimos had closer to seventy men than forty, and he flung them all up the path in one desperate assault. The archers made the best practice they could, but that was not good enough. They had no light save a few burning pine knots flung over the walls. Even those arrows that struck human marks struck armor as often as flesh.

Akimos's men reached the gateway with as many losses from falling off the path as from the defenders' arrows. They came up to the barricade with thrice the strength of the defenders there, rose up it like a wave, and threatened to spill over it.

As they did, Livia ran up, screaming words she had not thought she knew and waving her dagger in one hand, her tunic in the other. Facing what seemed a naked goddess of war, the attackers in turn stopped to gape.

That was more fatal to them than to the defenders. By now it no longer mattered greatly how Lady Livia chose to dress for the night's battle. It did matter that their lives and honor were at stake, and about to be lost. They took full advantage of their enemies' moment of confusion to shorten the odds by a good half score of men.

Then the attackers recovered and rallied, but another five or six went down along with three of the defenders. Livia herself leaped up on to the barricade, faced a man unsure of his footing, and remembered some of what Conan had taught her about real wrestling.

A shapely leg hooked the man's feet out from under him. He fell with a crash, denting his helmet and the skull under it on the stones. Writhing, he rolled down the barricade under the feet of two comrades trying to climb it. One went down, the other leaped over him to reach Livia.

But he reached her with one thought in his mind: this was the woman Lord Akimos wanted taken alive. So he ignored his steel and tried to grapple her about the waist. In doing this, he forgot that his throat was just at the level of Livia's knife hand.

He remembered this when a slash of the dagger opened his throat from ear to ear. Blood fountained as he slumped down, seeming to kiss Livia's feet in his last movement. Then Livia felt herself seeming to fly into the air, as Reza snatched her off the barricade and half dropped, half threw her to the scant safety lying behind it.

She went to her knees, tried to stand, then realized that she was in the middle of a battle wearing only sweat, dust, and the blood of a man she had killed with her own hand. She remained on her knees while her stomach rebelled and emptied itself, then lurched to her feet and groped for the tunic she vaguely remembered having in her hand.

While she searched, Reza and Sergeant Kirgesthes were turning the tide of the battle. Atop the barricade, Reza was at first mistaken for Conan himself. That frightened the wits out of those attackers who had survived the battle at House Damaos. Even when they realized who it was they faced, fear did not leave them. Reza, they remembered, had been nearly as formidable as the Cimmerian.

Another half dozen attackers died at Reza's hands alone before they could master their fear. As many more went down to other defenders. From walls and towers the women and children joined the fray, hurling stones with more abandon than skill.

Now the attackers' line gaped wide in places. Reza ordered his men through the gaps.

"Take them in the rear!" he thundered. "Take them in the rear, and we've the lot!"

Meanwhile, Kirgesthes was rallying the archers. Enough pine knots now blazed to make the courtyard reek of their smoke, but also to let archers tell friend from foe. Akimos had sent few opposing archers, and these were the first to fall. Then Kirgesthes himself shot down Akimos's captain, and his men began emptying their quivers at good speed.

With the counterattack from the barricade before them and arrows showering from above, Akimos's men had but one path to follow if they wished to live. They abandoned the attack and retreated through the gateway. It was a retreat, not a flight, although they did it with more haste than dignity.

By the time Livia had decently garbed herself (her tunic, with nothing under it save the towel wrapped around her loins), the gateway was secure. She was sitting on a fallen block, with her head in her hands, when Reza came up.

"My lady, we have beaten them off this time."

"Will they come again?"

"I may answer that when I have counted—"

A cheer interrupted him. Then another echoed it, and finally everyone in the castle was cheering with one voice.

"Livia of Damaos! Livia of Damaos! Long live House Damaos and Lady Livia!"

Tears that she had held back until now filled Livia's eyes. She needed the strength of Reza's arm to stand, wished for a moment that it was Conan's arm, then turned to face those she had led.

The cheers swelled until they echoed from the stones of the mountainside as well as of the castle. Livia contrived to smile and wave; she was weeping too hard to find words.

In the next moment the ground seemed to ripple underfoot, like a silken coverlet tossed carelessly upon a bed. The rippling came and went in the space of a single deep breath, but it thoroughly silenced the cheering.

Livia shook her head, brushed her tangled hair back from her face, and found her voice.

"Thank you, and the gods bless and keep you. Now, those sons of she-goats may come again. So let us be ready!"

The cheers this time were thinner, but only because a fair number of the defenders were already at work, gathering the wounded. Livia sat down again, discreetly drew the towel from under her tunic, and began cleansing her legs of blood and dust.

The third earthquake did not even make Harphos break stride. It was not strong enough to unsettle the boulders underfoot, and anything else he could ignore. Anything else, that is, except reaching Captain Conan in time.

When the dust settled and the remaining torches showed Conan in single-handed battle against six of Akimos's men, Harphos expected a general rush down the ravine. Instead only Talouf leaped forward. No one followed him, and even the archers held their shots.

Conan had taught Harphos enough for him to know what had to be done. His own honor told him the same.

"Follow me!" Harphos shouted, and drew his shortsword as he ran down the ravine. Men who might abandon a Cimmerian would not readily abandon the heir of House Lokhri, or so he hoped.

Harphos did not look behind him once as he plunged down the ravine. If the men would not follow, his eyes on them would not help. It would help even less for him to stumble and fall, to dash out the brains he sometimes doubted he had on the tumbled rocks. Harphos was only near-sighted, not night blind, but he had never tried to run downhill over boulders in a cloud of dust with enemies waiting at the bottom.

Somehow, simple will-power and the fear of making a fool of himself kept his feet under him. He still sighed with relief when he reached level ground. He sighed again, when he heard the scutter and rattle of the men coming down behind him. His swordsmanship might not be put to the test tonight—

Relief made him careless. As he watched the last of Conan's opponents flee, Harphos's foot sank into a crack in the rock. Pain shot up his leg as the rock scraped his skin and pressed his ankle bone.

Then Harphos's mouth gaped, as one of Akimos's dead men proved not so dead after all. Harphos drew his sword, but never had he expected to face an opponent when he had a foot almost literally rooted to the ground.

Sparks flew and sweat streamed from Harphos as he parried the man's dagger. By the gods' favor, the man was hurt and bloody, slowed by wounds and fatigue, and his blade was no longer than Harphos's.

As the heir of Lokhri fought, he felt the sweat on his skin reach his ankle. He heaved, and as if it had been greased his foot slid free. Akimos's man lunged in a final desperate effort, then died as Harphos's sword slid up between his ribs and Conan's broadsword clove his skull.

Harphos tried to laugh, contrived to smile, and did not faint. "Conan, had that stroke been only a trifle stronger, you would have split my—look out behind you!"

Harphos's shout had an echo, and the two warnings together made the Cimmerian whirl with inhuman speed. Instead of cutting down the man striking at his exposed back, he kicked him smartly between the legs, then kicked his legs out from under him. The man went down, gasping and writhing.

Harphos recognized one of Conan's men, whose name he recalled as Douras. A Damaos man, Mekhas, had dropped his sword and was looking in all directions save at Conan.

"What in Mitra's name—?" Harphos began.

"Listen to him, when he talks," Conan growled, jabbing a thumb in under Douras's jaw. The man writhed harder but said nothing.

"Captain Conan," Mekhas said, barely loud enough to be heard. "I—I thought you were going to slay Harphos next. We were warned against that. Then I saw I had been mistaken. I tried to stop Douras. Then all I could do was shout."

"Well, I'm grateful enough for that," Conan said. "I'll be more grateful if you tell me who warned you. Maybe even grateful enough not to serve you the way I'll serve Douras."

Mekhas looked at the ground. Harphos glared at him. "If Conan leaves anything of you, I'll warn Lady Livia to finish it off. Now—*who* warned you that Conan might be thinking to kill me?"

"Reza."

Harphos and the Cimmerian cursed together. "I'm going to geld that son of a sow with a red-hot knife," Conan growled, when he had done cursing. "That's one too many times he's put his nose in where it's not welcome. Unless—"

He broke off, and Harphos blinked at a sight he had doubted would ever be seen by mortal eyes. The Cimmerian seemed ill at ease. Then Conan laughed.

"Perhaps he only thought to save his lady from her

own folly, rather than my ambition. If so, then *she* can geld him.''

Harphos frowned. The Cimmerian no longer seemed ill at ease, but he was talking in riddles, which was hardly better.

''What folly of Livia's?''

Conan hooked both thumbs into his belt. ''Her—call it choice—to lie with me.''

For a moment Harphos felt as if he had been kicked in the stomach, not to mention slapped in the face and pounded on the back. His breath came in gasps. Then he remembered certain things, not least among them the way he had spent the first night at Castle Tebroth snugly wrapped in Shilka's arms.

Which, he realized, Livia had no doubt arranged, to keep him pleasantly occupied while she kicked Conan's feet from under him and leaped upon him! Harphos was certain that it had happened thus, and the picture in his mind made him smile, then laugh.

Conan frowned. 'What in the name of Erlik's pride is so funny?''

''The idea of my intended wife all but abducting you, Captain. I knew she had great strength of purpose, but not that much. Well, I shall have to say a word or two about it to her.''

The Cimmerian now looked almost bemused. ''So you're not angry?''

Harphos sighed. ''Had you sought to hide the whole matter, I might well have suspected you as Reza did. Since you spoke the truth, I have no further quarrel with you.

''My mother will be another matter. She will throw a royal tantrum. But I am past letting her tantrums strike me down, like a chamberpot flung from a high window.

Reza will be still another matter. I do not think he can remain in the service of—''

''If Reza lives out the night, we can settle with him then,'' Conan put in. ''For now, we spend time talking that we may need to save your—''

A scream that seemed to come from the bottom of a pit of demons interrupted them. Harphos spun to look uphill past the litter of corpses to the mouth of the Caves of Zimgas. Silhouetted against the flickering light stood a woman. Even seeing nothing but the silhouette, Harphos recognized his mother.

''It seems that my mother has saved herself,'' he said. He sheathed his sword and plunged uphill, toward where Lady Doris had now fallen on her knees, head bowed and shoulders shaking with sobs or exhaustion.

As Harphos ran, he saw the light in the caves dim, as if something had passed between the light and the mouth.

Between drugs, exhaustion, spells, and pain, Lady Doris remembered little of what passed the night of her rescue. She certainly never remembered that she owed her life to Lord Skiron.

But that was the truth. Skiron was the first man in the cave to sense the Great Watcher's approach. By the time he could hear the hiss and slither of its approach, he was moving. His slave already had the bags of magical apparatus on his back, and the sorcerer followed with staff and a phial for renewing the spell on Lady Doris.

As the hissing grew louder, they both began to run. They ran up to Lady Doris's pallet, and the slave tore the curtains aside while Skiron dragged the lady to her feet. She stared at him, eyes blank and wandering, making no effort to cover herself.

Then she pulled away. "I must stay here. Akimos will be coming to me. He will be here soon." She actually smiled.

"Akimos is outside, waiting for you there. You will be returning in state with him to Messantia. But you must come swiftly. My lady, please come, now! Come to Akimos!"

As he argued, Skiron heard the Watcher give tongue for the first time, a low rumbling cry. He flung the vial of potion at Lady Doris. It could pass into the body through the skin, if not as swiftly as by the mouth.

Doris ran a finger through the potion trickling down between her breasts, then licked at it. She smiled again.

"I come." Then she leaped to her feet and ran down toward the mouth of the cave, quickly outstripping even Skiron.

Conan saw half a dozen men appear at the mouth of the Caves of Zimgas just as Harphos reached his mother. He shouted a warning, but the men seemed more intent on flight than on attack. They ran past Harphos like rabbits fleeing a wolf, saw Conan and his men below, and turned sharply to either side.

"After those men!" Conan roared. "If they escape, I'll roast the ones who let them for breakfast!" He was almost certain, but did not care to say aloud, that one of the fleeing men was Skiron. If the sorcerer still had any spells at his command—

Then thoughts of merely human opponents vanished from Conan's mind, as the Great Watcher reached the mouth of the caves.

Some men who saw it fainted. Others knelt, to pray

or spew. Some merely stood as if their senses and limbs were all alike numb. Few could describe what they saw, other than that it was a translucent gray, shot with flowing lighter patches of crimson and a sickly dark gold.

If Harphos had been one of those men whose wits fled, he and his mother would have died on the spot. As it was, he saw the Watcher thrusting forward a tentacle ending in fanged jaws. He slashed at the jaws, chopped out a piece, saw it fly through the air—then land and begin crawling back toward the main body.

Yet the Watcher seemed to be capable of feeling pain, or at least sensing danger in its path. It drew back the tentacle, thrust out four more shorter ones covered with suckers, but did not itself advance. This gave Harphos time to half lead, half drag, and at the end mostly carry his mother out of danger.

At least for the moment. The Watcher took long enough to gather its strength for Conan to rally his men. They were mostly on their feet, alert, and with weapons in hand by the time the Watcher surged out into the open.

As it did, it flung part of itself well ahead and downhill. The mass of gray slime landed on top of two men, and their screams died swiftly as it absorbed them. As it did, horrified watchers saw it turn crimson with their blood and flesh—then sprout legs, a tail, and a head with more teeth than a school of sharks.

Before this monstrosity could move, though, Conan was up with it. His sword flashed in the light of the campfire, slashing down with a stroke that might have cloven a mountain to its roots. Half the head sheered off and flew through the air. It began crawling back toward the legged isolate, then sensed the Watcher itself uphill. It turned, careless of its path—and crawled over a hot ember from the scattered campfire of Akimos's men.

Instantly a high-pitched scream tore at everyone's ears. Conan saw the isolate jerking and twisting as smoke streamed out from under it. Seizing a burning brand in his free hand, he dashed forward and slashed at the isolate's back with his sword. It was like slashing at a sea turtle's shell, but the Cimmerian's strength was adequate to the purpose. The hard skin of the isolate's back gaped, and Conan thrust the brand into it.

Smoke poured up, and the scream came again, rising until even Conan wanted to clap his hands over his ears to shut out the sound of a world going mad. The isolate swelled up, until the skin began to crack, then burst like a gigantic pustule. Foul-smelling ichor and smoking fragments of skin rained down over the camp, but Conan's men ignored them.

They had seen that the Watcher was not invincible, and even how it might be bested. They ran to snatch up brands. Those who reached the campfires too late plucked handfuls of dry grass and used their flint and steel, or searched the tents for anything else that might burn.

Harphos cupped his hands and shouted, "Well done, Captain Conan! It stands to reason that there had to be some way of destroying those creatures without sorcery!"

Conan nodded. He had to admit that the ancient sorcerers who created the Watchers showed a trifle more foresight than most of their breed. Certainly more than Skiron, who had waked this monster with all the caution of a man building fires in a tinder-dry forest!

The Great Watcher sensed the isolate's destruction, but it had memories of isolates being destroyed before, without danger to itself. This was a situation that demanded more knowledge before a decision could be taken either to fight or to withdraw. The way to that knowledge seemed to lie forward.

So the Great Watcher surged entirely out of the cave, and onto the open hillside. Confronted with its full horror, some men once again lost command of themselves. Some even turned to flee, but Harphos stood in their path, his mother on one arm and his shortsword in the other hand.

"If you aren't afraid of dishonor, you'd best be afraid of me!" he snarled, and for that moment he looked as fierce and formidable as Conan himself. The would-be fugitives remembered themselves, and turned back to join their comrades.

From up the hill, arrows now whistled down into the Watcher. The archers had marched to the sound of the fight and were now shooting as best they could in the poor light, trying for anything that looked like an eye or a mouth.

"Fire arrows!" Conan roared, as loud as the Watcher itself. "Use fire arrows if you have them! If you touch fire to the thing, it burns like a haystack!"

Whether the archers heard him or not, Conan had no time to consider. His shouts drew the Watcher's attention, and it surged toward him, sprouting twenty stubby legs ending in five-clawed feet to speed its movements. With the slope to aid it, the Watcher came down on Conan so fast that three fanged heads were looping toward him on long necks before he realized it.

His speed saved him, though, his speed and a House Damaos man who ran in and thrust a spear deep into the nearest neck. The head stopped, and the man twisted the spear in the wound before withdrawing it.

Then a second man ran in as the neck writhed, darted aside from the snapping jaws, and thrust a burning brand into the wound.

The Watcher screamed from two mouths as the third head flew off in an eruption of smoke and stomach-turning fragments. The truncated neck writhed more frenziedly than ever, but the other two heads still had life, will, and sharp teeth. Conan saw one head seize a man, lift him high, then shake the life out of him and start absorbing him.

One of Conan's men ran in against a second head, wielding a tulwar with a strength almost equal to the Cimmerian's. The head flew into the air and landed on a man standing by the campfire, lighting an improvised torch. Both fell into the fire. The man screamed at the pain of burns and teeth sinking into his flesh, then the head vanished in a vast cloud of foul green smoke. A moment later the man lurched to his feet, scorched and bloody but cursing too furiously to be mortally hurt.

The Great Watcher now seemed bemused, even wary, at the vigor of its enemies. But Conan doubted that it had been seriously hurt. He wanted to alter that before it found some new method of attack less vulnerable than those fanged heads.

By now the men who had foraged in Akimos's camp were coming back, and Conan saw two of them carrying straw pallets. He quickly snatched up a fresh brand, summoned the pallet-bearers, and rallied a couple of spearmen. Then he led the whole party forward.

Conan's broadsword whistled, and the horny covering over the stump of one neck gaped open. The two spearmen lifted the pallets on the points of their spears, and Conan thrust the burning brand deep into the straw.

Then all three together heaved, ramming the pallet into the Great Watcher's wound like a cork into a bottle.

Conan said afterward that the end of all creation might well be quieter than the end of the Great Watcher. No man could stand close by and hear anything but the death-cry that began as a hiss and ended as a screaming roar.

Nor could anyone endure the smoke and stench that poured out as the Great Watcher exploded. Few cared to risk being struck down by razor-sharp fragments of skin the size of platters, or spattered with smoking ichor.

As one man, Conan and his party ran downhill and remained there until the last life had departed from the Great Watcher. Conan was prodding smoking fragments with the tip of his sword when he saw Harphos making his way up to join him. The young man was naked save for boots, loinguard, and slime-dripping shortsword.

"How fares Lady Doris?" the Cimmerian asked.

"Not well," Harphos said. "I have garbed her in my tunic and salved the worst of her hurts. But she will need a litter, and perhaps more. She cries out for Akimos, as a man dying of thirst cries out for water." The two men had no need to use the word "sorcery."

"Well, then, let us go find Lord Akimos," Conan said, sheathing his sword. "Oris spoke of more than one Watcher. If there's another about, perhaps we can feed Lord Akimos to it."

"Gods, Conan, have you no mercy? To poison even such a creature as a Watcher—"

"Will save my men and yours, as well as the villagers hereabouts." Conan was in no humor for jests.

"Then I will see about the men who are fit to walk, if you can contrive a litter."

It had been some time since Conan gave Harphos the formal Argossean bow, but now he did and not only because it was his "place." Tonight was finishing the work of turning Lady Doris's boy Harphos into a man and lord of House Lokhri—not to mention a fit match for Lady Livia.

CHAPTER 19

Akimos started as Partab loomed out of the darkness.

"Only I, lord."

So the Vendhyan swine knew that the lord of House Peram was uneasy! How long before all the men before Castle Tebroth knew it?

"Any news from the sentries?"

"They have heard sounds that might be the villagers moving about, wild cattle, deer, or many other things."

"Curse the city-bred fools!"

But if he had gone out to hire men wise in the ways of the country, his plans would quickly have been no secret. Then he would likely enough not have even come far enough to be facing defeat now in the mountains.

"The gods may do so in their own good time. For ourselves, I suggest that we strengthen the sentries."

Akimos frowned. He had lost close upon a third of his strength in the desperate battle in the gateway. That would have been a small price to pay for victory and possession of Livia. But instead the wench had fought bare from crown to toes and turned the tide of the battle, and now she was there sitting on that lovely arse and mocking him—!

Akimos cursed aloud, then commanded himself to cease. "How likely is an attack by the villagers?" He disliked asking an underling like Partab for advice, but the man had been leader of the raiding parties. He knew the villages and their folk better than any other man with Akimos.

"If they know our weakness, quite possible. If the men in the castle have ways of sending messages to the villagers, they will know."

"And how likely are the messages?"

"I do not think Reza would be likely to think of that himself, or Harphos, or Lady Livia. But Conan is a different matter."

Conan, it seemed to Akimos, had been a different matter since the day he came to Argos—and mostly in Akimos's path! He almost said that aloud.

But the words never left his lips, because from the castle above came a nightmarish din. First the rumble of falling stones, then screams and cries of fear and pain, and finally a hissing like all the serpents in the world at once.

The Lesser Watcher knew when the mind of the Great Watcher ceased. It was close to joining its comrade in search of sky-food when that happened.

It waited in a chamber of the Caves of Zimgas deep underground, until it knew that the Great Watcher would not wake again. Then swiftly it began to retrace its route through the Caves, and beyond that through other tunnels toward another opening to the sky.

Beyond that opening would lie more sky-food. The need for that was greater than ever, for the whole work of bringing into being more Watchers now fell to the Lesser Watcher.

But there was also another need that would be served by devouring the two-legged creatures that were the best source of sky food. In a man, that need would have been called vengeance.

The first men in Castle Tebroth to meet the Lesser Watcher were the sentries at the barricade to the cellar. There were only three of them and all bore minor wounds. Reza was ready to believe in the Watchers. He was not ready to believe in anything that could make its way through that pile of stones.

The three men paid for Reza's mistake with their lives. They heard a faint hiss, a louder rumble, and finally a crash like a mason splitting a stone block. Indeed, that was very nearly what they had heard.

The Lesser Watcher had transformed itself into a living battering ram, with a head hard as armor and massive legs to drive the head against the stones. The stones flew in all directions under the blows. One of them fell on a sentry, crushing the life out of him before he could even scream.

The other two sentries had time to grip their weapons before they died, without striking a blow. The Lesser Watcher's head divided, both halves opened mouths, and both mouths snapped shut.

The two sentries did scream as they died, and the screams warned everyone not already roused by the noise of the Lesser Watcher's emergence. One look at the Lesser Watcher as it lumbered into view persuaded the defenders that safety lay only in flight.

So some ran madly out the gateway, not caring who or what might lie ahead so long as they could flee what lay behind. Most ran for crumbling stairs and sprinted up them to the walls, towers, or keep.

When they had put twenty or thirty steps between them and the Lesser Watcher, they began to breathe more easily. After all, such a creature as that could hardly climb stairs, still less a wall or the outside of a tower.

Livia watched in horror as her men learned otherwise. The Lesser Watcher squatted beside one wall, and turned itself into a vast, hard-shelled, almond-shaped mass. From that mass a neck rose, until it reached the level of the top of the wall. Then a head with fanged jaws sprouted on that neck, like some hideous flower, and began roving up and down the wall, plucking screaming men like a boy stripping a bush of berries.

Livia tried to shut her ears to the cries of her men dying. She contrived to silence herself only by thrusting her fist into her mouth. Madness would have seized her, except for a lingering hope that the women and children might yet be safe.

At last the Lesser Watcher turned a deep shade of crimson and seemed to be less eager for prey. By now its shell was a pincushion of spears, arrows, and stones flung at it. Reza tapped her on the shoulder.

"My lady, there are tales that fire in some way had power against the Watchers."

"Do we have any fire arrows?"

"No, but there are burning brands."

Livia said nothing. Burning brands would need men to carry them close to the Watcher, and she could not see how such men would live—above all, Reza, who would surely lead them. But nothing else seemed to offer the slightest hope.

"Very well. I am going down to see to the wounded. If all else fails, I would not have them die alone."

If all else failed, she also was doomed. But at least in the sickroom she would not have to watch that doom approaching. With luck, the first knowledge she had of it would be the stones of the tower falling inward, to crush her lifeless before the Watcher began to feed on her—

Her stomach heaved and she leaned against the wall until the spasm passed. As it did, she was ready to swear that her ears were deserting her also.

Far down the hill, she heard warcries, the "Onward, ever to battle!" of House Lokhri, and even "Livia of Damaos!"

Conan and his men would have reached the castle about the same time as the Lesser Watcher but for one unlucky chance.

As they trotted the last quarter league toward the rear of Akimos's men, they encountered a band of villagers moving toward the same goal. Each thought the other was reinforcements for Akimos. Both went to ground, and their captains began readying them for both attack and defense.

It was only after some time had been lost this way that Conan recognized peasant garb, and some of the villagers recognized the Damaos badge. Then the two bands moved out quickly enough, but they were still on the hill when the Lesser Watcher struck.

For all the havoc it wrought in the castle, the Lesser Watcher was a blessing from the gods for Conan and the villagers. Akimos and his men were so bemused by what might be happening in the castle that they forgot to look to their rear. So Conan had the sixty-odd men who followed him in position for an attack before Akimos knew he had guests.

Then they went forward, and the hillside dissolved into the chaos of a night battle. Through that chaos stormed Conan, broadsword leaving red ruin everywhere it struck, warcries giving courage to his men and taking it from his foes. That night he was worth ten men in himself, and it was no shame to some of Akimos's men that they fled up the hill, crying that demons were upon them.

Then they reached the gateway and found themselves facing a real demon, as the Lesser Watcher thundered toward them.

Livia watched through the arrow slit in the tower as the Watcher sprouted legs and a spike-studded, eyeless head. Now it looked like a gigantic turtle with eight or ten—no, now twelve—legs. No tail, and the shell was as smooth as glass save where flung brands had left scars.

The legends were right. Thrust fire into the Watcher's substance, and it would suffer. Thrust deep enough, and perhaps it would die before it had eaten the castle bare of Livia's men.

The brands showered down until they were gone, but by then smoke rose from the Watcher in a score of places. Also until Livia and everyone in the sickroom were half deafened by the Watcher's cries.

Then it fell silent and began its transformation. Livia did not know if it was going to attack or seek easier prey elsewhere, prayed that it was the latter, and knew

that her prayers would do little enough. So she watched
the Lesser Watcher sprout three additional pairs of legs,
and lumber off through the gateway. Stones fell from
either side as the creature knocked them loose, and a
portion of the gateway arch crashed down. But stone
blocks larger than a man had no more effect than peb-
bles; they slid off harmlessly.

Then she crawled back down from the arrow slit and
returned to the work of bandaging wounds, salving
burns, and holding the hands of those who had taken
hurts only to their minds, not their bodies.

Akimos cheered his men when he saw them running
toward the castle. An attack now, when something dis-
tracted the defenders, might succeed. Then he cursed
them, as he saw them running back.

The curses died on his lips as he saw what made them
run. He planted himself on the path, waving his sword.

"Rally, rally, men! For the honor of House Peram!
For victory over the accursed—!"

The curses of his fleeing men drowned him out. One
man did more than curse. He slashed at Lord Akimos
with a shortsword. The blow was hasty and clumsy, but
chance guided it to Akimos's neck.

He felt the blood spurt, then flow down his shoulder
and chest. He felt the flow increase, and his strength
diminish with the flowing of his blood. In due course
he felt that it would be wise to sit down and stop shouting until he regained his strength.

Akimos had fallen over backward but was not quite
dead from loss of blood when the Lesser Watcher
marched down the path and devoured him.

* * *

Conan's men held their ground as the Watcher came down the hill toward them. The villagers were not so well led nor so wise in how to fight Watchers. They broke and fled, screaming.

Such of Akimos's men as were left mostly followed them. Some were still of a mind to fight, others were merely doing the same as the villagers—putting as many leagues between them and the monster as they could.

A few stout-hearted servants of House Peram tried both to hold their ground and to sustain the fight against Conan's men. But they were outnumbered three to one, apart from the worth of the Cimmerian. They were dead, taken, or in flight before the Lesser Watcher had finished consuming Akimos's corpse.

"Conan, we have to send men into the castle and bring Livia out," Harphos exclaimed.

"How are we going to send them around *that?*" Conan growled, pointing his sword at the Lesser Watcher. It had now sprouted three heads, with only small toothless mouths but huge glaring red eyes. It seemed content to remain where it was while it sought further prey, but Conan had no doubt what it would do when it found some.

"We cannot leave Livia!" Harphos all but screamed.

"We cannot, but *she* cannot leave her people and the wounded in the castle," Conan snapped. "It will be all or none with her, she's that kind of captain. Since it can't be all until we've killed that—"

"Conan, I will go alone if—"

Conan gripped Harphos's shoulder. The young man wriggled like a fish on a hook but could not pull free.

"You'll go nowhere. If you go up that path and end up eaten, Reza will have my blood if Livia doesn't. Stay, or must I have you bound?"

Harphos sighed. "Conan, there are moments when I think you understand my bride better than I do myself."

"Women being what they are, similar situations have been known to happen," Conan said. "But it's not the woman I know so much as the war captain."

He clapped Harphos on the shoulder in a friendlier fashion. "Now, let's be about finding the makings of brands and fire. A good bonfire up its craw, and this Watcher'll go the way of the first!"

Harphos nodded and began calling men to him. Talouf came up to stand beside the Cimmerian, as the young man went off.

"How long is that thing going to wait for us, Captain?" the sergeant asked.

"The gods only know and I haven't talked to them of late," the Cimmerian said with a shrug. "If it ate the castle empty, it may need to go slowly for a while, like a gorged lion."

He did not add what he'd heard, that when gorged the Watchers could split in two, each new Watcher with all the dreadful power of the old one. That was one reason he'd refused to send men up past the Watcher to save those in the castle. If no one stood between the Watcher and the open countryside and it then split, *two* Watchers would be roaming at large, devouring everything in their path.

It had not needed Captain Khadjar to teach Conan one important lesson about war. When you had your enemy before you, you fought him then and there if you could. You did not sit on your arse until he fled, then chase after him like an old hound after a young rabbit!

Conan and Talouf were almost alone facing the Watcher when Conan saw a dark-clad figure making its way down the slope above the monster. The moon was out now, giving just enough light to make out the figure as small and slight, with a hint of sharp features.

Skiron? Had the sorcerer come to take command of the Watcher, turn it from a witless monster into a weapon? Conan watched the figure's stumbling progress, measuring distances. He might—no, could—reach the sorcerer and slay him, but he'd never escape past the Watcher.

Well, any man's time came sooner or later, mostly the sooner for those who lived by their swords and wits, and that was no surprise to Conan. He had done his best, and if Crom did not call that best good enough, then that was the god's affair!

Conan stalked forward. He had gone ten paces, when Talouf called from behind him.

"Captain, look!"

A crack was showing along the Watcher's back. It reached the head, then stretched backward, toward the spiked tail.

Toward the spiked *tails*. Two of them, each with spikes longer than a man's arm, each flailing hard enough to drive those spikes through plate armor.

The Watcher was dividing.

Conan did not know what this did to his chances of escaping. He knew it made it even more important to cut Skiron down before he mastered both Watchers.

Conan broke into a run, bellowing the warcries of half a dozen lands as he flourished his sword. He did not see Talouf breaking into a run to follow him. His eyes were wholly on the Watcher and on the dark figure now close to it, raising its arms in the unmistakable gesture of a sorcerer about to cast a spell.

Skiron did not notice the Cimmerian until he began shouting warcries. Even then he gave the man little thought. Ten Conans together would be no match for two Watchers, each of them commanded by a spell to feed and divide, feed and divide, until they were as numerous as ants and as hungry as starving tigers.

Then they would plague the land of Argos until another spell brought them to heel. The man who cast that spell could command his own price, and the archons themselves would bestow enough gold to found a dozen schools of magic! Akimos might be dead, but not Skiron's hopes.

He felt the spell building in him, and he knew that as it did it was drawing its strength from his own body. He had few of the materials needed to cast it without draining himself. His mute servant had gone into the night, perhaps into the maw of the first Watcher, and with him all of Skiron's apparatus. That would not matter, if commanding the Watchers bought him the time to regain his strength and restore his apparatus.

So he poured out his strength, careless of whether he finished the spell-casting a drained husk or not. He was also careless of other things, such as the Cimmerian running up the hill toward the Watcher.

As Conan approached, two of the Watcher's heads sprouted teeth and lunged for him. He slashed at their muzzles with his sword, then danced back out of reach. Skiron saw only dimly the speed of Conan's arm and feet, and did not believe what he saw.

Then he saw clearly the Cimmerian running up the hill toward him. The Watcher's third head also sprouted teeth and lunged for the Cimmerian, but only struck the rocks behind him. Loose rock poured down the slope and dust rose to half-veil the Watcher.

Skiron felt sweat break out on his skin, carving paths

in the dust that caked it. While he built his spell over the Watcher, it had less than its usual swiftness. Was his spell also slowing its division?

The sorcerer continued the spell as he pondered these questions. What finally drew him away from the spell was seeing Conan's approach. A few more paces and he would be within sword's reach.

A simple spell would suffice, for a simple threat. Skiron's hands danced and Conan's sword flew from his hand. It arched high and one of the Watcher's heads darted at it, plucking it out of the air like a bird snatching an insect on the wing.

Unease filled Skiron. That was *swift* movement in the Watcher—and Conan was still coming.

Unease turned to fear. Skiron began to back away, but a lamb might as well have tried to back away from a wolf.

Conan reached the sorcerer and grappled him barehanded. Skiron squalled in terror as he felt himself raised high over the Cimmerian's head. Then fear stopped his mouth and breath as the Cimmerian flung him at the Watcher.

It did not blind his eyes. They saw all three heads dart up, the mouths gaping open. They saw the teeth coming down. They even saw the teeth sinking into his flesh before first pain and then death blinded them forever.

Conan drew his dagger and set his back against the rock as the Watcher's heads tore Skiron apart. No doubt the monster would be after him soon enough. The sorcerer could hardly be more than a morsel, and with the spell broken the Watcher would be too swift for even a Cimmerian to escape.

At least he had ended Skiron's life and, he hoped, lessened the danger of there being more than one Watcher. Those who came up the hill with fire and steel to finish the work would have an easier task, and some of them might live to tell Livia—

The Watcher shuddered, and the crack now stretching from head to tail widened. Smoke poured out, so thick and foul that Conan was too busy covering nose and mouth to see what was under it.

The smoke was heavy, like a sea fog. It flowed down around the Watcher as well as rising toward Conan. The Cimmerian felt a moment's inward chill as the reeking gray tendrils brushed his skin.

But there was no magic in the smoke, only a gagging odor worse than Conan had smelled even from the first Watcher. He tried to make out what was happening to the Watcher behind the veil of smoke, but it was now so thick that he might have been trying to look through a brick wall.

Then there was a sound like all the rotten fruit in Argos flung down at once on to a stone floor. Blue light seared Conan's eyes, piercing the smoke but blinding him at the same time. He pressed his face into the rock as a reeking wind roared past him, stinging his skin with gravel and grit and unspeakable fragments of the Watcher.

At last the blue glare died. Conan opened his eyes, brushed the grit out of them, and stared. Where the Watcher had stood was a vast pit of smoking blue glass, edged with blackened rock and a few charred fragments of Watcher flesh.

Whether or not Akimos had poisoned the Watcher, the sorcerer who had conjured it up from its long sleep certainly had. Taking him in, spells and all, had been too much for the Watcher.

The ledge was just wide enough for Conan to squat on his heels until he could breathe easily again. Then he began picking his way back down toward the path, in no particular haste. With the Watcher dead, it would be a witling's act to break his neck by falling into the pit it left behind!

Conan reached the path about the time Harphos led the men with brands and torches up to where Talouf was standing guard. At first they could not speak, only stare at Conan as at a man risen from the dead.

It was Harphos who broke the silence. "Conan, what in the name of—?"

"It ate something too rough for it," the Cimmerian said, forcing a laugh. "Our friend Skiron."

"Ah," the Lokhri heir said. "I'd be angry if his spell still bound my mother. But it seems it bound her only as long as Akimos was alive. She woke up, said that he was dead, wondered what I was doing with my healing materials, then fell asleep again."

"Thank the gods for small favors," Conan said.

"We'll need more than a small favor when she awakes and tries to rule again," Harphos said dubiously.

"No, we won't," Conan said. He gripped the young man by both shoulders. "All you need is to do two things. One is to ask Livia for her hand. The other is to be the kind of man you were tonight."

"Even with my mother?"

"Before all with your mother!"

Lady Doris had the courtesy to sleep until nearly the next evening, so much was accomplished while she slept. It was not long after she woke, however, that she summoned Conan, Harphos, and Lady Livia to her chamber.

Sitting up in bed, clad in a shift pieced together from the tunics of dead soldiers, she still had much of her old force. Conan watched Harphos refuse to meet his mother's eyes, as she rambled on about what she had heard, about him and Livia and Conan.

"The men clearly did not think I was listening, for they gabbled like so many geese, as foul and as witless. So, my son, I must ask you this. Are you proposing to wed a Cimmerian's leavings?" It seemed that more than Doris's wits had survived her ordeal. So had her determination to rule or ruin her son.

If Livia had been wearing her dagger, Conan would have snatched it from her. Anything short of murder that Livia did to Lady Doris, the older woman would richly deserve.

It was Harphos who restored peace, or at least prevented war.

"Mother," he said, with the same commanding voice Conan had heard him use in the fighting. "I will wed the Lady Livia of Damaos if she will have me. That is all I will ask of her. Nor will I permit anyone else to ask anything else of her."

"You cannot talk to me that way, Harphos! I must consent—"

"Mother," Harphos interrupted. "I am of age. I do not need your consent. I would prefer to have it. But by law I only need Lady Livia's." He looked at the younger woman.

"Lady Livia—do I have your consent, to wed me by the laws of Argos and of the gods?"

A moment passed, in which Conan had one eye on Lady Doris, who was rapidly rising to a hysterical rage.

The other eye was on Livia. He vowed by all the gods known and unknown that if she refused Harphos, he would turn her over his knee and spank her soundly.

Then Livia reached out and took Harphos by both hands. The look in her eyes said more than a day's worth of speech. Conan took his hand off his sword hilt.

Lady Doris was not yet beaten. "Her acceptance must have witnesses, Argossean citizens. I will refuse to witness her acceptance. Conan is not a citizen. Therefore—"

Livia used some of her soldier's words. Then she grinned wickedly at Harphos. "I remember that. But I also remember that if vows are followed by the consummation of the marriage, the vows need no witnesses. The marriage cannot be set aside."

"Con—?" Doris began, then lost the power of speech to sheer rage. The silence was merciful; it allowed everyone else to hear a knock on the door.

"My lady?"

"Come in, Reza," Harphos said. The big Iranistani entered, looking to Conan's eyes rather shamefaced. He had not saved his lady, and to make matters worse he had put his trust in a man who all but slew his lady's intended husband.

"Reza," Harphos said. "You have mostly done well, but not altogether. I will forgive you what you have not done well, if you will do me one favor."

"My lord, I am at your command."

"Excellent. *Confine Lady Doris of Lokhri within this chamber!*"

It took both Conan and Reza, as well as one of Harphos's sleeping potions, to accomplish this. By the time Conan reached Livia's chamber, the door was closed and locked. A few sounds escaped, however, to make it plain how those within were amusing themselves.

Conan set down the jug of wine and the two cups he was carrying and descended the stairs. He had thought of drinking the wine himself, but there was no doubt that Harphos would need restoring more than he would!

CHAPTER 20

Outside the Herdsman's Peace, the rain poured down on Messantia. Conan's table faced the door to the street, so he was quick to see the hawk-nosed man in a sodden Guardian's cloak enter. The man left a trail of water on the floor as he crossed the room.

"Talouf!"

"Captain Conan! I heard that you'd been seeking me, but not where to find you. We Guardians have our ways, the gods be thanked!"

The tavern wench was glowering at Talouf for dripping water on the floor. "More wine, for me and this good Guardian," Conan said. "Also, if you can go up to my chambers and ask the woman there for the silk bag with the red ribbon—"

"The red ribbon?"

"Yes." Conan slapped her bottom with one hand and passed her a coin with the other. She left smiling.

Roland Green

"Is that a new disguise?" Conan asked, pointing at the cloak and the Guardian's tunic now revealed as the cloak was thrown back.

"By Erlik's everlasting manhood, no. I'm truly a Guardian, and an Argossean citizen as well."

It was not altogether surprising. The rewards to those who had fought the battle against Akimos, Skiron, and the Watchers had been generous if discreet. House Damaos and House Lokhri had been open-handed, and so had the archons (although most of their generosity was at the expense of Lord Akimos's heirs).

"I hope that's no bar to you taking the silver I've been holding for you since we disbanded the company. You're the last man I owe anything."

"No, no," Talouf assured his old captain. "I'll want to put a bit by, and faster than I could on my pay. There's a wine merchant's daughter I've my eye on—"

"For herself, or for her father's barrels?"

"She's shaped rather like one of them, I'll admit, but she's one of twelve children and a cook the gods themselves wouldn't put aside. So if you come this way again, you'll likely find me fat and fatherly. I've reached the age where there's much to be said for that, in truth."

"Not me," Conan said. "I've a fancy to see Messantia, but when that's done I'll be bound onward."

Talouf was silent until the wench brought the wine and was out of earshot. Then he whispered, "Best be on your way quickly, then. You're not without enemies, and if you shed their blood even in self-defense—"

"I know, I know. The laws of Argos would fall on me like dung from a giant bull, and bury me back in the House of Charof. I'll be careful, Talouf. I swear it."

278

"Captain, you haven't a careful bone in your body. Have you thought of joining the Guardians yourself?"

"Don't you know? I was a Captain in the Guardians for all the time I was in Argos."

Talouf looked suspiciously at his wine cup, then likewise at Conan. "A Guardian?"

"It seems that they would have to bring the law against me for some of what we did if I were not a Guardian. So they wrote it down that I had been a Captain of the Guardians on a secret mission. But for going beyond the law and my authority, I was dismissed and barred forever from the Guardians."

Talouf started to spit on the floor, then remembered the wench's glare and instead spat into an empty wine cup. He shook his head. "The laws of Argos!"

"You're certain you want to spend the rest of your life under them, making others obey them?" Conan asked.

"Better that than the cold bed and scant rations of a free lance, or the short life of a thief," Talouf said. "But if you wanted to go free-lancing again, I can give you the names of a score of men who would gladly follow you."

The thought was tempting. Argos and Aquilonia still had no use for free lances, but Shem and Koth were hiring with a free hand. They feared that Moranthes II might try to prop up his shaky throne with a foreign war, and they would be first in the path of any such.

It was also futile. "I'd need more silver than I have, and there's no more to be had from the folk we saved. No, they're not ungrateful. But Livia and Harphos have learned that there's more to putting House Lokhri in order than sending Reza there with a club. They need all their silver and as much more as they can talk out of the archons.''

Talouf looked ready for plain speech about lovestruck Argossean lords when the woman from Conan's chamber came up and handed him a silk bag with a red ribbon around the neck. Talouf hefted it cautiously, smiled at the weight, then stared at the woman.

''Shilka!''

''Indeed, Sergeant—Talouf?''

''The same. How fared you to Messantia?''

''With my sister, when she entered Lady Livia's service. I thought I should like to see the city before I went home, and found a man with the same thought.''

''Well, I'll not quarrel with either of you,'' Talouf said, raising his cup. ''But remember this, Captain. There's too many folk in Argos who want to see no more of you than your back as you board an outbound ship.''

''I'll remember that, Talouf,'' Conan said, raising his own cup while pouring from the jug for the woman. ''Now, let's toast old comrades and pass on to more pleasant matters!''

Three cups rose. ''Old comrades!'' they said together.

''And new adventures,'' Conan added, under his breath.